INTERGALACTIC
GLADIATOR

Blacklantern swung drunkenly and saw the diving tly. Sunlight glanced on arrowed black wings, burned on crimson armor. The five-jawed mouth was a wide black chasm. Five great bright fangs unsheathed to strike. The tapered tail was whipping into a graceful curve already reaching to poison him. . . . With all his old cunning Blacklantern measured the dive. Deftly, at the ultimate instant, he flicked the sling to draw its black-tipped sting aside. He crouched to bring it lower, sprang to meet it. . . . The sting exploded behind him. A thin jet of venom spurted past. Recoiling from its acrid reek, he was suddenly afraid. . . .

THE POWER OF BLACKNESS
THE SAVAGE NEW SCIENCE FICTION SAGA
BY JACK WILLIAMSON

By Jack Williamson and James E. Gunn

STAR BRIDGE

THE POWER OF BLACKNESS

JACK WILLIAMSON

A BERKLEY MEDALLION BOOK
published by
BERKLEY PUBLISHING CORPORATION

To Blanche

with love

Library of Congress Catalog Card Number: 75-29508

Portions of this novel first appeared in *Fantasy and Science
Fiction Magazine*, *Galaxy Science Fiction*, and *Amazing Science Fiction*

SBN 425-03260-0

BERKLEY MEDALLION BOOKS are published by
Berkley Publishing Corporation
200 Madison Avenue
New York, N. Y. 10016

BERKLEY MEDALLION BOOK ® TM 757,375

Printed in the United States of America

Berkley Medallion Edition, NOVEMBER, 1976

1.

THE guide was a time-dried Nggonggan black, hopping ahead with dazzling agility on his one good leg and waving his single yellow-painted crutch like a banner to guide his company of tourists. They were a motley group of sun-burned other-worlders in bright shorts and black glasses. Nggongga was too hot for them, and most wore coolers that wrapped them in tiny individual cloudlets of condensation.

"Follow my crutch!"

He went bounding down the ramp to a reserved-seat section on the shady side, just above the barrier. His flock shuffled behind, grinning at his capers, squinting down into the painful blaze of the sun-flooded arena, gawking at the Nggonggan natives that packed the cheaper sunlit seats beyond it, a little apprehensively sniffing the rich scents of a world not yet fully sterilized.

"Respected guests of Nggongga, you are lucky today—"

Booming out of his scrawny frame, the guide's voice had an unexpected mellow resonance, but he had to stop for his listeners to adjust their translators and recorders to his Nggonggan clicks and gliding tones.

"Nggonggong-Nggongga smiles on you today," he resumed. "You are about to see a veteran champion risking his title and his life to an unknown challenger. Most of you on your own far worlds have heard of tly-

3

binding—or you wouldn't be here. If you know anything, you know that it is more than a very dangerous game. It is a traditional ritual that reflects the history and the spirit of Nggongga.''

Drums began to throb.

"The challenger!" The yellow crutch pointed. "A young man brave enough—or fool enough—to risk his life for glory. . . . What's his name? Madam, he has no name. He was born outside the Nggonggan clan system, by which we are named. If he upsets the champion today, he'll be asked to join. . . . Yes, sir, you could say he's fighting for his name.''

Marching to the measured drumbeat, he came out of a dark archway. A lean youth, quick and supple, head held high, sweat bright on sleek black skin. He wore a flat black hat, a brief black kilt, a short jeweled dagger in a jeweled belt. Two black attendants marched behind, one trailing a black banner from a gilded lance, the other with a white pack rolled on his back.

"His weapon-bearer," the guide boomed. "And his surgeon.''

The three marched in single file to a wide circle of smooth black sand spread over the glaring white at the center of the arena, knelt before it while the drums paused, marched on toward the flag-wreathed stand where the judges sat.

"I know the boy." The guide's voice rose against the drum throb. "He used to clean my boots. An abandoned bastard. Grew up on the streets. An independent sort. He asks no favors and takes no orders. He's got brains and guts. He's coming up on his own, and I wish him luck. See that, sir?" He chuckled suddenly, waving the crutch. "He has found at least one friend, I see. He'll be fighting today for more than fortune and a name.''

The crutch picked out a striking red-haired girl leaning from a box near the judges. She screamed and waved until the challenger turned, screamed again, and blew him a

4

kiss. Nodding very slightly, he knelt to the judges again and turned with his attendants to face the black circle.

"You have a good guide today." The crutch tapped the floor, accenting the rhythm of the drums. "I know tly-binding, because in my own youth I was once a tly-binder. That's the way I lost my leg." He hopped and bent to listen to a sun-broiled woman, grinned, and shook his head. "Another story, madam. Too painful to retell. But I do know tly-binding."

He waved away a grimy black urchin offering a basket of spiny native fruit.

"The last living relic of our historic—" He leaned again into the drifting condensation. "No, madam. He won't use the dagger. Or any modern weapon. Everything will be authentic. The costumes and the code have not changed in seven thousand years."

He hopped back to face his flock and raised his bugle voice.

"Respected voyagers of the eye, here you will find the real Nggongga. We've been touring our metropolis—Nggonggamba means Eye of Nggongga—but the city is not our world at all. These hotels and shops and tourists traps—they're an ugly scab, grown around the eye."

He scowled back into the fog.

"No, sir. I'm not speaking as a Nggonggan diplomat. Not even as a courier for Universal Travel. I'm only a native Nggonggan, saying what I feel. Nggonggamba, to me, is a rank thorn-weed, planted by the traders who came through the eye for our rich metals and the richer scents distilled from our desert muskweed. But it is not Nggongga. . . . You say the eyes bring progress, sir? What I call the eyes will not translate."

Listening, he fanned himself with the wide flat yellow cone of his Nggonggan hat.

"The machines of the eye, sir? . . . Yes, of course they are clever beyond imagination. Every man of reason must bow to those who understand how to fold our space

5

through other spaces, to bring a doorway on one world against another doorway a hundred or ten thousand light-years off. I know it takes brave and able people to carry a new transflection station on a twenty-year flight or a fifty-year flight to open another new eye on another new world. But progress—for that new world?''

Swaying on his single leg, he flailed the yellow crutch as if to sweep aside the clinging cloud wisps.

''As you say, sir. . . . But I don't speak of such new planets. I'm sure the eyes are fine for new worlds, where men have never been before. The colonists can step out into virgin lands with all the gear they need. They can step back again if they don't like what they find. But things were different, sir, when my own forefathers reached Nggongga, twelve thousand years ago. Space had not been folded then. Their starship had been in flight for forty years and its fusion fuel was gone. Most of them were killed by what they found, but they had to stay. They could not refit or refuel their ship. Four thousand years had passed before the next one arrived.''

He stabbed the crutch toward a fat man masked with white suncreams and harnessed with multiplex recorders.

''I speak of worlds like this one, sir. Worlds already old, rich with seasoned cultures of their own, when the eyes are opened on them. . . . Yes, sir, I've seen others. Couriers travel, too. . . . On every settled world it is the same. But look around you at Nggongga.''

He whirled the crutch above his head.

''We Nggonggans had been evolving here for many thousand years. We are black because our sun is hot. We live in communal clans because our deserts are too harsh for men alone. We had shaped a way of life to fit our world. A harsh life, you may think, but it was good for us. I am sad to see it lost. We used to know what was true, what was just, what was good. Now nobody knows.''

A quaver broke his mellow voice.

''Now, since those first galactic strangers in their star-ship brought machines to open the eye, our old world is sick. Hordes of sneering strangers came pushing through the eye, bartering bright new gadgets we never needed and spreading doubt of all we used to live by. They drained off our portable wealth and left such broken men as I am, grieving for the spirit of old Nggongga. When those first greedy robbers and desecrators went on to loot newer worlds, another wave of strangers came, like yourselves, to explore the wreckage they had left. To stereograph the ruins of our holy places. To record the relics of our lost culture. To toss a few coins at the broken human beings—''

The fat man's muttering checked him.

"No, sir, I'm not an anthropologist. I'm just an old Nggonggan. As poor as the boy yonder, except that I do have a name. . . . No, sir, it's nothing you could pronounce, but people call me Champ. . . . Till I lost my leg, I was a binder of tlys. Since, I've been escorting tourists for Universal Travel. Sometimes I long for my youth.''

The drumbeat had changed and he glanced into the arena.

"Here come the egg-bearers.''

They were two slim young black girls in crimson hats and crimson aprons, marching proudly to the drum, bearing the tly's egg between them on a cushioned litter. It was an ash-white globe, the size of a child's head.

"Listen.'' He held up the crutch. "You hear it screaming.''

The faint shrieks rose fifelike above the drums as the girls reached the black-sand circle. Moving to the rhythm of the drums, they placed the egg at the center of that circle and drew back from it. Gliding through a ceremonial dance, they swept out their footprints with green-wreathed brooms from the litter. They stood facing the young challenger, who now marched slowly back with his two attendants to face them across the black circle and the screaming egg.

"Our most ancient history is represented here,'' the guide was chanting, in time to the drums. "Our pioneer forefathers came near failing to survive. The sun was too hot, the whole planet too hostile. The ultraviolet wilted their crops and the native predators killed their animals. Some wanted to refit their starship, which was still out in orbit. But they could not reach it. Their shuttles had both crashed. They were desperate—until they found a hero.''

He waved the crutch at the young contender, who was kneeling now, facing the girls and the wailing egg.

"The stinging things they called tlys had been their most savage enemy. These winged predators had been spoiling their fields and killing their cattle and even carrying children off to dens in cliffs that men could not climb. Now a young hero caught and tamed the first tly.

"The domesticated tly kept the wild ones off. More useful than the legendary falcons of old Earth, it caught edible game creatures on the uplands and brought edible fish from the sea. Others were tamed, and they kept the pioneers alive. In gratitude they gave the young tamer a new name. They called him Nggugong—which means Skyman.''

Down in the arena, the kneeling challenger had risen. Removing the belted dagger, he buckled it on his weapons-bearer, who tossed him in return a short length of rope.

"Yes, madam,'' the guide said. "Skyman used only a rope. The dagger is not for the tly at all, but for the binder. The tlys disable their game, you see, with a paralyzing venom which causes unending agony. No antidote is known. If the binder should be badly stung, it is the surgeon's duty to give him comfort with the dag—''

The drums abruptly stopped. With ritual shrieks, the two girls fled into the archway. The surgeon and the bearer retreated hastily toward the judges' box. The young contender stood outside the black circle, swinging the short rope and facing the whining egg.

"He is not allowed to step into the black,'' the guide whispered hoarsely. "Or to use any weapons save the rope and his own body. However, tradition does allow him one advantage over the old hero whose role he plays.

"The keeper of the tlys is allowed to milk the venom from the sacs, so that the sting is not always disabling. In these days the daggers are rarely required. My own leg was lost because my tly had not been milked with care enough. The amputation saved my life."

The drums rolled briefly.

"Watch! The tly!"

An iron gate clanged open. Sunlight burned on crimson armor and the whole arena rang with a howling that seemed to have no source. On dead-black wings, the tly climbed and wheeled above the whimpering egg and the waiting man. Wings arrowed back, it dived.

The other-worlders gasped at its sleek deadliness. Burning scales flowed in graceful lines from five-eyed head to tapered tail. Its five-angled mouth yawned black to bellow, showing five flashing fangs spaced around a pentagon of jaws.

"The binder has a choice of several strategies," the guide was whispering. "He can try to mount the tly at a point above the wings, where the sting cannot quite reach. He can try to catch the sting itself, to break it off the tail. With clever footwork he can evade the jaws. His aim is to tie the wings flat and disable the sting, so that he can carry the creature out of the arena."

He grinned into the condensation cloud.

"No, madam. The tly is not exactly a mother. The female tly is a helpless slug-shaped thing that never leaves the burrow. The males watch the eggs and feed the young. This creature is male enough—the sting is also a penis. Yet it's fighting for its egg, as you can see—"

The black challenger bounded nimbly on the balls of his feet and waited almost casually. The egg churred behind him. The diving tly came level, sting reaching for him. The rope flicked upward—and a roar of triumph rolled across the hot arena from the packed sunlit seats.

9

The challenger was still easily erect, twirling the rope. The egg still squalled on the sand. The tly had flown on past. With a hollow yell that seemed to fill the hot sky, it climbed and wheeled to dive again.

"A cool man." The guide glanced briefly back at his staring flock. "He knows that the tlys strike instinctively at motion. He led its sting from his body to the moving rope."

As the tly came back from a new direction, the challenger danced and paused to wait between it and the egg. Again it came at him on black wings, a flashing red projectile. Again the rope flicked upward. Again it stung the air and hurtled on. The bright-kilted blacks were on their feet across the arena, roaring their approval. Thrown like boomerangs, flat bright conical hats began sailing out toward the wheeling tly and sliding back into the stands.

"No!" the guide breathed suddenly. "No—"

The roar of the crowd fell into a hush of taut alarm. The returning tly had dived lower. Now it came at the man not with its sting but with the scarlet-armored bulge of its five-eyed head.

The encounter was a blur of motion, half obscured by furious black wings. In fragmentary glimpses, the other-worlders saw him astride the tapered body, saw his rope whipping against the searching sting. Man and beast rolled on the sand, hidden in white dust rising.

The arena lay hushed till a drum throbbed once. The contender stumbled out of the dust, bent with the weight of the hissing tly slung over his shoulder, black wings bound against its armor, broken sting dragging crookedly. The drums were thundering now, and many-colored hats sailed like strange birds above the staggering man.

"I think we have a new champion," the guide was murmuring. "The boy has earned his name—"

The drums stopped. Silence froze the crowd. The contender had stumbled again, reeling backward into the forbidden circle around the wailing egg. He slipped to his knees and the tly flopped on the black sand. The last bright hats rained out of the air. In the stillness the egg uttered a shrill little crow.

"The boy was stung!" the guide gasped. "The venom sacs of his tly had not been fully milked."

He stood swaying with pain from the venomed scratch along his upper arm. It washed him in unbearable fire, choked him with dry nausea, bathed the whole arena with murky red. It howled in his ears like a desert khamsin. It spun him into a tight cocoon of raw agony and nothing outside mattered.

Yet he knew what was happening. He heard the egg chittering happily, heard the tly slithering out of the loosened rope, glimpsed it soaring away with the pipped egg safely wrapped in its quick prehensile tongue.

He watched the girl whose name-symbol was Sapphire. She had been halfway to him when he began to stumble. Red hair flying, white arms wide, green eyes smiling for him. Now she had stopped. Her bright eagerness faded into shock and pity and aversion. Suddenly she shrugged, bent to pick up a jeweled hat that someone else had thrown, scurried back toward her box.

His two attendants bustled past her. The bearer waved his lance foolishly after the tly, which was already gone. The surgeon swabbed at his wound, peered into his face, and reached for the mercy dagger.

No! I don't need that—not yet—

He thought the words, but his dry throat made no sound. Desperately he tried to shake his head. The effort made the whole arena rock and pitch beneath him, but he could not be sure his head had moved.

"Wait." Fragmentary words broke through the gusts of pain. ". . . relatively superficial . . . survival . . . amputation . . . a crime the venom had not been milked. . . ."

They took his arms, tried to walk him out of the arena. He resisted. Still he couldn't talk, but he tried to pull back toward the benches. He had to see what happened next. If

11

the champion had to take the dagger, he thought the judges might still be forced to declare him the winner.

"Come on, kid." The surgeon tugged at him. "If you want to keep your arm—"

But now he could hear the drums again, beyond the walls of pain. They were a faint, far rattle, like footsteps in dry grass. The two men muttered and helped him to the benches. Swaying between them there, blinking across the barrier, he watched the champion strutting in.

A man of the Wind clan, the champion had a name. It meant Storm Stalker. Perhaps he had once been as noble as that title, but time had began to overtake him now. His belly bulged too far above his dun-colored kilt and his massive muscles shone with too much sweat.

Yet the black stands screamed a welcome, and thrown hats swarmed like bright moths above a light. He knelt to the judges, knelt to the egg. The drums paused and the handlers released his tly. It looked smaller than the boy's had been, its flight erratic and slow.

"A sick one!" he heard his surgeon muttering. "Or perhaps underfed."

Through a dull haze of pain he watched the contest. Three times the tly dived at the black sand-circle. Three times the Stalker led it by with an easy flirt of his rope. Three times the hats sailed out from the roaring stands.

On the fourth slow dive the tly seemed to waver. The champion flicked the rope to lead it down and sprang heavily upon it. The thin red tail struck and struck but the stings had no effect. Man and tly toppled into blinding dust. Though what happened was hard to see, the boy thought the black wings had stopped flapping before they were bound.

His fat blackness splotched with wet white sand, the champion knelt to the judges, knelt to his shrieking fans. Panting through a gap-toothed mouth, he bent to hoist his lifeless tly.

"Stalker!" Sapphire was screaming. "Stalker—you promised the egg to me."

The boy turned his throbbing head enough to see her scrambling down from her box. The champion nodded to his men. The bearer picked up the egg and brought it to meet her. She brushed it aside and ran on to seize the Stalker's sweaty arm. In a final hail of hats he stumbled out of the arena with the clinging girl and his drag-tailed tly.

As the cheering died, the boy limped stiffly after them. Dirty urchins were picking up the hats, but they paused to mimic his painful gait. His bearer had to push them aside with the black-bannered lance.

The sun was suddenly too hot, the air too thick to breathe. His feet began to drag the sand. The jeering of the urchins became a senseless howling. The walls of pain turned dark around him and he knew that he was falling.

He waited for the dagger.

But then the sun was gone. Dimly he recognized the low gray walls of the dying room—the surgery beneath the stands. Vaguely he wondered how much time had passed. Faintly he could remember the tiny hiss of red-hot needles thrust into his wound and the choking reek of burnt tly scales that was supposed to drive away the venom.

He remembered fragments of a quarrel. His surgeon's voice, shrill with anger, protesting that his clan had handed down their secret remedies five thousand years. The worried chief handler, insisting that the new doctors who came through the eye had better medicine than the dagger.

He didn't know how the quarrel came out. He lacked the life to care. But a pale young stranger in white was bustling around him now. He felt cold metal that stung like the tly, heard the click and hum of unknown devices, relaxed at last beneath a warm red glow. The pain began to drain away. He wanted to thank the pale man, but he was too sleepy to say anything.

He woke again in the dim cool stillness of the dying room, somehow quite alive. Stretching himself, he found no pain. Even his arm felt smooth and sound, where the scratch had been. His body moved well when he sat up, and he felt a pleasant stab of hunger.

His attendants and the pale man were gone, but an old black came shuffling toward the bed. A handler he knew. Although the man had never been a binder, his leathery skin was seamed with accidental scars, his gaunt frame stiff and palsied from accidental stings.

"Lad—lad!" His shrill voice cracked. "I've been waiting to beg your forgiveness." He knelt beside the bed. "It's all my fault you are not the champion."

He ducked the boy's clutching hand.

"There's a stranger—a gray-skinned other-worlder called Wheeler. One of those rogues who come through the eye to prey on Nggongga. An importer of forbidden drugs. A crafty gambler. He bet on the champion. Arranged for you to lose."

"You—" The boy slapped the bent bald head, before he could check himself. "What did you do?"

"Mercy, lad!" he whimpered. "I'll tell you everything. I was the milker. They had come to the arena to look over the tlys. Wheeler and the champion. A whore with them. They whispered together, with their translators set for privacy. Then the champion spoke to me.

"He made me promise to leave poison enough in the sacs to cripple you. In return he promised that Wheeler would bet five hundred gongs for me and take me along to a richer world beyond the eye when he went on—don't hurt me, lad!"

His gnarled hands lifted, twisted and trembling from old stings.

"I did try to put them off. Believe me, lad! I had always been an honest handler. I like your courage and your style. But I'm an old man, remember. I've been stung too many times. When I tried to say no, Wheeler promised that his other-world doctors could stop the pain that twists me. So I did what they wanted."

"I—I forgive you," the boy whispered. "But not the Stalker!"

"Now they won't—won't pay me!" Bitter tears burst out. "Wheeler says he never saw me. The champion kicked me out of his way and his whore laughed at me. They say the stings have curdled my brain. That's why I came back to you."

"Why tell me?" The boy laughed harshly. "I have no clan, no name, no rights. The entry costs took all I could raise. All except my hat and dagger. What can I do?"

"Kill the Stalker!" the old man gasped. "Kill Wheeler, too!"

Trembling suddenly, the boy slid to his feet. He shoved the old man aside, snatched his dagger-belt from its hook behind the bed, buckled it around him.

"Why not?" he breathed. "What have I to lose?"

"Wait, lad!" The old man whined. "What I've told you is only half the story. Both tlys were fixed. Yours unmilked. The other drugged and dying."

He turned back, staring.

"Another handler told me. Wheeler's girl promised him money—three hundred gongs bet on the champion— to slip the Stalker's tly a black capsule with its last feed. When the handler pushed it out to meet the Stalker, he says it was already weak and twitching. But now he says the whore won't pay."

"So I should kill all three?" The boy chuckled. "Perhaps I will."

He clapped on his black hat—the color of the clanless man. He thumbed the dagger's edge with a bleak black smile and strode out of the dying room into the clangor of Nggonggamba. Somehow, in spite of the tly's sting, he felt quite fit. All his pain was gone. Each bounding stride felt good, as if that pale outsider had oiled every joint, restrung every muscle.

An open freightway gave him a heady whiff of musk-weed. He breathed deeper and walked faster. The gaudy towers all looked brighter, the rush of the rolling ways sounded louder, the tly-pens behind him stank with a sharper fetor, as if his senses had all been renewed. He found himself peering aside into the glittering perfume shops and ahead at the mobs of black-skinned workers and the paler troops of merchants and shoppers and lovers and tourists, as if they had all been new.

The odor-lure of an eating place wet his mouth and stabbed him through with hunger—the quickest, keenest, brightest hunger he remembered. Searching his belt, he found one worn iron five-gong coin and a bright two-gate bit of portal money. Enough for dinner and a tip. He walked inside to eat. Stalker and Wheeler could wait. After all, he felt too good to kill anybody. Perhaps, over good food and drink, he might decide to forget—

"Hold up, boy!" The black doorman stopped him. "See that sign?"

It was the swirling disk of rainbow color that meant *clansmen only*. Beyond it he saw old Champ hopping nimbly about the tables, waving his crutch at the bowing waiters seating his pale other-worlders.

"They aren't clansmen."

"They're honorary clansmen," the doorman snarled. "You get out."

That turned his hunger into anger. He clutched at his dagger, let it go again. It was not the stupid doorman but the Stalker who had earned it.

In the native market he shopped for a weapon. Wistfully he tried the balance of the sleek man-guns, weighed the tapered rockets, peered at the cunning booby-bombs. Each was priced at many hundred gongs. So were the night glasses, the seismic traps, the chemical trackers. He was fingering the lower-priced knives and poison darts and lethal baits when a clerk frowned at his black kilt and began asking who a clanless man had any right to kill. He spent his five gongs for a hunting lantern, and the two-gate bit for glasses to see its light.

The builders of the eye had chosen an arid site on the arid planet. The portal itself stood on a rocky ridge between a dry salt lake and a narrow arm of Nggongga's single landlocked ocean. The new city ringed it now with enormous looming towers that mixed the styles of a hundred other worlds. Power plants and rolling ways honeycombed the rock beneath. New barge docks lined the ocean inlet, and new airpads dotted the ancient lake.

Only the arena was old. It stood southward on the same ridge, with an awesome view of infinite desert and land-bound sea. Once it had been the common ground of a dozen roving clans, with domesticated tlys allowed to burrow in the cliffs around it, but the mirror-domed suburban villas of wealthy other-worlders shone on the slopes below it now.

Storm Stalker was a nggugong of the Wind clan, and his loyal clansmen had long ago rewarded his prowess with the historic fortress of his clan, which perched like a resting tly on a naked peak above the arena. Though it was two thousand years older than the eye, he had opened it to progress. The new robot keeper at the street door ignored the boy when he asked to see the champion.

Yet the boy was not defeated. Growing up in Nggong-gamba without clan or rights or name, he had learned to use the dust-traps beneath the rolling ways. He rode a freightway, climbed a disposal shaft into the castle, crept past the Stalker's sleeping attendants into the tower where he lived.

Nothing stopped him until the flitting ray of his lantern shivered and came back to the long rows of black heads grinning at him from the trophy cases in the hall. For one frozen instant he felt as if the tly had stung him again. As he tried to breathe, his last qualms faded. The Stalker had also been a hunter of men. He dimmed the lantern and gripped the dagger and moved noiselessly on.

The bedroom door was locked, but a roving other-worlder had taught him how to deal with bedroom locks before he was eight years old. Inside he turned up his hunting light to fill the great stone room. He heard the Stalker's wheezing breath and found the ancient bed.

17

Thick-pillared, covered with a khamsin canopy, it loomed like a dark inner fortress.

The old floor took all his skill, but he had almost reached the bed without a creak when an odor checked him—the rose-tempered musk that Sapphire wore. Though he tried to tell himself that he should not have been surprised, her scent shook him like an unfair blow.

He stopped where he stood, breathing carefully. When he dared move again, he pushed up the hunting glasses to make sure his light could not be seen and pushed them back to survey the huge room again—the massive old armoire that towered like a second fort beyond the bed, the alternating tly's eggs and black heads that decorated the high stone mantel, the window-slits that looked out across islandlike airpads on the dark sea of desert.

Calm again, he framed his plan. He turned the black lantern high, its whole globe glowing, and placed it gently on the floor. He drew back into the shadow of the bed, lest the Stalker have hunting glasses of his own.

"Stalker!" His hand settled on the dagger. "Wake up, Stalker."

Sapphire screamed. Stalker's last snore became a grunt. His fat-jowled head thrust through the heavy curtains, darted back. The girl gasped something about "the stung man."

"You pitiful kid." The hoarse startled voice had a rasp of seeming sympathy. "A bad break you got." Behind the curtains there was motion. "What are you doing here?"

"Asking—asking questions, Stalker." He had thought he was calm enough, but his voice tried to stick. "Why was I stung? What killed your tly? If I like the answers, I'll let you live."

"Fool kid!" That croaking shout failed to cover a click of metal and a scrambling in the bed. "You've been listening to some brain-stung handler—"

White light blazed. Feet thudded beyond the bed. The kicked lantern clattered across the floor. The Stalker loomed where it had been, crouching and blinking, swinging a heavy man-gun. The boy slung his black glasses away, threw his poised dagger, dived aside.

The rifle crashed once, rattled on the floor. With a soft, childlike cry the Stalker toppled backward. Inside the canopy Sapphire choked back another scream. The boy scooped up his lantern and the gun, got his dagger back. When he stood up he found Sapphire trembling beside the bed, clad only in her long red hair.

"No Name—" Huskily she breathed the half-mocking term she had found for him the night after he first saw her in a tourist group old Champ was leading through the arena. "No Name, you know I always—always wanted you to win."

"Once I thought you did." Half afraid to look at her, he bent to wipe the dagger on Stalker's naked belly. "But we're done with your game. If you still want to play, we'll play mine."

"With you, No Name—"

He felt her flowing motion toward him and her rose-tempered scent turned him giddy. For a moment all he could hear was his own blood pounding.

"I'll play any game with you."

"I won't kill you, Sapphire." He pushed her back with the muzzle of the man-gun. "I'll even play fair. Show me his winnings and you can keep half."

"You hurt me, No Name." She cringed backward. "There's forty—forty thousand gongs. There in his safe under the hearth. I said I'd play your game." She tried to smile, swaying toward him. "Just tell me, No Name."

"I'm sliding through the eye—"

He heard pounding boots and shouting in the hall.

"Your part is to get me out alive," he whispered. "If these seed-eaters know you're here, convince them the Stalker isn't hurt. Maybe he shot at something in a dream. Dig up the loot. Find me a cooler-cloak to cover the gun. If you try one trick—"

"Trust me, No Name!" Her white arms opened. "Take me—take me with you."

"Not yet!" Grinning at her, he waved the man-gun toward the door, where the Stalker's people had begun to hammer. "First we've got my game to play."

Old Champ was guiding a group of native black Nggonggans around the terminal complex. Members of the Sand clan, in brown hats and kilts, they were rare-earth miners and muskweed cutters and crawler drivers from the equatorial uplands half around the planet. Rollways and towers and the eye itself had humbled them with awe, and he was snappish with them, suspecting that they disapproved the other-worlder custom of the tip.

"See that dome?" He waved the yellow crutch. "It covers the transflection portal."

They marveled at the dome, which was wide enough to cover the largest village in their desert highlands. They stared again at his agility as he hopped up a rolling ramp and led them along the high gallery that belted the dome above the terminal doors. They gasped when he turned a section of the inner wall transparent to let them look down into the dome.

"The portal," he bugled, in their own tonal dialect. "The eye itself."

The floor was a vast circular plain. Rollways entered it from hundreds of terminal entrances three levels deep, spaced all around the rim of the dome. They flowed together into six broad trunks, all at the same level, that converged into the actual eye.

"Monstrous!" A hulking miner shivered. "Forty yards wide—and looking straight at me."

"An optical effect," old Champ said. "The same from every direction. The blue iris is a circular image of all the other portals—some of them ten thousand light-years off in ordinary space. The black pupil—the engineers call it a circle of inversion—reflects the darkness of all the unknown spaces collapsed between the open eyes."

He waved the crutch at the unending streams of traffic

—piled freight containers and crowded passenger floats—flowing into the eye on one side and out on the other.

"Ring-fields around the iris push the traffic through—"

"A forbidden thing!" A stooped weed-cutter shrank fearfully back. "People and things go into that eye and come out—different! Bales of weed turn to big black boxes."

"It only looks that way." Old Champ rapped the deck impatiently. "What goes in is scattered through other eyes to destinations on many thousand planets. What comes out here has been gathered from those same far eyes. A ticket through costs more than you have, but it does save travel time. A thousand gongs can save you a thousand years in a starship—if you could live so long."

He paused to let them gape.

"The operators and the inner guards are stationed on those six islands." He pointed at the triangular platforms that stood between the converging rollways. "They sort and watch the traffic. But what you see is less than half the eye. The computers and the power installations fill nine more levels under the floor."

"Sir!" A curious crawler driver stopped chewing the sweetseed that colored his mouth vividly orange. "Can we go down there? I want to see—"

"Not without your ticket." Old Champ snorted. "Not without your exit visa. Not without being screened for weapons and contraband and bad ideas."

"Why?" The driver looked for a place to spit and gulped uncomfortably. "I don't see why—"

"Eyejackers!" snapped the guide. "A lot of con men and bigger thieves do get through the eye with loot collected on Nggongga—but they're the slick ones. The eyejackers are the fools. They rob somebody and turn up here with a gun or a bomb for a ticket. Every one gets caught, but more keep coming."

"How do they catch them?" The miner squinted through the crystal wall. "I don't see any guns."

21

"You won't see—"

The wall turned suddenly opaque, now the color of polished steel.

"Trouble inside—but we won't see it." Old Champ rapped with the crutch and hopped toward the ramp. "They've cut us off. We'll have to move along. Your good luck. Our next stop is a perfume factory, and now we'll have time enough to shop. The manager is my clan-kin. Highly reliable. If you decide to purchase anything I can get you wholesale rates."

The boy had never been inside the portal dome, but he had begun cleaning boots and sometimes picking pockets on that sight-seer's gallery before he was seven. Tourists had told him of other worlds where all people had rights and a name was not too hard to earn. Never expecting to have the money or the right to buy legal passage, he had brightened many an hour of hunger and despair with schemes for illegal transit to some kinder place. That converging web of rollways was mapped in his mind, and off-duty workers had told him how the eye was run.

Now, with twenty thousand gongs in his belt, he might have paid his legal way, but he could not expect the dead Stalker's fans to leave him time enough to comply with legal regulations. He rode a low-level freightway into the dome, crouching between piled bales of cured muskweed.

When it slowed to pass an inspection station he dropped off the rollway behind the bales and slipped into a washroom. He waited there for an inspector, took the man's uniform and eye-badge, climbed a ramp to the main level, sprang boldly on a passenger float.

The man-gun slung across his back as if it had been official equipment, he moved briskly between the files of standing passengers, asking to see their departure papers. With a hardwon deftness, he extracted transit coupons from one folder, the visaed passport from another, gathered a medical clearance and a credit disk and a universal translator, working his way along the float until

22

it was entering the slot between two control islands, within moments of the portal.

"Documents," he was rasping. "Departure doc—"

When he glanced up toward the eye, his voice caught. Already overhead, the brilliant blue flicker of the iris was many yards across. The black stare of that vast solitary pupil struck him with a terror as keen as his breathless hope. All around the iris was a haze of colorless nothingness—already swallowing the front of the float. In a few heartbeats he would see a new world—

The rollway stopped.

"Get off!" That amplified command thundered from somewhere above and blinding searchlights blazed down on him from the island wall. "Get off that float!"

Plunging into a knot of startled tourists, he unslung the man-gun.

"Eyejack!" He fired a short burst upward at the island's crystal wall. "Cut the light!" he screamed through the slam and howl of his ricocheting bullets. "Take me through. I won't hurt anybody—unless you stop the float."

Crouching, he swept the shrieking passengers with the muzzle of the gun. The searchlights went out. The float lurched ahead. The eye swelled till it was half the world. Men and women ahead toppled into the hueless nothingness around the iris. He would be next.

"Keep it rolling!" he screamed at the island. "Take me through—"

The rifle tore itself out of his hands to vanish into that flickering blankness, drawn by some savage force he could not see. Desperately he plunged to follow it. Something smashed him back as if he had struck an invisible wall.

Something hurled him off the float, crushed him to the floor. The searchlights blazed again. He was groping for his dagger, but heavy boots came thudding down around him. A gas-gun thumped. He caught one bitter whiff and the blinding lights dimmed again.

He lay sprawled on a wet metal floor, too numb at first to move. He was bruised, naked, drenched. His chest felt raw where the gas had burned him. When he moved his throbbing head he struck a steel cell wall. Dagger and money and clothing were gone, even his translator. He sat hunched and shivering on the edge of the bare metal bunk, waiting miserably for anything to happen.

"Wake up, lad." A big paunchy black in the blue kilt of the Sky clan rattled the bars and hailed him in his own dialect. "So you're the rascal who stabbed the Stalker and tried to eyejack your way off the world?"

The boy nodded dully.

"Idiot!" The scolding tone was oddly mixed with kindness. "You never had a chance. I guess you got closer than most, but the operators can work those ring-fields like their own hands. I hear they grabbed your gun with a magnetic vector and tossed you back to the eye-guard gang."

"They got me."

"I see you've had a working over—but don't blame me. I just came on. I'll get you a towel and something to wear. Wait right here."

Chuckling heartily, he vanished and came back with the towel and a tattered black kilt.

"I saw you in the arena." He held the kilt while the boy dried himself. "Lost ten gongs on you—but don't mind that. I like the cool way you played that tly. I think you earned the title fair enough. I guess old Stalker stung us both."

"I killed him, anyhow." The boy grinned with a brief satisfaction. "But they've got—got me."

Something like a sob caught his voice. "What will they do with me now?"

"Nothing good." The guard clucked with sympathy. "The eyejack by itself would probably get you a free trip to the world they call Bottom Nine. But the Stalker's fans won't let you get off alive. A mob of them is marching on the municipal tower. They want you hunted."

"That's their old tribal law." The boy nodded bleakly. "Stalker was a hunter himself."

When the guard was gone the boy sat trying not to think about the grinning heads he had seen in the Stalker's trophy cases and arranged with tly's eggs on his mantel. He reviewed his eyejack attempt, trying to pick out his blunder, but he could see no blunder. He simply hadn't known how the ring-fields could be used to disarm a man and toss him to the cops.

"Come along, boy!" That cheery shout broke into his dismal abstraction. "Good news! Maybe a chance to save your head. An agent of the Benefactors wants to talk to you."

"The Benefactors?" He sprang upright and sat heavily back, resolving not to hope too much. "What's a Benefactor?"

"You'll find out." The guard returned his translator, squinted sharply at him, nodded in bland approval. "I think you'll do. Just speak fair to the agent. If you please him he can take you through the eye to a better place than Bottom Nine. Now come along."

Two levels up, the guard let him into a bright, quiet room where two others waited.

"No Name!" Sapphire ran to greet him with a hot wet kiss. She led him to meet her companion, a pale outsider with a puffy face and glassy eyes. "My friend Wheeler."

The other-worlder gave him a sullen stare.

"Don't mind Wheeler." The girl made a face. "Of course he blames you for his own arrest. But we're all three in this together—and we can all get out together if we can only play the Benefactors' game."

"I think I've played too many games." The boy wiped his mouth with the back of his hand and stepped back from the hostile other-worlder. "What are Benefactors?"

"Friends of humanity, they say." Wheeler spoke in a raspy whisper. "No friends of mine."

"Play along." The girl glanced at the farther door and dropped her urgent voice. "Both of you. Promise to befriend the human race, if that's what the agent wants. Let him get us off Nggongga—before these black hunters take our heads. We can walk out later—"

Wheeler hissed softly to stop her. The farther door slid open. Two uniformed blacks stalked through, gas-guns ready. A pale, worried portal official appeared behind them, the blue eye-symbol staring from his silver tunic. He scowled at the prisoners, called the policeman sharply out.

A tall man walked in alone. Wheeler flinched away from him with a startled grunt. Sapphire gasped. The boy blinked and stared, trying to resolve his confused emotions of dread and wonder and even delight.

Standing very straight in a queer, close-cut uniform of some blood-red stuff, with a black weapon-shape at his belt, the stranger looked severely stern till he smiled at the three. With the snowy hair flowing to his shoulders and the lines around his penetrating eyes, he looked old, until the boy saw the firmness of his deep-tanned flesh and his youthful ease of motion. His quiet voice carried invincible authority, somehow mixed with appealing warmth.

"Call me Thornwall." He paused to greet each of the three with a searching look and an oddly casual nod. The boy shrank a little from the blue directness of his eyes. The girl darted impulsively toward him, but Wheeler snatched her back.

"Sit, please." He waved them toward the chairs. "Before you speak, you should know that I'm here as an agent of the Fellowship of Benefactors. We've arranged this meeting to discuss the possibility that you might join us."

"We're ready, sir!" the girl cried. "You'll find us willing—"

"Not yet!" Wheeler rasped. "Let's hear the conditions."

"We've time enough." He leaned against the desk, smiling easily. "First of all you should understand your

26

difficult legal situation." Sterner than the smile, his blue stare probed them one by one. "Here in Nggonggamba, you are subject to a triple jurisdiction. The portal complex has laws of its own, in force on many planets, recognized here by both the city and the adjacent clandoms. The city has its own legal authority, created by the treaty of entry. Under the same agreement the aboriginal clans retain certain paramount rights to which city and eye must yield."

The boy waited blankly for meaning to emerge. The words were a frightening jangle, yet he wanted to trust the voice that spoke them. Wheeler sat staring glassily when he looked at the others, and Sapphire was wetting her full red lips.

"Each of you is charged with grave offenses against all three jurisdictions." Thornwall's young face was warm and brown and casual, yet his old eyes froze the boy. "Yours include the killing of a treaty clansman, not yet avenged, armed robbery and transportation of stolen property within the municipal limits, and numerous violations of the portal code, even space piracy."

The boy gulped. "Guilty, sir."

"We're not concerned with guilt." A lean red arm waved his words aside. "Only with the truth."

The boy sat back uneasily and Thornwall turned to the girl.

"My name-symbol is Sapphire." Very pale, she stood up as if somehow lifted by his pointing finger. "I was with Stalker when he was killed. I was caught at the portal with part of his stolen money."

"I believe you're also involved with him."

The finger moved on to the puffy man, who sat in stubborn silence.

"You face a long list of charges, Wheeler. You are accused of misusing the portal on many occasions, to ship illicit drugs, to dispose of stolen property, to avoid arrest. Here on Nggongga the clans and the city officials suspect

27

you of controlling a dope ring, adulterating perfumes and counterfeiting containers, even of fixing the tly-binding contest that led to this boy's arrest.''

"No comment," Wheeler rasped. "My lawyers will speak for me."

"You have no lawyer here." Thornwall shrugged. "If you wish to petition for fellowship you'll have to speak for yourself."

"No comment—"

"Don't be a lunatic!" the girl flared at him. "The Wind clan will get us all if the Benefactors don't decide to save us. The clans don't like other-worlder lawyers and you know how their law works. They'll turn us loose in some salt sink, naked in the sun and five hundred miles from water. They'll hunt us down with trained tlys and manguns—and mount our heads for trophies!" She glanced at Thornwall and sank back into her chair. "Sorry, sir."

"I'm afraid that's an accurate statement of your situation." The tall man nodded with an unconcerned emphasis. "Under the treaty agreement the portal municipal authorities will be compelled to release you to the jurisdiction of the clan."

"But you can save us?" The girl's green eyes searched him desperately. "You will save us?"

"That same treaty does grant the Benefactors a superior jurisdiction," Thornwall said. "But only over our own people. We are not yet ready to offer membership to any one of you. Perhaps some of you are not yet ready to accept. I want to explain what we are. Any invitation to join our fellowship will depend on your own responses."

Old Champ was guiding a new tourist group into the perfumers' quarter when the rollway stopped, the street blocked ahead by a mass of chanting blacks in dun-colored hats and kilts. Most of his flock clustered uneasily around his lifted crutch, but a bold few ran ahead to multiplex the

28

scene. One pale gangling youth picked up the chant in his translator:

"Kill! . . . Kill the killers! . . . Kill! . . ."

That brought the strays scurrying back and he led the apprehensive group to a quiet concourse on the level below.

"Respected guests, you're in no danger." He waved the yellow crutch to collect the stragglers. "What you glimpsed is a unique survival of our native culture. One of our folkways not yet destroyed by the invasion of civilization."

He helped a flushed, perspiring woman turn on her cooler-cloak.

"No, sir, that's no mob." His mellow voice rose again. "Those are Wind clan people, demanding ritual justice. A clan nggugong has been murdered. The people are simply asserting their right to punish the killers—a right guaranteed by both the city and the portal."

He hoped to hear some muttered protest.

"Madam, that's our law. Accused criminals are released out toward the center of our traditional hunting lands. Their accusers are permitted to pursue them to the death. . . .

"Never, sir!" He banged the pavement for emphasis. "Our sacred hunts never endanger the innocent. We Nggonggans don't bring false charges, sir. If an innocent person should ever be accused, the holy hunters promise that our ancient deity would save him. Nggong-Nggongga would guide him to a temple of refuge only nine days away across the hallowed lands."

He held his hat behind his ear to catch a voice.

"Yes, madam? . . . Most certainly. Any of you can arrange to witness our ritual of justice. In fact, our Golden Desert Safari allows full participation. Competent bush guides escort our desert tours, with weapons and all equipment provided by Universal Travel. . . .

"Legal? Of course it's legal. The holy hunts are sanctioned under the treaty of entry. The safari fee covers your special initiation into the Wind clan, and several of our field guides are visiting anthropology students who can help preserve and mount your trophies. . . .

"Yes, madam. By all means. We guarantee a kill. . . . You'll be living in the open, quartered in a flying camper, but there's no actual danger. Our people are competent and the accused are given no arms. You can trust us, madam. Universal Travel has never lost a hunter!"

Sunk in a sullen apathy, Wheeler had been fingering his puffy jaw. Suddenly he cleared his throat and sat up straighter. From the faint sour reek of his breath, the boy knew that he had been triggering a stimulant implant under his skin.

"We're listening." His lax gray flesh flushed and his hoarse voice rose stronger. "We're interested in anything that will get us off Nggongga."

"That depends on you." Blue as the iris of the portal itself, Thornwall's eyes roved slowly over them, dwelling warmly on the boy, resting sadly on the girl, keenly probing Wheeler. "I must tell you about our fellowship.

"To begin with our reason for being, I suppose you are all aware that the human race has not yet reached any very lofty cultural level. A philosopher might say that technology has outrun ethics. We invent the transflection portals—then let them import crime and pain into such worlds as Nggongga."

Wheeler stirred angrily and the girl hissed at him.

"I get your point." Thornwall tossed his long hair back. "We humans aren't ready for utopia. We aren't all alike. We're still more animal than mechanical. We need excitement and uncertainty, perhaps even violence. Even what we have is no doubt better than any static ideal state."

His eyes ranged over them again.

"From my survey of your separate cases, I know that

30

you are all individualists, all in conflict with society. You need not conceal your hostilities from us—nor even past behavior classified as criminal. In fact, social independence can help qualify you for our fellowship.''

Wheeler sniffed and stiffened.

"I don't mean that we're outlaws." The blue eyes stabbed at him. "If admitted, you'll be retrained—at one of our schools on some other planet. You will be required to obey our code. You'll find that strict. We aren't criminals."

He had seen the boy's protesting gesture.

"I know you dislike government. But we are not a government. We don't try to be. There has always been too much government. What is sometimes called the empire of man has now become too vast and too various to be governed at all, by any central authority."

"If you have no power"—Wheeler squinted at him shrewdly—"how can you save us from the clansmen?"

"We do have authority," Thornwall said. "But only what is granted to us freely, in fair exchange. We are committed not to use it to coerce anybody. I am here on Nggongga because we happen to agree with the portal people. We regard the portals as a way to continued human progress and local portal officials often need our aid. We work together. If the clans should order us to go, the eye would be closed."

"That's what I understood." Wheeler raised his raspy voice as if he had scored a point. "So what do you do with this curious authority?"

"We defend individuals"—Thornwall's brown smile warmed the boy—"from other individuals. From unjust societies. We support a code of individual rights. A right to learn. A right to choose. A right to act."

"So you spread anarchy?"

"An ideal anarchy, perhaps." He gave Wheeler a quizzical nod. "An individual who learns his own rights also learns the rights of others. When he is allowed a liberated choice, he commonly chooses humane paths of action."

31

"Noble noises." Wheeler snorted. "But I don't see the payoff. Where do you collect?"

Thornwall tossed his white hair back with a puzzled gesture.

"We don't collect taxes, if that's what you mean. We don't sell protection. What we offer is a way of life. You may fail to understand, but most of our fellows do feel adequately rewarded, simply with the way we serve mankind. We sometimes call ourselves the humanistic volunteers."

The boy sat tense with a troubled alertness, watching Thornwall the way he had once watched a tly's egg hatch. Even in his translator the words rang strange. The swirl of ideas was hard to grasp. Yet, for all his confusion, the youth and strength and warm goodwill of Thornwall drew him like sweet water in the great salt waste.

"We're a volunteer legion of progress." The red-clad frame leaned toward the boy and the soft voice spoke to him alone. "We believe in man's great future. Armed with science—the weapon of reason—we champion the human cause. Sometimes we fight a hostile cosmos. Sometimes man's own backward nature. Often a fossil society, no longer alive—"

"Magnificent!" Sapphire was on her feet, flushed and eager. "I pledge—pledge my life to that ideal. I volunteer. I think we all do." She swung urgently back to Wheeler and the boy. "Don't we?"

"I want to keep my head," Wheeler muttered stolidly. "I'll go along."

The boy saw the girl's quick green wink, but still he hesitated. He felt her flash of puzzled anger, found Thornwall surveying him sharply. He was suddenly trembling, the way he had trembled in the hot arena while he waited for his tly.

"Young man"—Thornwall spoke very gently—"how do you feel?"

"Sir—" The word came strangely, and he had to get his

breath. "I've never belonged to anything. I see that you mean well, but I'm afraid your fellowship is not for me. I don't like to take orders. Not from anybody. I think I'll take my chance with the hunters in the desert. I know how to deal with them."

"Simpleton!" the girl hissed at him. "You'll be killed." She caught Wheeler's arm and whirled back to Thornwall. "We two will go. We'll agree to anything you require—"

Her breathless voice faded when she saw him still looking at the boy.

"I see that you don't quite understand the Benefactors," he was saying. "We don't require you to take orders—or to give them. We hold that nobody belongs to any society he didn't join or doesn't accept. You may leave us when or if you please. We don't compel anybody."

Wheeler snuffed.

"Perhaps you feel compelled now." Amusement flickered on his dark-tanned face. "But the threats you face come from others, not from us. What we offer is life—a way of life—for those who qualify."

"Do we?" Desperately, Sapphire caught at his hand. "What do you want us to promise?"

"Nothing." Thornwall looked hard at her, his amusement fading. "All we need is to know what you are."

She met his eyes silently, her fair skin very white. Suddenly she gasped and reddened.

"If you don't take us, don't—don't trust him!" She swung on the boy, green eyes blazing. "We were speaking before you came in. We all agreed to say we'd go along, to save our heads. But we planned to desert you as soon as we were safe."

"Such motivations are common enough." He paused to glance at Wheeler, who was again massaging his puffy jaw. "I haven't rejected anybody, though we do need to know more about the two of you."

33

The girl sank back into her chair.

"As for you, young man—" He paused while the boy's heart thudded. "Would you accept a student fellowship?"

"Not—not yet." The boy gulped. "It's hard to tell you how I feel. But you see, I've never really had anybody else. I've always been alone. Whenever anybody offered me something I wanted, it turned out to be bait—bait for a trap." He glanced at the girl and her bright image blurred. "Whenever I trusted anybody, I got hurt. You other-worlders have never done much for me."

"We aren't all alike. Remember your doctor? The man who cleared the tly venom out of your body? He was one of us."

"I didn't know." The boy looked resolutely away from the girl. "He was gone before I woke."

"Did you know you yourself have other-worlder blood?"

The boy squinted doubtfully.

"Perhaps we know more about you than you know about yourself. Your grandfather came here through the eye when it was new. A muskweed trader. He lived with a native girl, one from the Sand clan. Of course they couldn't marry here—he was not allowed to join the clan system. When he could retire, he took her on to a more flexible society."

The boy sat tense and scowling.

"They had one son, who became your father. He stayed here to manage the business. Died before you were born. An official report says he was caught in a salt storm in the Great Salt Rift. There's better evidence that a rival weed trader bribed a Sand clansman to take his head.

"Your mother was a Water clan girl who worked in his office. Soon after you were born, she married a Wind clansman. The clan had no place for you. She gave you to a blind beggar."

"I remember her!" The boy caught his breath. "Actually, she had one good eye." He sat silent for a moment, watching Thornwall with a fixed intentness. "What are

34

the duties?" he asked abruptly. "What exactly does a Benefactor do?"

"Nearly anything to aid an individual. I've helped a lost child find its home. We operate schools, labs, hospitals, libraries, communication webworks. Our agents have often come to the rescue of people falsely accused of crime—"

The girl was jabbing Wheeler's ribs.

"I'm afraid you can't qualify for that." Thornwall gave her a glance of wry apology. "There's evidently nothing false about the charges against you."

"Or against him!" She glared at the boy, green malevolence in her eyes. "I saw him murder the Stalker in his own bedroom."

"He has not denied it."

She shot a warning glance at Wheeler, who had begun to rub his jaw again.

"We defend individuals," Thornwall was murmuring. "Sometimes against the aggression of other individuals. More commonly against a bad society—bad in the sense that it subverts the rights and cripples the lives of those we seek to protect.

"Yet our defense is rigorously restrained. We use no violence except in our own defense. We do supply knowledge—commonly that is enough. Sometimes we offer tools, very rarely weapons. If other means fail we can often avert violence by arranging escape through the eye. Does that appeal to you?"

"Sorry, sir," the boy muttered. "But I've never been beyond the eye. I can't see what you're talking about. Not the way I can see those hunters in the saltlands with their rifles and their tlys."

"You'd like the work," Thornwall promised. "I've never found it dull. The assignments keep you moving. They're always different and most of them are exciting. For one example, the portal people want one of our agents to go along with an expedition they're sending back to Old Earth—"

35

"The mother planet?" The boy sat up. "So it really does exist?"

"But it's in trouble," Thornwall said. "It slipped backward after the colonists were gone—sending out the starships had used up its best resources. It soon turned back from science and the notion of progress. Now its people have been isolated from all other worlds for many thousand years. When a portal was set up there a few centuries ago they wouldn't let it open. Since that seemed to be their own free choice, we felt we had no right to interfere. But things have changed. We have since discovered a shadow of danger over the planet. The people must be told about it. The eye must be opened, for those who elect to leave. That's the duty of our agent."

The boy had risen slowly to his feet.

"Could I go?" he whispered. "If I join?"

"Perhaps." Thornwall shrugged. "All I can do now is accept you for training. Your assignments can't be decided until you have passed the final tests for full fellowship—which aren't easy. But even if you don't get to Old Earth, you'll find other missions with the same sort of challenge."

The boy stood looking down at himself, shuffling his feet on the thick rug. He shot an unwilling glance at Sapphire and Wheeler, who sat with heads averted, whispering together. He pulled up the tattered kilt and frowned again at Thornwall.

"I think—I think I'll take a chance," he muttered. "On one condition."

"Watch him, sir!" Wheeler rasped. "He's the vilest scum of Nggongga. He knows every dirty trick there is. He'll con you if he can."

"I warned you what he was planning." Sapphire glared through the red disorder of her hair. "I know him, sir. I saw him butcher the Stalker. He's a slick black rat."

The boy flinched.

"You'll be surprised, sir." His voice was breathless and uneven. "I'd like to help save their heads—in spite of

36

all they're saying. I'll go along, if you'll take them too. That's my condition, sir."

"No Name!" The girl stared blankly, red mouth wide. "I never get you." She whirled desperately to Thornwall. "Will—will you take us now?"

"Sorry, young man." Thornwall's face turned stern. "I can't make that sort of deal. Every Benefactor has to prove himself." He raised a lean red arm to stop the boy's impulsive protest. "Yet perhaps we can agree."

He swung to Wheeler and the girl.

"We can't yet accept you two for training, but you can still be useful. I can offer you at least temporary shelter in return for what you know about implants traffic. Agreed?"

"Agreed!"

Later, when Thornwall was preparing their exit papers, he looked up at the eager boy.

"Name?" A quizzical smile lit his eyes. "We need a name for you."

"Sir, I never had a name."

"We'll find you one." He tossed his gleaming hair and his eyes dwelt on the boy. "Something the translators can handle. Something reflecting your color and your past— and the future I see for you in our fellowship. Darkness, perhaps, and light—"

"I had a hunting lantern."

"Your emblem!" he murmured. "The black globe of the lantern, on its square black base, set against a field of glowing light. For your name—"

He gave the boy a strong brown hand.

"Welcome, Blacklantern!"

2.

IN the Sand clan suburb of Nggonggamba, the one-legged guide waved a yellow crutch to lead his sunburned tourist flock off the passenger slideway to a sun-parched ramp. Before them stood a blank stone wall, broken only with a tall iron door, black from smoke.

"What's this?" A fat and dewlapped other-worlder mopped at his sweat and scowled up and down the empty platform. "What's to see here?"

"The tragedy of our planet."

The old guide's voice boomed out of his black-leather face with an unexpected eloquence. Hopping vigorously ahead, he swung the crutch toward the fire-bombed door and the crude native script splashed in red across the wall.

" 'Nggars beware!' That's what it says. 'The Night clan warns you! Sunsdeath is coming! The just wrath of Cru Creetha must be cooled with alien blood.' "

The crutch dropped to indicate a rough drawing placed like a signature, the outline of a red-eyed angular creature, dangling snaky tentacles.

"So some vandal paints a slogan on a wall," the fat man grumbled. "We've seen the same red scrawl all over the city. What's that to us?"

"For one thing," the guide said, "it means our tour is over. Because of the Night clan terrorists and the near approach of Sunsdeath, all tourist visas have been can-

41

celed, effective at sunset. I stopped you here to show you why."

"Swindler!" A rawboned blonde turned up her translator till its bellow echoed off the fire-scarred wall. "I'll have you know I've paid in advance for the Black Desert Safari. Five days and four nights at air-camps or full service hotels with spotters and beaters included and a trophy kill guaranteed."

"Respected visitor," the guide said gently, "I advise you to take your own head away while you have it."

"I'll have you know that I'm a professor of exoethnography." She bridled indignantly. "I demand my trophy kill or a full refund."

"You may speak to the office," the guide said. "But I won't be there. You few people are my last tour group. The terror has ruined our business and I've had my fill of fire and bombs. . . . Where am I going, sir? To an old town named Krongkor, off at the far end of our long sea. A busy trading center in the old days before the space gate opened, but a quiet refuge now, well out of the terror. I have spent my savings to buy a hotel there."

His voice became a droning chant.

"A noble landmark, respected guests. A monumental relic of our historic past. If our darkened star is indeed restored—if you ever return to Nggongga—I hope you will plan to visit me there. I promise you the hospitality of the old desert clans, as it was before the shadow of terror fell upon us. We offer full service, with the latest cooler equipment, and we feature the local seafoods and wines."

"Don't hold a room for me!" shrilled a scrawny otherworlder, cloaked in the fog from his cooler suit. "Frankly, I'm baffled by all this talk of terror. I happen to own a few shares of space transport, and I came here to look at my investment. We've brought you people all the benefits of technological progress. I came here expecting gratitude. Instead it seems you want to run us off your backward planet."

42

"Respected sir, you state our situation precisely." The lean old black gave him an ironic bow. "We've had several generations of your sort of progress. Most of us are sick of it. That's what makes this coming Sunsdeath so dangerous to you."

"Sunsdeath?" the fat man wheezed. "What's Sunsdeath?"

"A failure of our star. The cause is not clearly known, but the event has happened perhaps once in a long lifespan, ever since the colonists landed. There are rains of meteors. The darkness is commonly complete. It lasts sometimes for a whole day. On past occasions, however, the star has always been restored."

"An eclipse!" the scrawny man scoffed. "Don't you know about eclipses?"

"I know the lunar theory, sir. But Nggongga has no moon."

"Have you another theory?"

"Our priests do," the guide said. "They say the star is eaten by the red-eyed dragon-god Cru Creetha, whose symbol you see on the wall."

"You mean the hunger of Cru Creetha is predictable?" The tourist squinted skeptically into the glaring sun. "Like the motions of a moon?"

"The priests do have foreknowledge, sir. Cru Creetha is believed to act from wrath. His present anger is said to be directed at the other-world invasion of Nggongga, which has led so many of our people to forget their ancient ways. His most fanatic followers are preaching that the sun will not come back until the head of every alien has been piled around his altars."

"Superstitious nonsense!" the fat man muttered. "I say your priests are ignorant fools—or more likely they are cunning rascals deceiving ignorant fools."

"I myself am no believer in Cru Creetha." The old guide shrugged blandly. "Yet I can show you reasons for the revival of his cruel faith. That's why I brought you here."

43

His crutch spun toward the smoke-darkened wall and its red-painted slogans.

"Here you see a chapter of our sad history, written in flame and blood. The tragedy of the Nggars. They're a foundation family—the first Nggar was one of those bold adventurers who opened the space gate and came through to build Nggonggamba. He grew fat on the sweat and blood of a million poor blacks gathering muskweed in the desert to make his famous perfumes. The generations of Nggars have always ruled that rich trade. Though they've married native women, they're still other-worlders, using their alien know-how to plunder Nggongga. That's why we don't love them."

With a startling savagery, his crutch slammed the smoky stone.

"That's why today you find NggeeNggar, the current family head, hiding in his compound with these marks of terror on the wall. That's why he has run off his black retainers and brought queer green speechless people from another world to be his bodyguards. That's why he has sent his son away to be educated on another planet. The Night clan fanatics are howling for his head."

"I think your whole stinking planet is sick." The professor of exoethnography elevated her sun-blistered nose. "If you want my professional opinion, you're too primitive for uncontrolled contact with civilization. You're suffering from technological shock. I think you need the doctors of progress. The Benefactors."

"I've known Benefactors." Unimpressed, the old guide shrugged. "Sometimes they keep a resident agent here. They have taken two of our young men to be trained on Xyr. I suppose they mean well, but what can two men do for a hundred million?

"Or against Cru Creetha?"

His crutch stabbed at the red-eyed dragon god.

"One of our cadets on Xyr is Lylik, the heir of Nggo Nggar. The other is now named Blacklantern, who fought

44

tlys in our arena here before he had a name. They are brave young men. I'm sure the Benefactors are training them well. But I'm afraid they'll find Cru Creetha harder to conquer than any unmilked tly.''

Xyr was a newfound ocean world whose islands held the administrative complex of the Benefactors, with the schools and labs and computers and everything else that made it the nerve center for the planned new universe of galactic man. In the first year there Blacklantern had chafed unhappily under the discipline of his instructors and the sophistication of his fellow cadets.

Things had gone better since Lylik came.

Fellow Nggonggans, they decided to room together. He liked Lylik's shy modesty about his family and his fortune, and Lylik admired his skills in the arena. They soon discovered more things in common—impatience with authority and pleasure in a fight.

At an off-limits bar in the interworld zone, they disabled a gang of cargo handlers who didn't like their color. On disciplinary probation for that, they exchanged daggers in the ritual of brotherhood he had learned in the arena, and Lylik began to share the native nuts and sweets that his mother sent from Nggonggamba.

In all his hard climb from the alleys and gutters of his childhood, he had never enjoyed such a genuine friend. He was distressed when he found Lylik worrying about trouble at home.

"There's always trouble on Nggongga." He tried to be cheerful. "We're too primitive to produce much but poverty and pain. That's why I want to be a Benefactor. To help bring civilization."

"The trouble is my parents." Lylik was chewing a saltflower seed and its narcotic sweetness filled their study room. "I can't find out what is really wrong. My father's too badly crippled to write and he won't make tapes because his voice is bad. My mother was hurt last year

45

when a Night clan terrorist tried to kill them. I don't know how badly. The nurse keeps writing that she's better, but I want to go home to see for myself."

Before he got permission to go, however, the shadow of terror fell across the long light-years from Nggongga. Classes were over that bright afternoon. Blacklantern had been teaching Lylik the weaves and feints and vaults of the arena and they were jogging across the hexangle toward the gym for another lesson. A queer high voice quavered behind them.

". . . Nggar!" Their translators took a moment to pick it up. "Cadet Lylik of Nggar! Spacemail parcel for you."

They waited for the yellow-clad carrier, a squat, pale, hairless man so massive that he looked monstrous. He gave Lylik the parcel and bounded away. Blacklantern glimpsed the stark ferocity on his face and sprang to intercept him. He snatched a dagger from beneath his flying cloak. Blacklantern danced in, grasping and twisting at the dagger arm as if it had been a tly's venomous sting. They grappled and recoiled. Blacklantern stumbled backward, the red-dripping dagger in his hand. The dwarf slumped toward Lylik, all his ferocity erased.

"My good mother!" Still unaware of their silent brief encounter, Lylik was tearing his parcel open. "Never too ill to send more Nggonggan goodies. She must think the Benefactors are starving—"

A thunder-crack cut off his voice.

A pale flash dazzled Blacklantern. A sudden gust slammed him forward. In the ringing calm that followed instantly, he turned to look for Lylik and the dwarf. Where they had been, a raw new crater was cut through turf and gravel and clay.

In the aftermath he stood in a tower office above the hexangle, relating that shattering incident to Benefactor Thornwall.

"Am I to blame?" He saw disapproval in the old man's eyes and felt a surge of indignation. "The dwarf was killing Lylik and attempting to escape. As Lylik's dagger-brother I owe blood for blood." A defiant satisfaction drew him erect. "The way things happened, I killed the killer."

"Which has unfortunate consequences," Thornwall said. "As violence commonly does. If the man had survived, he might have told us who sent him here."

"Lylik's parents have been attacked by the terrorists on Nggongga. I suppose the bomb came from there."

"Evidently." Thornwall nodded. "Though the device was not exactly a bomb. Our experts say it was part of a space gate. An ejection field circuit. Stolen, maybe, from some repair crew."

"So Lylik was thrown somewhere out of space?" He scowled at the red-robed Benefactor. "With no nexus bonds or receptor ring-fields to bring him back anywhere." His black hands lifted as if to grapple with a tly. "When I get out of training I want duty on Nggongga. I want to hunt the terrorists down—"

Thornwall held up a blue-veined hand.

"Cadet Blacklantern." His tone turned formal. "I have something painful to say. Your mentors have voted to terminate your preparatory fellowship. That means your training here has ended. We're sending you home—but not as a Benefactor."

"Why?" He found breath at last. "Because I killed that murderer?"

Slowly, sadly, Thornwall shook his silvered head.

"The error was mine when I brought you to Xyr. Or perhaps a blunder of the whole fellowship when we offered our aid to Nggongga. I'm afraid the planet is still too primitive for us."

"You promised," he whispered bitterly. "Promised to make me a Benefactor."

"But look at yourself." The old man paused, biting thin blue lips. "Remember that we condone no violence—and think of the blood we found on that dagger. I do admire

47

your courage. Even your skill at killing. But the mentors feel that you have always been too ready with every sort of weapon. I'm afraid you're violence-prone.''

"Where I grew up—" He drew a long uneven breath. "Where I grew up, you had to fight or die.''

"So I know.'' Thornwall's time-worn face twisted as if with actual pain. "But, as Benefactors, we are pledged to solve our problems with intelligence and compassion. I had hoped that our training might change you, but the evidence shows you killed that man with no thought at all, almost as a reflex act.''

"I—I don't understand.''

"That's the trouble,'' Thornwall said. "Precisely.''

"I want to be a Benefactor.'' Desperation shook his voice. "I—I'll try to learn, sir.''

"It is not only you.'' Thornwall frowned at the winking signals on his computer terminal. "Your whole world seems prone to excessive violence. We've just received distressing news from Nggongga. When our resident agent there unlocked his office this morning he triggered another implosion device.''

Blacklantern shivered inwardly from a sense of secret and implacable evil more deadly than any peril he had ever faced in the arena.

"Sorry.'' Thornwall gave him a stiff little bow of farewell. "The fault is only partly yours. We ourselves are not prepared to cope with terror. I might add, too, that I wanted to keep you here. I was overruled. There are too few of us and too many worlds where our aid is wanted.

"The Benefactors are pulling out of Nggongga.''

The girl spoke to him as he left the portal dome in Nggonggamba. In the moment before his translator picked up her language there was only the low-pitched music of her voice, which somehow recalled the midsummer songs of the Sand clan women. Eyes wide, he forgot that he had come home friendless and planless and almost desperate.

"—waiting for you," she was saying. "Did you know a cadet Benefactor named Lylik of Nggar?"

She was nearly his own height, with red-golden hair, pale-golden skin, green-golden eyes. Her garb was bright and oddly cut, too scant to shield her from the harsh Nggonggan sun, but he liked the way it displayed her clean athletic grace.

"Lylik was my dagger-brother." The words stabbed him again, like an actual blade. "His killing is a debt of blood I hope to pay."

"Perhaps I can help you."

He stepped backward warily, recalling the traps for newcomers he had sometimes helped to set. Travelers to and from a hundred worlds were hurrying past, but he saw no eyes on them. Sharply, he peered at her.

"I am *Dzanya Dzu*." That was the sound of it in her own melodious language, but his translator said "Snowfire." She showed him the name emblem of her ring: a gold flame rising from a white snow crystal. "You are Blacklantern?"

"Maybe," he admitted. "What do you want?"

She moved so close he caught her faint perfume, a cool sweetleaf scent.

"We could be watched," she murmured. "Let's go where we can talk."

"Why not?"

He followed her off the concourse into a wide arcade walled with shops. She stopped beneath a sign that winked NGGONGGAN EXPORTS—TAX FREE!

"Stand close," she whispered. "Act like you admire me."

Still distrustful, he eyed two young blacks inside the shop. They were haggling for an antique man-gun and he wondered if he might be their intended target. An old woman in white-fringed mourning was sniffing and selecting dry yellow stalks of muskweed incense. Breathing the familiar heavy bittersweetness, he was swept back

49

into his boyhood. Xyr was suddenly far away and old Thornwall's parting words no longer hurt so much. If he was really violence-prone, Nggongga was where he belonged.

"Now what?" He tried to recall his caution. "What about Lylik?"

"I know how he was killed."

She caught his hand to lead him along the displays. A tly's egg—or the dusty shell of one—crudely painted with the black-fanged grimace of Cru Creetha. A tray of hand-forged table daggers. Rough brown pottery bottles of seaberry wine. A shriveled black trophy head.

Cheap trash, he thought, laid out to trap arriving tourists. The egg was probably plexoid. The daggers were brittle cast metal. The wine would be a weak and evil-flavored imitation. The head had never been human. Yet he followed the girl, playing her game.

"I don't like terror." Her murmur was almost too faint for his translator. "Others don't. We're planning action. We need your talents and your training. If you really want to pay that debt of blood, you will join us."

The old woman had paid for the muskweed sticks. He inspected the trophy head while she shuffled by.

"Perhaps," he said then. "I need to know more."

"That's all I can say." She studied Cru Creetha's dusty snarl. "Until you have decided."

When he looked around the old woman was gone. One young black was testing the action of the old man-gun while the other paid. Drawing a deep breath of the fragrant muskweed cloud, he smiled at the girl.

"I'll go with you," he said.

Holding his hand, or walking so near that their hips and shoulders collided slightly, she led him out of the arcade into a long triangular park between two diverging ways that carried traffic from the portal. As they came into the open he felt her flinch from the sun's blinding glare, but he raised his face to it and inhaled again, enjoying the dry heat and the rich scents he had always known.

50

The park was almost empty, abandoned to the sun. At the far end a tiny knot of listeners were gathered around a shouting speaker. Nearer, a big man sat alone on an unshaded bench. Like lovers strolling, they approached him.

"Hello," the girl said. "I've found a friend."

Fair-skinned, the man wore the bright shorts and sandals of an unwarned other-worlder. With neither the enormous flat hat the natives had invented nor the cooler cloak the tourists wore, he was already burning. His head was a huge bald egg, now pink on top.

"Clayman," the girl murmured. "Blacklantern."

The man looked up through multiscopic glasses. They had heavy black rims around wide blank lenses. They whirred faintly, changing focus to inspect him.

"I hate terror." Clayman's voice clinked like metal. "We fight it. I believe Snowfire has invited you to join us."

"I—" Before the cold stare of those humming lenses he had to catch his breath. "I want to join."

"You understand our terms of enlistment?" The round pale face was almost genial, but the lenses looked inhuman and cold. "When you join us you're in for life. Beyond this point you cannot withdraw."

"I understand."

With no show of approval Clayman nodded at the opposite bench. They sat. Snowfire slipped her golden arm around Blacklantern. He breathed her slight, exciting scent.

"We call ourselves Counterkill." Clayman's voice was hushed, harsh. "Our emblem is lightning striking a coiled snake. We have all suffered from terror, but we strike back with a greater terror. Our discipline is strict. You will obey me absolutely. Is that clear?"

He glanced into the girl's bright face, troubled at the contrast between Clayman's flat deadliness and her appealing charm. When the lenses hummed, as if for a better focus, he realized that he had hesitated.

"Afraid?" the translator rasped. "You have already come too far to quit."

"I won't quit," he muttered hastily. "I've a debt of blood to pay."

Snowfire moved closer and murmured something, playing her role.

"One thing more," Clayman rapped. "We protect ourselves. Our cells are small. We kill snoopers. You are not to ask about anything beyond your duty. You will never reveal anything you happen to learn. Understand?"

"I do."

"A few facts you must know." Savagely, Clayman slapped a fly on his fleshy knee. "We operate elsewhere. Recently we learned that a shipment of twelve ejector field units had failed to reach a new portal under construction. We knew they could be modified to make implosion devices. When they began detonating, we came here to offer our services. We are already in contact with people who need us. We'll be meeting them later today."

"So the terrorists have ten more bombs?"

"I'll make the inferences," Clayman snapped. "You'll obey my orders.

Blacklantern felt an urge to hit him, but the girl was clinging to his arm.

"We're tourists here," she chattered gaily. "With historic sights to see. Let's begin."

"You had better get out of the sun," he told Clayman. "Or you won't be fit for anything."

Strolling down the park to the passenger ramps, they passed the white-robed speaker and his audience, all sweating beneath wide flat hats in the colors of their clans.

"—again I say it." The hoarse shouting arrested him. "The dark god Cru Creetha has appeared to me. I was alone on a sacred hill outside the city, lighting a dawn-fire to aid the return of the sun, when he came down from the sky."

52

Clayman went tramping on, but Blacklantern caught Snowfire's waist and stopped to listen.

"He appeared as a bodiless head. Larger than a man's. It had two great eyes, ringed with red fire. Floating in the smoke above the sacred fire, Cru Creetha called to me with a voice like monsoon thunder. He gave me the message I bring to you."

Snowfire tugged sharply to follow Clayman, but he swung her back to hear the speaker.

"Sunsdeath is coming—that was Cru Creetha's warning. He gave us nine days—and that was nine days ago. Tomorrow, friends, the sun will die! It cannot shine with Nggongga in bondage. When we drive the other-world exploiters out, it can be lit again. That is Cru Creetha's promise—"

"Come!" Snowfire whispered fiercely. "Our enemy is the man who operates the remote manipulator, not the superstitious dupe."

Walking on with her, he began to see the impact of terror on Nggongga. Ugly new concrete guard boxes stood along the portal ramps and the streets beyond had a gritty shabbiness he didn't remember. Armed police rode the traffic ways, and the passengers looked hurried and grim.

Clayman asked the way to a cooler shop, where he bought suncreams and cloaks for Snowfire and himself. At a gunshop he selected an expensive long-range man-gun. While they waited for him, Snowfire played her game of young love so attentively that Blacklantern began to wish it had been real. Clayman kept silent about their destination until he led them off the passenger way at the Nggar terminal.

They crossed the ramp and Clayman thumbed the keyplate at the bomb-scarred gate. The portal system had brought many strange races to Nggongga, but Blacklantern was startled by the guards who opened a wicket.

Naked except for gun belts and short black kilts, they

53

were hairless and darkly green. Even their bulging eyes were green. Half his height and twice his weight, they looked as monstrous as the dwarf he had fought on Xyr. Their evolution, he thought, must have been shaped by a singular environment.

Though they wore translators, they didn't attempt to speak. One stood watching, man-gun drawn. The other vanished and soon came back with a heavy, slow, light-brown man who dragged one leg.

"The Nggar," Snowfire whispered. "Nggee of Nggar."

He opened the bottom of the gate to let them in and came limping to meet Blacklantern. His kilt was Sand clan red. Half his face was smiling, the other half scarred and frozen, hideous.

"Blackie!" His voice was a hollow whisper. "Lylik used to speak about you on the tapes he sent from Xyr. I'm glad you're going to be with us."

He held out his sound hand in the Nggonggan greeting and they touched palms. Blacklantern tried not to look at his face. Lylik had seldom spoken of his father's disabilities, but now he recalled a story he had heard long ago from an old tly handler—that the young Nggar, trying his courage in the arena, had been badly stung by an unmilked tly.

"I hope you aren't alarmed at my people." He waved at the froglike guards. "They look that way because they're off a heavy planet, one with lots of copper and a hot blue sun. I've got them here because I can't trust the blacks. They're contract labor. Slaves, actually. Their masters don't recognize the Benefactors. I get them through a barter deal. Their translators are set only to mine, to save them from corruption."

As he talked he had led them into a wide, brick-paved yard, walled with crowded and ill-matched buildings erected by three generations of Nggars. A bright new business tower overlooked the loading docks of a rust-streaked sheet-metal warehouse that exhaled a rich muskweed fragrance. The huge stone residential palace had been enlarged several times in clashing styles. A squat green woman stood waiting at the door.

"My friends are coming later to meet with you," Nggar said. "While we wait, Kopopo will show you your rooms."

Mute, she beckoned with a green enormous hand.

"Wait, please." Blacklantern turned back to the lame man. "May I speak to your wife? About Lylik? My dagger-brother—"

"My wife is ill." Pain clouded the live half of Nggar's face. "She was hurt last year, when the terrorists booby-trapped our flyer. Badly hurt. She has never recovered. We were afraid to tell her that Lylik is dead. She requires sedation and she never leaves her room."

"I'm sorry," Blacklantern muttered uncomfortably. "I didn't know."

The green woman had waddled away and he ran to overtake her. On an upper floor of the rambling palace she gave him a key-strip and pointed at a door. Inside, he discovered that the room had been Lylik's.

Brown images of Lylik smiled out of a long stereo tank, standing with arena heroes or with glamorous girls. A crystal case held athletic awards he had earned. One whole wall was hung with family portraits, heavily framed. Of the grandparents, only one had been a light-skinned other-worlder. The rest were mixed or black.

Studying the portraits, Blacklantern felt a darkening shadow of mystery and tragedy. He looked longest at Lylik's mother. No darker than Snowfire, she sat proudly, almost defiantly erect. Her dark eyes looked stricken, desolate.

Why? The picture must have been made before the terror, before her own injury, long before her son's death. What had she foreseen? Her ivory face became a tantalizing riddle.

He prowled the room, searching for clues to that sad puzzle. Beyond the bed he found a heavy inner door.

Somewhere beyond it must be the room that held that tragic prisoner. Suddenly he felt that he had to see her in spite of Nggar.

With his ear against the door he heard no sound at all. It was locked, but his hard childhood had taught him how to cope with locks. On impulse, without stopping to weigh the consequences, he masked and fingered his key-strip to open the door.

What he found was no sickroom. Rather, it must have been Lylik's playroom and hobby room. Shelves along one wall held toys and games, long outgrown. Newer metal-working tools lined another wall. One long bench was cluttered with half-assembled electronic and transflection gear. Model spacecraft hung from the ceiling. Toward the end of the room an old study desk had been rebuilt into a flight simulator with viewscreens and controls.

A normal boy's room, it told of Lylik's boyhood but offered no clue to the mystery of the Nggars. He found another locked door behind the flight simulator. Listening again, he still heard nothing.

He froze a moment there, key-strip already against the contact plate, hesitant to go on. He knew he shouldn't enjoy the risks of adventure as much as he did, but then, he reflected, he was violence-prone. Though he shouldn't be violating the house of a friend, he had his debt to Lylik. He listened again and opened the door.

A short dark stair led three steps down to an older level of the rambling palace. He found himself in a huge wardrobe. One side was hung with kilts and cloaks and hats in Nggar's Sand clan rust-color. A woman's clothing hung along the other side, fragrant with rose-tempered musk.

Nothing stirred in the huge, high-beamed bedroom beyond. Anxiously he crept around the big antique canopy bed. The curtains were lifted and the bed was empty. If Lylik's invalid mother were confined any-where—

He heard a gasp.

Whirling, he found a startled girl framed in the open bathroom door, still dripping from the tub, her long red hair dark with dampness. Her wide eyes as green as Snowfire's. She was not Lylik's mother.

After one breathtaken moment the woman laughed.

"No Name!" She made no move to cover herself. "I was expecting someone else." She glanced swiftly at the other door. "What are you after?"

"I was looking for Lylik's mother."

"You won't find her here." Her cool green gaze came back to him. "I thought you were learning to be a Benefactor."

"I was." He eyed her again with unwilling admiration. "You were under arrest the last time I saw you."

"My luck is running better now." She made a possessive nod at everything around her. "I have a friend—and a new name of my own. If we happen to meet don't call me Sapphire. Now I'm Diamond Dust."

"Fitting." He gave her a small ironic bow. "Your old friend Wheeler—where is he?"

"He too has discovered better luck. With another name to match. Squaremark. He's a banker."

"He's a crook."

"We've all had our troubles." Her eyes narrowed, probing him. "I suppose you're here with Counterkill. Even so, you have no business in my room. I'll make a bargain with you." She smiled in a way he remembered bitterly. "You'll forget Sapphire and Wheeler. I'll forget that you were here."

With a painful grin he shook his head.

"I know you too well, Sapphire—or whatever. I couldn't trust your promise. I'm afraid I couldn't keep mine. Because I am with Counterkill."

For an instant her face looked dangerous.

"I can destroy you—" Suddenly she smiled again, turning slowly in the doorway to display herself. "We're old friends. Perhaps you'll be back at a better time. If you survive the terror—"

Her head cocked to listen and her low voice died. Silently she beckoned him into the closet. He returned to Lylik's room, relocking the doors behind him. When he opened the corridor door he found a squat green female planted outside, a silent sentry. He retreated to reflect again on the dark plight of the house of Nggar.

Nggogga's rotation was slower than Xyr's. No longer used to thirty-hour days, he had fallen into an uneasy sleep before Snowfire called him. She had changed into a clinging crimson sheath that accented her hair and eyes in a way that made him wonder if she had already met Nggar's other green-eyed guest. His silent guardian was gone.

"You'll be meeting the people who hired us." She was guiding him down a great stair toward a lower floor. With no audience for her game of young love, she was now crisply impersonal. "Friends of Nggar's who have been threatened by the terrorists.

"Yava Yar comes from another rich foundation family. One brother owns mines. Another has airways and factories. He's an astronomer, the one who found the cometary dust cloud. He showed it to us last night with a little telescope Nggar's son built.

"Longbridge is a churchman. An other-worlder, as you'd guess from the name. Head of the All Worlds Mission. The terrorists dislike him because his church is uprooting the native faiths. He doesn't believe in Cru Creetha.

"The third man is Squaremark—"

He almost missed a step.

"Another other-worlder," she went on. "A banker. He has made an enormous new fortune speculating in muskweed and the exported perfume made from it. The terrorists seem to feel that he's exploiting the native muskweed industry."

He followed her into a huge dim room massively furnished with Nggonggan antiques. One gloomy alcove was filled with racked man-guns and grinning trophy heads. Nggar came limping across the tly-wing patterns of a fine old Sand clan carpet to escort them to the heavy table where Clayman sat facing three troubled men.

In his voiceless rasp, Nggar introduced them.

Yava Yar was a short brown man, evidently of mixed ancestry. His small dark eyes were darting everywhere, at Snowfire and Blacklantern, at Clayman, at the two men beside him, as if in tormented apprehension.

Longbridge looked too pale and lean and tall for Nggongga. He must have come, Blacklantern thought, from a world with a cooler sun and weaker gravity. His hollowed eyes had a remote, unseeing stare, as if fixed on unpleasant things beyond.

Squaremark—once called Wheeler was flabby and shapeless and gray. His bulging glassy eyes rested on Blacklantern with no hint of recognition.

Clayman sat bolt upright across the table from them, his hands and arms and hairless head all smeared white with suncream. Masked behind the opaque multiscope lenses, he looked more mechanical than human.

"Blacklantern is a native Nggonggan." Completing his introductions, Nggar smiled with half his face. "He has been trained for the arena and trained to be a Benefactor. Perhaps he can help us locate the hiding Sun Lighter."

He waved Snowfire and Blacklantern to chairs beside Clayman. Bending painfully, he opened a safe hidden under the table and sat up to show a heavy little device the size of his fist.

"This was tossed through my bedroom window last night," his strained whisper hissed. "As you see, it didn't operate. In the light from the room I glimpsed the thing that threw it. The god Cru Creetha, as the native fanatics describe him. A huge black head with blazing red eyes and snaky metal tentacles."

Voiceless, his sardonic laugh rattled like dry gravel.

"Actually a remote manipulator."

"A proxy box," Clayman agreed. "Common enough

on advanced planets. Used for work too hazardous for men. I'm surprised to find one here."

"Can you trace the control signals?" Nggar asked. "To locate the master station?"

"Probably not." Clayman shook his white-plastered head. "The beam would be tight and shielded. In use only briefly. We couldn't hope to intercept it."

Nggar pushed the fist-sized device across the table to him. "Does this tell you anything?"

"A modified ejector circuit." Clayman turned it in chalk-white hands, his blank lenses whining. "Modified to make an implosion bomb. Expertly done by a workman who understands transflection technology. Fortunately the detonator jammed—damaged, probably, when the device struck the window."

"That's how close I've come." The hoarse whisper quivered. "But we're all in the same danger."

Nggar looked along the table, at the restless little astronomer, the far-staring churchman, the impassive banker. None of them spoke.

"This terror is—intolerable!" His dry wheeze had a savage force. "With Sunsdeath upon us, we're desperate." With a pause to recover himself, he twisted painfully to give Clayman a stiff Nggonggan bow. "Counterkill is our one hope. We've met your terms, costly as you are. We'll do anything you advise."

"Before we start we need information." Clayman's audible syllables clinked like coins. "We can't act without facts."

"You'll have to find the facts," Nggar whispered. "We've failed. Sun Lighter has too many friends. There are two hundred million blacks on the planet. Every one enjoys ten times more wealth and comfort than the clan chiefs did before the portal opened. Yet I suppose most of them feel they have been somehow robbed or wronged by other-worlders. There has always been a secret war against us. Just look at me."

A withered hand lifted to his blighted face.

"I was a whole man once. Being the heir of a foundation family, I had to try my luck in the arena. I was tly-stung. A tragic accident—but not entirely accidental. My tly had not been properly milked of its venom. The handler who failed to milk it was a black who didn't love me."

The live half of his face twitched with pain.

"I should have died, but I suppose there are blacks who enjoy each tormented breath I draw. When I was young, such events were rare. Year by year the war has grown more open and more grim. Two years ago I had to send my son away to what I thought was safety. Last year my wife was crippled hopelessly."

"Now, Sunsdeath!" Little Yava Yar was abruptly on his feet, too nervous to sit. "Something more than a silly superstition. I'll show you the cometary dustcloud which obscures our star on some of its returns. Sun Lighter and his fanatics have made it a signal for the blacks to rise. The end of civilization on Nggongga. Unless—"

"Unless we defeat the terror." Clayman looked up and down the table. "We expect to win, but we do require your aid."

His whirring lenses settled on the anxious astronomer.

"Respected Yava Yar, you can help deflate the panic." Though the translated words were courteous, the audible tone was coldly commanding. "Invite the media to observe the dustcloud. Convince the people that this eclipse is a natural thing."

"I—I tried to announce my discovery," Yava Yar stammered fearfully. "People won't believe. The street fanatics threaten me with the wrath of Cru Creetha."

"Speak out," his hard tone rang. "You're fighting for your life."

Clayman's blank stare moved on to the churchman.

"Respected Longbridge, you will join this effort. Instruct your clergymen to explain the eclipse. Ask them to pray for compassion and peace."

61

"We have done so," Longbridge said. "The terrorists have burned out missions."

Clayman looked at the banker, who sat hunched in his chair, rubbing at his puffy jaw.

"Respected Squaremark, you will offer rewards for information. Generous rewards. For the taking of any terrorist. For any fact to help us find the hiding leader."

The banker grunted and inclined his head. Blacklantern caught the stale salt taint on his breath and knew that he had been triggering a narcotic implant.

"Respected Nggar"—Clayman swung again—"you will provide supplies and support as the need arises."

"Done."

"That's our part." The gaunt churchman's stare came suddenly back from nowhere to rest darkly and briefly in turn upon Snowfire, Blacklantern, and Clayman. "What is yours?"

"To fight the terror we must first find the terrorists." Clayman glanced down at the glinting metal and yellow plexoid of the bomb. "This is the only clue you have given us. The missing Sun Lighter is the only suspect you have named. I understand he has been in hiding for years. If you want action, tell me how to hit him."

Before his humming lenses, the table was silent. The banker massaged his jaw. Yava Yar bobbed up and sat down again. The churchman looked back into his own dark infinity. Nggar twitched and quivered as if to a spasm of pain.

Blacklantern spoke. "I can look for him," he offered. "I used to see him begging on the streets. He had a friend—a man who sometimes filled his bowl—who might know where he went."

Hope rustled around the table.

"Who?" Nggar bent painfully forward. "Who's the friend?"

"I never knew his name. An old man who had lost a leg in the tly arena. A tourist guide—"

"Old Champ!" Nggar wheezed. "I knew him around

the arena long ago, though he's no friend. It was his brother who should have milked the tly that stung me."

"No matter," Clayman rapped. "Where is he now?"

"Retired. Gone to Krongkor—that's an old Sea clan city. I believe he owns a hotel there. The Pilgrims Rest. I used to stay there when I was buying muskweed. I can call him, but I expect no favors."

"We'll see him," Clayman snapped. "We can persuade him."

Nggar offered a flyer and Clayman mapped their strategy. He would be an other-worlder journalist, doing a Sunsdeath story. Snowfire would be his pilot and they would leave at once. Blacklantern felt cheered to have a plan for action, but Snowfire called him and Clayman aside as they left the hall.

"I'm afraid we're on a false trail." Her voice was hushed and troubled. "That old native priest may hate other-worlders bitterly enough. But I don't think he'd have the use of remote manipulators and implosion bombs."

"We're fighting paradoxes." Staring blankly, Clayman shrugged off her objection. "Perhaps the Night clan priests have learned to fight technology with technology, as we fight terror with terror. In any case we must follow the trail. It's the only one we have."

A mute green woman escorted them up a long stair. When they climbed into the night, Snowfire gasped with awe. The moonless sky was alive with streaks of vivid fire, blazing and fading, all radiant from a point in the north.

"Meteors!" shouted Yava Yar, who had followed up the stairs with Longbridge. "From the swarm around the cosmic dustcloud. We're already in its fringes." He beckoned them toward the small telescope that must have been Lylik's on a railed platform beyond the airpad. "Come along if you want to see the cloud."

"No time," Clayman rapped. "We're just waiting for my luggage."

Snowfire had climbed into the little flyer. She was inspecting the controls. Blacklantern and Clayman stood outside, watching the meteor-fall. Twenty yards away Yava Yar and Longbridge approached the telescope. A green woman started from the stairwell with Clayman's heavy bag—

A deafening concussion slapped Blacklantern's ears. A hot gust brushed him. When he could hear again, the green woman was wailing strangely, running for the stair. Where the telescope had stood, there was only broken rubble. Yava Yar and Longbridge were gone.

That cruel concussion left a frozen hush upon the roof platform. Soundless, the meteor needles still stabbed down the night sky. Nothing moved until Nggar came limping up the stair followed by a handful of his green retainers. Circling the pit in the roof where the telescope had stood, he shuffled toward the flyer.

"Another implosion!" His crippled whisper shook. "We can guard the gates, but we can't stop that proxy box—which they must have used to plant the bomb." He stared at Clayman. "What are we to do?"

"Find Sun Lighter." Clayman's audible voice crackled with confidence. "Recover the rest of the bombs—eight of the missing devices are yet to be accounted for. Smash the terror group. Trust Counterkill!"

They took off.

Blacklantern had an eerie sensation of escape. All he could hear was a muffled rush of air. The dark compound dropped away and they climbed into the silent wonder of the firefall. Snowfire sat quiet beside him, the light of the meteors dancing on her ivory loveliness. For a moment he felt that they had risen out of terror into a world of winking splendor.

But his head still rang from that near implosion, and Clayman sat close behind them, the new man-gun under his cloak, watching everything. The terror flew with them.

Snowfire's silent presence tantalized him. He thought

she looked too clean and fine for Counterkill, with none of Clayman's ruthless coldness. If anything had ever wounded her, as Lylik's killing had wounded him, she showed no scars. He wanted to penetrate her cool reserve, to learn what she was and why she was here, but, caught before Clayman's humming lenses, he could say nothing.

The flight was brief. They dropped out of the blazing sky, toward the fainter lights of old Krongkor. Snowfire set them on the new airpad built above the old hotel. They emerged into a cool dank sea scent, and unhurried blacks escorted them down into a monumental lobby. Champ had been out on his beach, watching the meteor storm. At sight of Blacklantern, his seamed face lit.

"The nameless challenger! I was in the stands the day you were tly-stung." His dark eyes sharpened. "Are you already a Benefactor?"

"I'm afraid I'll never be."

Blacklantern turned to present Snowfire and Clayman.

"I'm an interworld mediaman," Clayman announced. "I'm here to do the Nggonggan story. I know the other-worlders and I've met the foundation families. Now I want to see the black side."

"I'm black." Champ had met ten thousand egotistic tourists, and he didn't look impressed. "Look at me."

The dark lenses whirred, blindly peering.

"I'm searching out the secret soul of black Nggongga," Clayman boomed, his loud audible voice as smooth as oil. "Now, with Sunsdeath coming, I want to explore the hopes and terrors related to it. I believe the old Night clan shaman is still alive. I hope you can help me find him."

"Sun Lighter?" Astonished, the old man swung to Blacklantern. "You're looking for Sun Lighter?"

"I used to see you filling his bowl," Blacklantern said. "I told the respected Clayman you had been his friend."

"I knew him." Champ swung on his good leg to study Clayman's white-painted strangeness. With an inquiring side glance at Snowfire, he shrugged and continued, "But he has gone home."

"Where's that?"

"Brongeel. A sacred place of the Night clan." Reserved at first, the old man spoke with growing animation, almost as if he were escorting tourists again. "In the legends of the clan, it was the nest of the monster gods. Cru Creetha was hatched there. But the first fathers of the Night clan killed his monster mother and purified the spot so that he can never return—unless he is able to destroy Sun Lighter and bring back the everlasting dark."

"Do you know where Brongeel is?"

"I used to guide tourists to the old ruins of the old holy city. It's below the equator, in the highlands of our dry hemisphere. In a region too dry for muskweed or even for wild tlys and nearmen. The priests used to live on the pilgrims who came to beg them to keep the sun alive."

"Can you guide us there?"

"I'm retired." Champ moved one thin black hand in a native gesture of weary negation. "The old pilgrim trails are gone—so are the pilgrims. The Night clan cult was almost dead even before the other-worlder astronomers and preachers came through the portal to break our old beliefs. Besides, I think Sun Lighter would have no time for visitors now. When he saw Sunsdeath coming, he went home to be ready. He'll be at work tomorrow fighting Cru Creetha and restoring the sun."

"That's what I want to see," Clayman urged. "We'll pay well."

Champ waved a firm refusal.

"What of the new Cru Creetha?" Hopefully, Blacklantern tried another angle. "The one who is haunting Nggonggamba now, throwing implosion bombs and calling on the people to wash the streets with the blood of other-worlders?"

"I left the city to get away from that." Champ looked both puzzled and indignant. "It makes no sense to me, using other-world inventions against other-worlders. But it is no work of the true Sun Lighter. He has no love for the gifts of the portal, but he's no terrorist."

"Many people think he is," Blacklantern objected. "If you would help the respected Clayman reach him, the truth might help us end panic and terror in Nggong-gamba."

Champ leaned on his yellow crutch, frowning solemnly.

"I'll show you the way," he decided at last. "But the distance is long and the landmarks are dim. We must wait for daylight."

Blacklantern was glad to stay. In the beginning he had expected to meet the terrorists like tlys in the arena. If he was really violence-prone, he needed a target to attack. With no visible opponent he felt frustrated. The terror had become a baffling nightmare, the mystery of the Nggars a hopeless riddle he longed to forget.

After Clayman had gone upstairs, he sat with Snowfire in a long, high-ceilinged dining room that overlooked the beach. They ordered seafood. The waiter was elderly and slow, unalarmed by the rain of meteors toward the sea.

"Sunsdeath comes." He shrugged and refilled their glasses with dark seaberry wine. "Perhaps the sun is eaten by a god. Perhaps it goes behind a cloud. No matter to me. I think the sun has winked before."

Snowfire liked the food and wine. She exclaimed at the dancing splendor in the sky. She asked about the dishes they were served, about muskweed trading and perfume making, about man-guns and trophy hunts, about wild tlys and nearmen, about his own adventures in the arena.

At first he was slow to speak of himself, but her interest seemed genuine. It began to arouse him. Even though he had been born nameless and clanless on this backward planet, even though he was black, she accepted him. As they finished the wine, he felt excited again with the game of young love she had played when she met him, and suddenly he hoped to make it real.

Yet he had learned on Xyr that customs of sex and marriage differed vastly in different cultures. Afraid of

67

anger or laughter, he asked again how she came to be in Counterkill.

"A long story." She rose abruptly to leave the table. "Too long for tonight."

In the corridor upstairs he tried to kiss her. She slipped away from him, green eyes wide. Yet she smiled at his look of dismay and turned back to touch his forehead with one golden finger. Before he could learn what that gesture meant, she was gone into her room.

With daybreak the meteors vanished, though the sky had a copper-colored dustiness. The same calm and ancient black served their breakfast.

"Perhaps the sun winks today." The windows were open, and he nodded almost casually at the ominous sky. "Perhaps it does not. Either way, men must eat." He shrugged. "The fish is a fresh catch, sir."

When Champ was ready they boarded the flyer. He sat with Snowfire in the forward seat to show her the way. On his last trip to Brongeel, he told them, he had been with other-world anthropologists, digging up sites along the old pilgrim trail and among the ruins of the holy city itself. He had been a young man then, with two good legs.

They flew south from the sea, over the dark-green fingers of watered valleys, over the wooded coastal range, over vast brown highlands dotted here and there with clumps of purple muskweed, over dry salt lakes and red clay hills.

The dust storms of centuries had erased the actual roads. His landmarks were the bend of a dry canyon, the shape of a white salt pan, the outline of a distant peak. Lost, once, he had Snowfire circle lower until he found his bearings.

Clayman raised a partition behind the forward seat. Leaning back as if to sleep, he whispered harshly to Blacklantern:

"Listen! We must be ready for action. First, perhaps, against the black. If he moves when I pull my gun, you cut his throat."

He slipped a long dagger into Blacklantern's hand.

The empty land slid back beneath, until a black cinder-cone like a volcanic islet rose from a sea of yellow sand ahead. Champ pointed. Snowfire rapped on the partition. When Clayman sat up to open it she said the mountain was Brongeel.

The dagger had become so hot and heavy in Blacklantern's sweaty clutch that he began to doubt that he was really violence-prone. Watching for signs that the terrorists' stronghold would be defended, he saw none. No lasers stabbed them, no missiles met them, no shells exploded.

Circling the dead volcano, they flew across the time-shattered walls and sand-drowned domes of the old temple town. At a signal from Clayman Snowfire brought them down inside the broken crater.

Even then he saw no sign of man till old Champ pointed out a squat black tower, crudely built of mortared lava blocks on the farther rim. A spiral path wound around it to the top.

"The holy spot." Champ sounded wearily ironic. "We've reached the womb of all creation. All life springs from here. When the sun must be rekindled, Sun Lighter climbs to the altar and burns three sacrificial sticks."

"Is this all?" Lenses whining as the focus changed, Clayman was peering about the crater, looking for the master station that controlled the remote manipulator, for the hidden arsenal that still held eight implosion bombs. "Isn't anybody here?"

"There." Champ pointed. "The holy family."

They came out of a cave in a lava cliff. A thin old man stumbling blindly over the rocks, a dirty bandage around his head. A tattered black woman, holding his arm to guide him. A naked boy who clung to the woman's other hand.

"Are you sure?" Clayman hissed. "Is that Sun Lighter?"

"An old friend." Champ was reaching for his crutch preparing to leave the flyer. "He was still the holy child when I brought the anthropologists here. That was before he had to give his eyes—''

''Quiet!'' Clayman snapped.

With a sharp nod at Blacklantern he slid his window down. His man-gun rattled. The blind man staggered. The woman shrieked. The naked boy tried to run. All three crumpled.

''Why?'' Snowfire gasped. ''Why do that?''

Clayman's gun swung toward the forward seat. Trembling, Blacklantern gripped the dagger. He saw Champ touch the yellow crutch, saw him freeze.

''I fight terror,'' Clayman rapped. ''I don't take chances.''

His gun gestured at Blacklantern.

''Get out. Look for implosion devices.''

Shaken, Blacklantern climbed out into furnace heat. He crossed incandescent sand to the lava cliff. Beneath a narrow ledge he found a dwelling—a pile of filthy rags, a few bits of dried fruit and meat in a battered metal pot, a brown leather bag that held a worn fire-drill and three dry sticks.

There were no implosion bombs.

When he came out of the cave the sky had begun to change. All around the horizon the copper dust had darkened to the color of the sun's blood, shed in the mythic battle with Cru Creetha. Overhead it was purple-blue.

The sunlight in the lava cup was pale as Xyr's moonlight, its heat gone. He stopped to form a pinhole with his fingers, to cast the sun's image on the sand. Half its disk had disappeared.

Plodding slowly toward the plane, he paused beside the holy family. Sun Lighter lay face upward. For the last time his wide blind eyes gazed at the sky. His blood stained the yellow sand, queerly blue in the failing light. Flies buzzed around him.

''—grateful, I think.'' He heard Champ's voice, oddly quiet. ''He had no real believers left. If there are Night clan people in Nggonggamba now, they never followed him. I think he knew long ago that he would never live to light the sun. Bullets, I think, are kinder than starvation."

Clayman shouted at Blacklantern, asking what he had found.

"Nothing."

The man-gun swung to beckon him aboard.

"So this is Counterkill?" He stood beside the dead family, quivering with a hot contempt for Clayman and himself. "I once thought we had a worthy cause. But we've done nothing"—his sick eyes fell to the dead family—"except to cross half a world of desert and kill three harmless people. We're red-handed fools!"

They touched down twice again before they left Brongeel. On the black altar tower whose fires had burned to rekindle the sun. On wind-rippled sand beneath a shattered dome in what had been a temple court. They found no master station, no bombs, nothing else alive.

The sun by then was a thinning reddened ember, so pale they could look directly at it. The purple night around it was falling toward the strange-hued horizon, and a sudden wind whipped dust around the broken columns.

"So we lost one toss." Clayman's flat cold voice held no audible regret. "We may win the next."

He moved to the forward seat before they took off and ordered Snowfire to fly straight to Nggonggamba. In the rear seat with Champ, Blacklantern tried and failed to wash the blind staring image of the dead Sun Lighter out of his mind.

Since Clayman dropped his journalistic mask, Champ had been told about Counterkill and informed that knowing made him a member, willy-nilly, under Clayman's command. He took the situation philosophically, as if he had seen too many other-worlder follies to be upset by anything.

"If I were hunting terrorists I wouldn't be shooting ignorant blacks." He offered Blacklantern a saltflower seed, crunched one himself, chewed contemplatively. "I'd look for a clever city man. An interworlder, maybe.

71

A money pirate looking for the loot he can find on backward worlds like Nggongga.''

"A man like Squaremark?" Blacklantern speculated. "I knew him when his name was Wheeler. He was selling illegal implant drugs and fixing tly fights." Bitterness edged his voice. "I might have been an arena champ myself but for him."

"But his money's paying us." An expressionless robot in his thick white suncream, Clayman twisted to look back. "Perhaps he had an unfortunate past, but he's a respected banker now."

"I can tell you how he got his money," the old man answered. "I got the story from the gossip of the muskweed dealers who put up at my hotel. He robbed Nggar."

"Impossible!" Clayman sniffed. "They're still friends."

"Perhaps Nggar doesn't know who hit him." With a quiet relish, Champ licked his purple lips. "The theft was cunning. Even the muskweed dealers don't know how it was done."

"What was stolen?"

"A priceless secret," Champ said. "A way of making perfume. The Sand clan chiefs had always been perfumers, before the portal opened. The art was their great treasure. The first Nggar got it when he married the daughter of a chief.

"He built his fortune on the essence and passed it to his son. Other clever other-worlders tried to analyze and imitate it but they never quite succeeded. With the secret the Nggars were masters to the muskweed industry and the kings of all perfumers.

"Till Squaremark got the essence!"

Champ rubbed his lips with a handkerchief, and the sharp sweetness of his spittle began to fill the flyer.

"Squaremark keeps under cover," he added. "There are native agents who buy the weed—with funds borrowed from his bank. There is an interworld syndicate that makes and sells the essence—and his bank owns the syndicate.''

"A wild accusation.'' Clayman snorted. ''I see no proof.''

"I have none,'' Champ admitted. ''Just muskweed talk.''

"You haven't connected Squaremark with the terror,'' Clayman persisted. ''He may have been unethical but he is still an other-worlder. What could he hope to gain by turning the blacks against his own kind?''

"We're only talking.'' Champ shrugged. ''But I think Squaremark brought a habit of using terror when he came to Nggongga. From the time the syndicate got into the business, Nggar's buyers have been ambushed in the desert. His water holes have been poisoned. His ricks of curing weed have been burned. He had to turn his own compound into a fortress and send his son away to Xyr. His wife was murdered—''

"Murdered?'' Blacklantern echoed. ''I thought she was only hurt.''

"Killed,'' Champ said. ''By explosives planted in their flyer. About the time the son was sent away. That was when Nggar locked out his own blacks, because he didn't trust them, and brought in his green dwarf slaves.''

"He never told Lylik she was dead,'' Blacklantern muttered. ''I wonder why?''

"A strange man.'' Champ wiped his purple mouth. ''I hated him once. When we both were young braves about the tly arena. Still whole men. He was part white—and too proud of it. Sometimes nasty. Perhaps I was glad to see him stung.''

His eyes rested on the darkened desert, where red-black shadows had begun to clot.

"I've pitied him since,'' he went on. ''Because he has suffered too much. I would like to know how he came to lose the Sand clan essence.''

"There's a girl''—Blacklantern leaned sharply forward—"living with him now. She used to be with Squaremark when his name was Wheeler. She's—she could have been beautiful. She has been a thief."

"What girl?" Clayman stared, lenses buzzing. "Why didn't you tell us?"

"Her new name is Diamond Dust," he said. "I decided that Nggar's private life was none of my business."

"She's *my* business," Clayman said gratingly. "I'll find what she's up to."

The unnatural dark grew denser, until meteors streaked the sky again with Cru Creetha's whiskers. Snowfire snapped a switch as they neared Nggonggamba and a tight voice blasted from the cybernet:

" . . . sabotage! The portal is closed. Disorder is reported on the traffic ways. Though municipal authorities will not confirm rumors of an extremist plot to destroy the portal and massacre aliens, police are urging light-skinned individuals to avoid public places. . . ."

Pillars of smoky flame stood here and there about the city. As they came down toward the Nggar compound, Blacklantern had a glimpse of passenger ways jammed with people in panic flight.

"Wait here!" Clayman rolled clumsily out of the flyer. "While I find Nggar and get the truth about this woman. If she has been a spy for Squaremark, I think we'll find the master station in the tower of his bank."

They waited. Nggar's green guards had disappeared. The dusty sweetness of cured muskweed drifted from the dark yard below, mixed with a bitter smoke-reek. Shrill voices came faintly from the traffic way. Champ calmly chewed his seed. Snowfire sat very quiet; again Blacklantern thought her too clean and fine to be involved in Counterkill—

He saw her start. Her mouth gaped open. She crouched back from the window of the flyer, pale hands lifted. Jumping out, he heard a descending roar in the meteor-needled sky. In a moment he found the proxy box, diving at them.

An armored oval, painted like that tly's egg in the shop with Cru Creetha's black-fanged grin. Two wide-spaced camera eyes, ringed with red lamps. Two manipulator arms hanging from it, one steel hand clutching the small bright implosion bomb.

He clutched for a weapon, but all he found was Clayman's useless dagger. Snowfire and Champ had scrambled out behind him, the girl unarmed, the old man waving his yellow crutch.

"Champ!" A great metal voice drummed from the fiery sky. "Your gift from Cru Creetha!"

The manipulator hurled the implosion device.

For an instant Blacklantern felt nakedly defenseless. If he had ever been violence-prone, this was too much violence. But the twin lamps were flashing red as the armor of a fighting tly, the black-and-yellow bomb came slashing down like a stabbing sting.

He vaulted past old Champ as if to meet a diving tly. He reached to seize the sting. Very gently, yielding to the force of the falling bomb and letting its own mass move him, he pivoted and tossed it back. He saw it strike the black-fanged head.

The darkness winked and crashed.

A smoky gust struck him and the proxy box was gone. His head ringing from the blast, he turned to lean against the flyer door. His knees were quivering. He saw Snowfire speaking but he couldn't hear what she said.

Smiling palely, she bent to place one finger on his lips. Again he had to shake his head, wishing he understood the folkways of her world.

Clayman came back across the airpad at a stumbling run. He was breathing hard, gripping his man-gun. His lenses whirred as if hunting for a focus in the flickering dimness.

"The bomb?" he panted. "What got hit?"

"The proxy box." Snowfire's voice came faintly through the roaring in his ears. "With its own bomb. Thanks to our Benefactor."

"But we're too late—too late to help Nggar." Clayman's lenses lifted toward the fire-bearded sky, and Blacklantern heard the quivering desperation beneath his stiff white mask. "Can't find him. Can't find the girl. Only those green slaves—some of them scared white —barricaded in a muskweed warehouse. They took a shot at me!"

He wheezed for his breath.

"Another implosion crater. Down in the freight yard. A hole in the wall of the perfume factory." The multiscopic glasses settled on Snowfire. "The way I see the picture, Squaremark and his girl were trying to escape. Alarmed, I think, by Counterkill. Nggar tried to stop them. They hit him with a bomb."

"I think I see a different picture." Blacklantern turned. "I think I can find Nggar—if we're quick enough."

Clayman muttered doubtfully, but followed him at Snowfire's urging. He ran down the stairs, hurried through the echoing corridors of the vacant palace. His masked key-strip let him into Lylik's old room, where he had stayed, unlocked the farther door.

He flung it open.

In Lylik's childhood playroom beyond, they found Nggar standing at a workbench beneath the hanging model spacecraft that Lylik must have built. On the live half of his scar-hardened face shocked surprise became a sheepish grin.

"More terror than I can take!" His voiceless laugh rattled like dry seed in a manskull pod. "When that last bomb crashed I ran in here to hide."

"I know why you're here." He was shuffling toward the flight simulator built on the old study desk, and Blacklantern sprang to block his path. "This is your master station for the proxy boxes. You came in here to kill us."

"You can't think that!" Wildly, his mismatched eyes darted to Clayman, to Snowfire, back again to Blacklantern. "You're the terror-fighters I hired!"

"The riddle now is why you hired us." Blacklantern

76

danced to keep him from the simulator. "Maybe you will tell us that?"

"I brought you here to stop the secret war that has been waged against me," his harsh whisper hissed. "We Nggars had been princes of Nggongga, owners of the muskweed trade, perfumers to the galaxy. For two years now, some unknown enemy has been killing my agents and burning my posts, stealing my secrets, harming my wife, murdering my son. I brought you here to defend me, not to make insane accusations."

His eyes rolled at Clayman.

"You left me naked here," his plaintive hiss went on. "Today I was robbed again—by a man I trusted and a woman I loved. Squaremark and Diamond Dust. I found the wall blown out of my strongroom. They're gone with a fortune in perfume. Into the desert or more likely through the portal before it closed. If you can catch them for me—"

"They're dead," Blacklantern broke in. "Killed. Like your wife and Lylik. You are the killer!"

"How can you imagine that?" His harsh whisper fell. "My son's best friend!"

"I didn't want to think it." Blacklantern shook his head. "But the facts are pretty plain."

"He's crazy!" He was scuttling painfully toward Clayman. "Dangerous! You're in command here. I order you to kill him."

Clayman retreated uncertainly toward the shelves of Lylik's old toys.

"We're employees," he muttered at last. "We were well paid. We have invaded a private room. Perhaps we have no business here." His man-gun wavered toward Blacklantern. "Your accusation lacks any visible basis—"

Nggar's sound hand was creeping beneath his cooler cloak.

"Don't do it!"

Blacklantern swept the dagger back to throw and

77

watched Nggar's twitching hand drop into view. In his peripheral vision Snowfire's sudden movement was only a blur. Her voice held a cool force he had never heard in it before.

"Counterkill has changed command!"

When he glanced at her, she had Clayman's man-gun. Clayman was staggering backward, still off balance.

"Another traitor!" Gasping with his startled fury, Clayman swung to Nggar. "Believe me, sir! I'm still loyal. Counterkill is loyal. Trust me to deal with this incredible treachery—"

"Quiet!"

He looked at Snowfire and stood still.

"You may speak." She nodded at Blacklantern with a new authority. "Make it brief."

"Nggar used to travel," Blacklantern said. "To peddle perfume. His story of his perfume war with Squaremark is probably half true. When the syndicate began to hurt him, he brought back the dwarf slaves and the proxy boxes and the ejector circuits. All three, I imagine, from the same construction site. He didn't know that Diamond Dust was Squaremark's spy, and he was pretty desperate. Built his master station in this room, out of Lylik's old flight simulator—"

"Liar!" Nggar crouched closer to Clayman. "Stop him!"

"State your evidence," Snowfire commanded. "Keep it brief."

"When I found the girl here, I suspected Squaremark. I began to guess the rest today when I learned that Nggar had lied about his wife's death. I wasn't sure till just now, when Clayman said he found the green slaves scared white."

"The man's insane!" Nggar hissed. "That makes no sense."

"A white dwarf killed Lylik. With the hint that these don't have to be green, I was able to finish the picture. A

78

master station here couldn't operate a proxy box on Xyr. When Nggar wanted to kill Lylik, he had to send a dwarf to carry the bomb. A dwarf somehow bleached—''

"Natural, more likely," Snowfire said. "I believe the green is an artificial pigmentation against the sunlight here."

"Lunatics!" Nggar clutched at Clayman's chalky arm. "Why should I kill my own son?"

"Because he was coming home," Blacklantern said. "Because you had to keep him from discovering that you had murdered his mother. I suppose she objected to Diamond Dust and you put her out of the way?"

Nggar swayed away from Clayman, shaking his blighted head.

"Monstrous nonsense!" His unmatched eyes rolled toward Snowfire. "You're still sane. You can't believe such flimsy lies. Look—look at the holes in the story! There were no implosion bombs before I employed Counterkill. If you want the true terror-master—there he is!"

His sound arm thrust toward Clayman.

"We're no dupes!" Clayman plunged at him, glasses buzzing. "If you hired me for a sacrificial fool—''

Clayman's dagger flashed.

Nggar reached beneath his cloak.

Darkness flickered.

Groggily Blacklantern sat up. His head ached and a fading gong rang in his ears. His mouth was salt with blood, the air sharp with dust. Lylik's old toys and the wreckage of Nggar's master station lay scattered around him. Broken beams fringed a dark crater in the floor where Nggar and Clayman had stood.

He looked for Snowfire, but he was alone. Both doors had been blown in. The rush of air must have carried her into the ejection field, he thought, into some unknowable void beyond visible space.

79

Desolation fell upon him, as cruel as that abrupt implosion. Now he could never discover what sort of world she came from, or how she had been trapped in the savage madness of Counterkill, or why she had acted her role of lover with such warm zeal. Now they could never really love, and he felt a deep ache of loss—

Sounds broke faintly through the roaring in his ears. Lights flickered over the wreckage. Turning dully, he saw men in uniform. They pushed into the shattered playroom, peering at everything, calling to him, pointing into that dark pit.

They tried to lift him onto a stretcher. He pushed them away, stood up unsteadily. He staggered again when he saw Snowfire.

Blood had oozed from a scratch on his chin, but she looked alert and well. He swayed toward her, trying clumsily to take her in his arms. She caught his hand to keep him from falling. Gravely she put one finger on his lips. He saw her speaking, but all he heard was the din in his ears. A black policeman tried to help him toward the splintered doorway, but he stood fast, holding to her.

Other men searched the demolished room and came back to her with empty hands. He saw a black officer shouting to her.

"No bombs left." Faintly, now, he caught the words. "All ejected. The end of the terror." The man gave them both a formal Nggonggan bow. "Thanks to you Benefactors."

Startled, he peered at her.

"Yes, I am a planetary fellow." Her voice came through the ringing, still whisper-thin. "When we learned about Counterkill, I was asked to infiltrate it. For all of Clayman's talk, I think his cell was the only one. We're done with Counterkill."

He had leaned to listen, and she bent closer to help him hear.

"Your mentors on Xyr told me you were violence-prone." She gave him an odd small smile. "If that was ever true, I think Nggar and Counterkill have cured you. I think you've proved that you're a fine potential Benefactor. If you like I'll ask Thornwall to restore your preparatory fellowship."

He swayed unsteadily from the impact of that; again he had to wave away the men with the stretcher. Her voice was clearer now, and a bright hint of her sweetleaf body scent was mixed with the stinging smoke and dust.

"I'd like that, " he told her. "Very much!"

When he felt like walking, they left the imploded room and climbed back into the fire-needled night. They found old Champ impatient to get home. When the police were done they flew him back to Krongkor.

The meteor-streaks had begun to fade before they landed, and a rose-colored patch was growing in the west, around a faint red spark of the rekindled sun. The roaring was gone by then, and he could hear the husky softness of Snowfire's voice when they sat again in the old high-beamed dining room with a bottle of Champ's tangy wine.

Alone with her he felt his pulse quicken. Yet, when he leaned eagerly to exchange their wineglasses, she merely looked perplexed. The Nggonggan signal meant nothing to her, and he had a sudden painful sense of the wide gulf between their cultures.

Her expectant smile puzzled him.

"Of course you had to be mysterious." Hopefully he sipped the glass that had been hers, set it back before her. "But now, with Clayman gone—"

He faltered again, afraid of losing her. If she had been a wild tly, he thought, he would know better how to act. Yet, when he looked up, her green eyes told him to go on.

"You're still a mystery," he whispered. "I want to know about your world and you. About your customs and your language and your gestures." He moved a hesitant finger toward her mouth. "What does this mean?"

"Nothing alarming." Laughing, she leaned to touch his lips again. "In matters of love our ways are not so rigid as yours. As a woman I enjoy more freedoms than the clans of Nggongga allow. The touch—let me show you what it means."

They went upstairs together.

3.

HE had been dozing through a long seminar on culture clash and cosmopolitics when the signal ring stung his finger. The three quick tingles meant *Report to Benefactor Thornwall—now!*

Outside he paused in the cool green hexangle to shake himself awake. Lean and straight and black, he stood there a moment, enjoying the clean bright plant-scents of Xyr until a needle of unease pierced his pleasure.

The last time old Thornwall had called him violence-prone. Too savage to become a Benefactor. What would it be today?

With a supple shrug he breathed deeply and hurried on. The blind tly of time stung men at random. With Nggong-gan fatalism he was ready for whatever came.

"To you, Blacklantern!" In the high tower office, Thornwall surprised him with the two-fingered ritual salute of the Benefactors. "You are now a lunar fellow."

"But, sir—"

Unbelief checked his voice. He wanted to be a Benefactor—wanted it so hard his blood was pounding now. But the semester wasn't over. His training wasn't done. He couldn't help suspecting some ugly trick of circumstance.

"Come." In the control alcove, from which he directed agents of the fellowship on a hundred scattered planets, Thornwall waved him into a seat and bent gravely to siphon hot black liquid into two ruby cups that were inlaid with the golden sunburst of a stellar fellow. "Stonevine tea." he murmured. "From my own home world. Let's drink to your mission."

"Where?" Blacklantern peered at the red-robed Benefactor, not quite daring to hope. "To Old Earth?"

"Not yet." Smiling soberly, Thornwall tossed back his long silver hair. "When you ask for that adventure you'll have to be at least a planetary fellow. But all that's still far off. Our slow probe hasn't yet arrived in Earth orbit. You're needed now on Nggongga."

He had learned to love the stern old man, but a restless impatience gnawed at him now while Thornwall moved with a ceremonial deliberation to seal the siphon and savor the tea.

"Needed to deal with something strange," Thornwall told him at last. "A report of something hard to believe. Big metal worms, eating up the planet!"

He was about to grin, but the Benefactor's face reflected no amusement.

"I think you know our resident agent there. A planetary fellow named Snowfire."

"*Dzanya Dzu?*" He breathed the sounds of her name in her own native tongue. "I loved her once," he said. "Till I found that the meaning of love is not the same in our two cultures." Alarm struck him. "Has anything happened to her?"

"We don't know." The old man shrugged. "She's our only fellow there. She called last night. Xyr time. She was on her way to find the native who encountered the planet-eating worms. A clan chief named"—he leaned to touch a computer terminal, glanced at the flicker of green symbols—"Flintbreaker. Elder Huntsman of the Game clan."

"Old Tlongga Tlong." Blacklantern nodded. "I've seen him. He keeps his own striker tly and he used to visit the arena. His clan claims half the planet—the waterless highlands in the dry hemisphere. Beyond the reach of progress. They still hunt nearmen. Sometimes men. Do they''—his breath caught—''do they have Snowfire?''

"I hope not." Thornwall sipped his scalding tea. "No word today—her ensign is dead. I talked just now to a native office clerk. He's incoherent. Afraid of something. That's all we really know. You're to replace Snowfire and clear up the situation."

"I can't replace her." He sat for a moment staring at his own image of Snowfire's lean yellow loveliness. "She's too—different. From a world unlike Nggongga. One where the old starmen never slid back into darkness the way we did. I could never understand her. She's delicate, sensitive—everything I'm not."

"That's why we're arranging for you to skip the graduation ceremonies," Thornwall told him. "I suspect that she's in trouble precisely because she's too high cultured to cope with the primitive. You aren't."

"Must I go alone?"

"We nearly always work alone. We're too few. Needed too much on too many planets."

"I wish—" The complex duties of a Benefactor seemed suddenly appalling. "I wish you were coming too, sir."

"Nonsense!" Thornwall lifted the crystal cup as if to toast him. "You're a fellow now. Perhaps before you go I should remind you what we are."

Silently he bent to listen.

"We aren't a government. Galactic man has outgrown government. We're volunteers with no authority not freely given us. We maintain ourselves without demanding taxes. We aid and advise, but we cannot coerce. When our agents get into trouble it's commonly because people aren't ready for us."

"I'm afraid Nggongga isn't—"

The console chimed softly, calling for Thornwall's attention, but he touched a key to quiet it and swung in his chair to open a safe.

87

"Your ensign." As formally as if they stood before the graduating class, the old man rose and bowed to present the small oval plaque. "On worlds where we are recognized it will sometimes get you aid. Anywhere within range of a portal relay it is your link with us here."

At the touch of his thumb the symbol of his lunar fellowship glowed within its gleaming blackness—a tiny golden crescent inside a galactic spiral of silver frost. He held it silently, trembling a little before all it stood for.

"It is sensitized to your fingers and your voice and your call word," Thornwall added. "For this mission the word will be *wildworm*."

He had to hush the impatient console.

"On arrival you must register with the Nggonggamba police, but I'm afraid you can't expect much help from them. As other-worlders, we're suspect. Until you find Snowfire, you'll be our resident agent."

With a quick salute, as if to end the meeting, he turned toward the red-flashing console.

"Sir!" A painful uncertainty shook Blacklantern's voice. "Can't you tell me—tell me what to expect?"

"Trouble." Smiling bleakly, the old man paused. "I'm afraid your black brothers never really liked us. They accuse us now of destroying their ancient culture. Even of importing those metal worms!"

"You think the worms do exist?"

"That's your problem." Thornwall shrugged. "Snowfire found facts hard to get, and she has been too busy for long reports. Now go along."

Blacklantern went along, elated to be a Benefactor and haunted with Snowfire's smiling image: the red-gold hair and pale-gold skin, the green-gold eyes that reflected every puzzling mood. That afternoon, as he packed and stored what he wanted to keep, he twice found himself standing motionless, whispering the syllables of her untranslated name. Her bright image was too painful to remember, yet he couldn't forget.

"You want to possess me." She had raised one long

yellow finger in her odd little gesture of negation. "Among my people nobody is owned."

When he tried to explain what she meant to him, she refused to understand. Laughing at him, she told him to change his ways if he wanted her. In his hurt bewilderment, he told her that she would never see him again. Now, with that old pain awake again, he wasn't certain what he wanted.

The things he kept were few. The dagger and the binding rope from his last adventure in the tly arena. A few books and spools of tape. The formal crimson robe, woven with the golden crescent of his lunar fellowship, that now he would not be wearing at graduation.

Along with those few articles, he felt that he was storing his youth and all his years of training in the locker. Three friends walked with him across the hexangle to the slideway. He left them, with his new two-fingered salute, and rode to the portal. His doubts began to fade before a growing eagerness. He was a lunar fellow now.

A traffic officer beside the ticket vender warned him that tourists were advised to avoid Nggongga because of a cosmopolitical crisis. One flash of his ensign changed the protest into affable aid. The officer waved him on into the dome.

The glideway swept him into the enormous midnight pupil of the staring eye and out again instantly. He almost felt that he was still on Xyr until he began inhaling the muskweed pungence that awakened all his recollections of his native world.

Near the exit he found a police office.

"No good." The squat black inspector squinted at his ensign and stared blankly back at him. "The city elders want no more Benefactors."

"But we have an office here. I'm to be the new agent."

"Your office has been closed. The elders have withdrawn their recognition. Xyr is being informed."

"Why?" He studied the flat black face. "What's wrong?"

"I think some of the elders don't like the way you Benefactors claim to be above our laws." The officer frowned at his face. "You look native. You should understand."

"I'm a Benefactor now. But we don't ask favors. We got our rights here in a fair exchange. In return for what we brought. We never defied your laws."

"Then you have nothing to fear." Impassively the officer pushed his ensign back across the desk. "With this for a passport you may enter Nggongga. But only as a private tourist. If you break our laws you are subject to our justice."

A thick black hand waved him on.

"One more question." He stood where he was, searching that dark stolid face. "Our former agent here is missing. Benefactor Snowfire—"

"That has been reported." The officer shrugged. "A hundred people disappear in Nggonggamba every day. Commonly for reasons of their own. They are seldom traced. If we do find this woman Xyr will be informed."

"But—please!" He tried not to show a jolt of anger. "I want your help to find her. She came here as a Benefactor. Under the treaty of entry you have obligations to aid and protect—"

"The elders have revoked those obligations," the black man growled. "Wherever she is, her special rights are gone. Like you she is subject to the justice of Nggongga."

The black man waved again, as if to brush away a fly. Blacklantern picked up his dishonored ensign and walked outside. On Xyr it had been sunset. Here, he emerged into the scorching noon of Nggongga's thirty-hour day. Under the "white night" of the traditional siesta the whole city slept.

Only the freightways were moving, a string of locked containers creeping past the ramp. He was still waiting for a passenger float, bathed in the hot fragrant brightness of his boyhood, when a high-pitched voice spoke beside him.

"—newcomer?" His translator took a moment to uncode the alien speech. "I said, are you a stranger here?"

"Not quite." He turned to face a huge copper-colored man in a blue cooler suit. "I was born here."

Through pale wisps of condensation, yellow cat-eyes scanned him. "What's your clan?"

"I have no clan."

"Then you're in trouble." The big man swayed clumsily forward, his voice falling familiarly. "No clan, no job. No clan, no girls. No clan, nothing. These clumsy natives don't like other-worlders."

Blacklantern edged cautiously back along the empty ramp. The blue giant shambled after him, grinning without mirth. When the arrival gong sounded he swung off the ramp into a roofless passenger float. The big man followed.

The lone passenger on the float was the big man's twin, cloaked in fog-veiled black. Both had the same massive angularity, the same copper skin, the same rawboned alien face.

"Got a twenty, friend?" Barging to meet him with the same tipsy-seeming arrogance, the second man thrust a horny red paw out of his cooling cloudlet. "For portal fare—"

Caught between the two, Blacklantern moved warily aside. He sniffed the cold mist. High as they seemed, he got no scent of drink or drugs.

"Where to, friend?" the blue cloak was whining.

"Anywhere." The other answered with the same alien nasals. "Away from the worms. I hear they're boring under the city. I want to get away before it all caves in."

His yellow eyes flickered at his twin. Glancing behind him, Blacklantern found the blue cloak reeling oddly backward. Silence exploded in the blinding heat and the stifling air had a sudden sour taint. Struck with a real alarm, he stopped breathing and reached for the buckle of his heavy belt.

91

"Listen, friend!" The black cloak's squeak turned frantic. "D'you want to feed the worms—"

That was all he heard. The narrow float had become a sun-washed arena, and the identical giants were unmilked tlys. He knew what to do. Spinning, he found the one behind him tossing back the stiff blue cloak to pull an odd, thick-tubed handgun.

He slashed with the belt. Like a tly-binding rope, it whipped around the gun hand. He hauled on it, grabbed the gun, twisted the muzzle upward. The gun coughed softly. The giant yelped and folded to the deck, the mist from his cloak soiled with a spreading cloud of yellow paragas.

Still not breathing, Blacklantern whirled out of the gas cloud. His eyes stung and blurred, but he heard a squeal of rage, saw a dim shape charging, caught the hot glint of sun on steel.

The dagger became the sting of a tly. He lunged and grasped and thrust to make the tly sting itself. A cleated boot kicked at his head, but he ducked as if it had been a tly's hard claw. With all his will he fought the need to breathe. With all his strength he wrestled the descending blade.

His eyes streamed scalding tears. His lungs caught fire. The float began to tilt and spin. But the giant faltered first. Blacklantern heard him gasp for breath, felt his muscles slacken to inhaled paragas. The twisted dagger slid home.

With a dying moan, the giant wilted down. In Blacklantern's blurry eyes his blue shadow dissolved into the spreading yellow cloud. Side by side the alien twins lay very still.

Blacklantern had to breathe. With one last savage act of will he vaulted out of the sour cloud, over the wall of the float. He came down on his feet, staggered into the empty passenger way, stopped at last to gasp for air.

When his burning eyes could see again, he looked for the float. It had glided on, followed by another string of big containers. He saw no movement from it. Stumbling on to the wall of a wine bar, he leaned weakly against it, drinking great gulps of clean air.

Before he could go on, brakes squealed beneath the freightway. The line of containers rumbled to a halt. Police sirens began screaming in the brassy sky. Dazzled men and women began straggling into the street, squinting at the police flyers dropping.

He pushed past an off-duty streetcleaner into the dark tunnel of the bar. Folded in its thick scents of alcohol and seed spittle and sour piss he felt safe until he reached for a coin and felt his belt missing.

He had left it on the float with the gassed giant and the dead one. Dismay chilled him. On the ornamental buckle the police would find the fire-drill emblem of his college on Xyr. If they caught him now he could suffer Nggong-gan justice.

He found a dark booth in the barroom and ordered a beaker of seaberry wine. When the waitress had gone he thumbed his ensign and whispered, "Wildworm."

Instantly his golden crescent lit the sleek black oval. Leaning to whisper his report, he waited for the computer signal that Xyr was standing by. What he heard was the dull drone of a recorded voice, "Portal relay service suspended by order of the elders."

He sat a long time staring into the dark beaker. After all, he reflected wryly, he really had nothing to report. He had failed to learn who those identical other-worlders were or what lay behind their paragas attack.

A blind musician in the entry hall was chanting the saga of Nggugong the Skyman, who tamed the first tly. Beside the complex hazards of his own mission, those ancient heroics seemed childish. Abruptly, impatient with himself, he gulped the wine and walked back into the street.

The white night was ending. Though the hot air held a bitter hint of paragas, the police were gone. The passenger ways were moving again, still nearly empty. He boarded the radial way, changed to an arc strip that took him toward the fellowship office.

The agency was on the top floor of an old stone tower in the interworld sector, built in an earlier era of insecurity. As he swung to the unloading ramp, he saw two white-kilted police officers inspecting people at the street door.

Feeling tly-stung, he jumped back to the moving strip. If the police were here, they would also be watching the residential compound where Snowfire lived. Shut out of the office and that compound, he knew only one way to turn—to Flintbreaker.

From his own boyhood he knew the Game clan sector. A radial way carried him out of the central city toward a range of bare brown hills. The lower slopes were lined with native markets and rock-walled compounds, but the clan elders camped like nomads on the high flat mesa beyond.

He left the glideway at the last dusty terminal. When two sleepy lancers in the dust-colored kilts of the clan came out of a tent, he asked to see the Elder Huntsman. They searched him for weapons and sent him up a rocky trail.

No longer used to the cruel Nggonggan sun, he was breathing hard when he came to a low flat building, just below the mesa rim. High barred windows overlooked the trail. He heard the animal grunts and squeals of stabled nearmen, hurried on through their foul smell.

A sudden whistled bellow triggered responses he had learned in the arena. He crouched and ducked aside, snatching for his missing belt and felt a little foolish when he couldn't see the screaming tly. In a moment, though, it squalled again.

Beyond the bend he found it perched above the trail on a lancegrass log between two upright posts. Though its five eyes were hooded with nearman skin, it had sensed him. Red armor blazed when its black wings spread, and the hot air was thick with the odor of its fury.

He walked on beneath it, avoiding the green slime of its droppings. The mesa beyond lay open and flat, scattered with a few white tents. He waited at the gate, as courtesy required, until a sun-parched clansman came down to meet him, saddled on flexing poles between two trotting nearmen.

He stared at the creatures. In his boyhood the treaty of entry had outlawed their use inside the city as well as all traffic in their hides and flesh. The first he remembered were a mangy pair in the park zoo, hardly equal to the horrifying tales of their cannibalistic ferocity. Still fascinated by their dark-furred half-human strangeness, he was almost startled when the clansman asked what he wanted.

"I beg water from the Elder Huntsman." Bowing, careful to use the Game clan dialect, he recited the formalities he had learned long ago. "I beg shadow. I beg wisdom."

"The Huntsman is admired for wisdom, loved for generosity." The clansman bowed with an equal formality. "His proper name is Tlongga Tlong, which means Flintbreaker. He will ask for yours."

"He knew me in the tly arena before I had a name."

"Come."

The clansman flicked the lead nearman with his whip. Blacklantern followed across the rocks to a long white tent. Its skirts lifted against the heat, it was empty.

"Wait."

The clansman trotted his nearmen away. Blacklantern entered the tent, grateful for shade. Bedrolls were laid for seats around a worn brown carpet of nearman hair. He sat down to wait, wondering what to say. Roaming and claiming the most hostile highlands of the planet, the Game clan people lived on their nearmen hunts and the profits from their traditional games of justice. They had never welcomed the interstellar culture and they seemed unlikely to be helpful to him now.

Three nearman teams came clattering across the rocks. Two armed riders remained in their saddles. Unarmed,

Flintbreaker walked into the tent with a wary readiness, almost as if Blacklantern were some dangerous prey. Ridged and seamed with clan tattoos, his face wore an appalling scowl until suddenly his white teeth flashed.

"The nameless challenger!" His formal bow held a sudden respect. "We saw you in the arena. You worked your tly well till the accident when you were stung. We welcome you to shade and water."

They sat on the bedrolls. His eyes still searched, but he asked no questions until one of the clansmen had brought a ritual water-skin. When they had drunk, Blacklantern bowed his thanks and asked if Benefactor Snowfire had come to speak with the leaders of the clan.

The tattooed mask stopped trying to smile.

"We don't converse with women out of the clan." The voice turned bleak as the mask. "It's true the female other-worlder came here. She spoke with one of our women. We are told that she asked impertinent questions about the justice of the hunt, which has been our law for five thousand years."

"Do you know where she went?"

"She came to beg permission to visit the sacred game grounds. We denied that permission. We also sent her a warning. If she is caught in Game clan territory, she will be subject to Game clan justice."

Blacklantern blinked.

"She was investigating—" A sense of absurdity checked him. "Some wild tale of big worms! Eating up the planet."

"We ourself have seen the worms." Flintbreaker shivered, his black eyes dilating. "We do not wish to see them again." A bitter violence shook him. "They're a curse on us all, brought by the greedy men who sold our world to strangers."

He paused to offer a little pouch of nearman leather. Blacklantern declined with a bow of thanks. Tlongga

Tlong rolled a small purple seed into his palm, licked it into his mouth, crunched it hungrily. The sweetish odor filled the hot tent.

The lips of his mask turned savagely purple. "Our own foolish elders! Back in our grandfathers' time when the portal was new. For a few guns and toys and tales of other worlds they sold mining rights to all our lands. The buyer was a clever other-worlder named Ironforge. They thought he wanted gold. Now the worms are eating everything. Soil and rock. Our sacred water holes. The world itself!"

"So the worms are mining machines?"

"If machines can be so large." A fearful wonder hushed his voice. "If machines can make a pit deeper than the sea. If machines can eat so much."

"Did Benefactor Snowfire know about Ironforge?"

With deliberate skill, Flintbreaker spat a bright purple jet at a rock outside the tent.

"She asked many questions. She was told about Ironforge and his heirs. His son was called Copperforge by their queer way of naming. His grandson is Goldforge. She was told of him."

"Perhaps she went to him?"

"His ways are not ours." The mask of scars turned grimmer. "Even when he hunts he uses neither nearmen nor tlys. Perhaps he does talk to women." He spat again, expertly. "If you wish to see Goldforge, his firm is the Deeplode Mines."

"Your water revives the body, your wisdom the spirit." Murmuring the ritual words, Blacklantern bowed and rose to go. "I'll look for Goldforge."

"You are still our guest." With a bleak black courtesy, Flintbreaker waved to detain him. "For yourself, do you desire hunting rights?"

"I have never hunted nearmen," he answered. "Nor men."

"Perhaps you don't approve?"

97

"I grew up here," Blacklantern answered carefully. "I knew about the hunts and I accepted them. But now I've been away to other worlds. I've learned what other peoples feel—that they are wrong and cruel."

"We affirm our ancient justice." The old huntsman stiffened with a measured indignation. "The accused has always been remanded by preliminary trial. He is always hunted fairly, according to all the old tradition, with every right of escape to the refuge oasis."

His angry lips were stained with purple froth.

"We may seem stern to your female agent and all the prying other-worlders, but justice should be stern. The ritual of the games has been good for Nggongga. It weeded out the evil and the weak for many hundred generations. It taught our people to fear the law and love the truth—until strangers came to corrupt them. As long as I live the games will go on."

He offered the water skin once more as a sign of dismissal. Under the savage sun, Blacklantern picked his way back beneath the tethered tly and down the rocky trail. The shriek of the baffled tly echoed after him.

Deeplode Mines was one of the great "first companies" that had guaranteed traffic when the new portal opened. As a boy he had cleaned boots and sometimes picked a pocket on the narrow ramps below the Deeplode building, a huge cube of plain stone and steel.

A gold-kilted guard stopped him now at the door, frowned haughtily, let him in at last to see a slim black girl in a bright gold skirt. With a distantly arrogant smile, she informed him that Manager Goldforge was out. He saw nobody. He accepted no messages. He made no gifts.

"I'm a Benefactor." Blacklantern decided to risk what she might tell the police. "We are investigating a report that your company is consuming the planet with big metal worms."

She nodded loftily. If he wished to discuss mining operations he might speak to Engineer Toolcraft. A tall black boy in a stiff yellow kilt escorted him down a cavernous hall into a huge room that didn't belong on primitive Nggongga.

The floor was crystal, nearly invisible.

Three walls were stereo tanks. One contained an enormous solid model of a planet, cut away to show its inner structure in color-coded layers, from cool blue crust down to red-glowing core.

The opposite wall was a window into space. It showed a queer machine—a bright silver disk spinning like a slow wheel against starry darkness, sprouting black and angular wings from its hub. It looked toylike until he saw a spaceliner docking at the hub and felt a dazing sense of its immensity.

The third tank was shallower, set back behind a long computer console. It was alive with shapes and signs he didn't understand—glowing lines, sheets of color, geometric solids, luminous symbols, all appearing and vanishing in a fluid dance of bewildering information.

The crystal underfoot covered yet a fourth tank. Glancing down, he saw an enormous excavation, walled with fractured cliffs and long slopes of broken stone, floored with a thick brown haze. Its bottomless depth turned him giddy.

"Here he is, sir." The black boy pointed at a man walking across that dizzy pit from the console. "Engineer Toolcraft."

Blacklantern caught his breath and stepped out across nothing he could see. Toolcraft himself looked nearly as strange as the room. Too fair for Nggongga, he was splotched with yellow freckles and peeling from sunburn. His sparse hair was short and stiff and white. His eyes were shaded with huge blue goggles that bulged like the compound eyes of a giant insect. Yet he nodded readily when Blacklantern showed his ensign.

"Of course we recognize the Benefactors." Though his accent was odd, he spoke fluent city Nggoggan, needing no translator. "I regret the wave of feeling against your fellowship here. I'll help if I can."

99

"I do need help." Blacklantern smiled gratefully. "I'm looking for a missing agent."

"The girl Snowfire?" He frowned with a quick concern. "She was here yesterday, asking for Manager Goldforge. I spoke to her."

"Do you know where she went?"

Toolcraft spread his sun-reddened hands in a falling gesture that meant nothing to Blacklantern. "She was inquiring about our mining operations. She wanted to inspect the site. I told her I couldn't take her there without permission from Manager Goldforge."

Despite the air of sympathetic candor, the blue goggles still looked like insect eyes. Toolcraft began to seem a clever opponent in a strange arena. An angry tly might have been simpler to cope with.

"I'm new here, of course," he was saying. "I've taken over a good deal of routine. Manager Goldforge spends most of his time with his hobbies, but he still holds control. Without his approval I can't do much for anybody."

"Do you think—" Blacklantern flinched from a sudden stab of alarm. "Do you think Snowfire tried to enter Game clan territory?"

"I advised her against it." Toolcraft repeated that falling gesture. "I warned her that the natives have become pretty hostile to our whole operation, but I'm afraid she wasn't impressed. If she's caught out there of course she'd be subject to their peculiar justice." The blue goggles stared. "I suppose you know what that is?"

"I know." But he didn't want to think of that. "One more question." His throat felt rough and dry. "Can you tell me about this—this mining operation?"

Toolcraft waved a casual sunburned hand at the cutaway planet in the stereo tank.

"Our material." He gestured toward the opposite tank and its image of that enormous black-winged silver wheel spinning against the field of stars. "Our product."

"And that?" Shaken, Blacklantern glanced into the appalling pit projected beneath their feet. "Your mine?"

"The initial excavation." Toolcraft nodded. "We're only beginning. But we're miners. We own mining rights here. We're mining the planet."

"How much of it?"

"As a matter of fact—" The engineer hesitated, blue goggles unblinking. "All of it."

"So it's true?" With a shiver of awe, Blacklantern looked down again into the image of that bottomless chasm. "Your big metal worms are really eating up Nggongga?"

"A naïve description." Toolcraft shrugged. "I know the story has disturbed the natives, but there's not much they can do about it. Their own ancestors sold us legal rights to do what we're doing. We aren't stopping now. Not even to please the Benefactors."

"Did Snowfire ask you to stop?"

"She implied that she might. She wanted to investigate. She was worried about the native population when we use up the planet. I told her we've made plans for that. We've been here for generations now, with a heavy investment in preliminary surveys and special equipment. We can't afford to quit."

"What will you do with a whole planet?"

"Because of native ignorance and superstition, we've never discussed that here." The blue goggles studied him. "Your own agent found it hard to understand. Yet, as a Benefactor, you're entitled to know. We're swarmfolk."

Blacklantern stared uneasily at the mad dance of changing forms and fiery symbols in the computer display, but he found no meaning there.

"You appear puzzled." Toolcraft turned. "Come along. Manager Goldforge is out, but I can show you a model swarmworld in his office."

The office was enormous but Nggonggan, stifling with a heavy stale sweetness of chewed saltflower seed. A purple-splashed spittoon flanked the great desk of

101

polished dark-red hardroot. One big window overlooked the narrow harbor and the docks. Blacklantern turned from that to the opposite wall, where tall cases held trophies of the hunt.

"Manager Goldforge is three-fourths native," the engineer commented affably. "The family has always embraced the native people and their culture." He waved at the racks of antique man-guns and shrunken trophy heads. "The ritual hunts are his special hobby." He turned. "But here's what I wanted you to see."

Opposite the spittoon, a thin pedestal was topped with a small bright globe. A tight swarm of tiny silver particles surrounded it, crawling along orbital circles. Blacklantern leaned to peer, but their shapes were too small to be distinct and their moving glitter was almost hypnotic. He looked back at the engineer.

"A model of our solar system," Toolcraft said. "It was colonized twenty thousand years ago by one of the first starships from Old Earth."

"That cloud of sparks?" Blacklantern stared again. "Where are the planets?"

"Used up," Toolcraft said. "You see, our forebears made a lucky planetfall. With a good environment for technological progress, they never fell back into savagery the way your own people did. In a few thousand years they were overcrowding all the worlds of their system and exhausting all the surface resources. Their solution was the swarmworld."

He waved at the cloudlet around the model sun.

"They discovered something that the Game clan elders are still too savage to perceive. A planet, seen as a dwelling for men, is fantastically inefficient. Most of the mass, with nearly all the useful metal, is buried out of reach. Most of the solar power is wasted, escaping past the planet into empty space."

Blacklantern blinked into the bulging goggles.

"So we turned to space. We rebuilt the moons and then the planets into space vehicles—like the one you saw back

102

in the tank. They spin to simulate gravity. Their vanes catch solar energy. Using them, we've multiplied our living space and our resources many thousand times. But a few generations ago we saw another crisis coming. Our last planet was nearly gone. That's why we're here.''

"To turn all Nggongga into space machines?"

"In time." Toolcraft nodded blandly. "We look ahead. This planet was carefully chosen. An excellent mass composition, mostly nickel-iron. Light elements for water and air, in a cometary object. A stable and powerful sun. A tiny population, too backward to matter."

"But it was—ours!"

"Don't upset yourself." Toolcraft stooped to pull an elaborate bar out of the desk. "Help yourself to the manager's best and let me tell you how it is."

Blacklantern waved the glittering bottles away. "Just tell me."

"We aren't demons." Toolcraft stopped to pour himself a drink. "Our excavators aren't the monsters old Flintbreaker imagines. It will take them several generations to reach any important settlements. When that time comes we'll take care of the natives. Retrain them for survival. Subsidize migration. We'll even build vehicles for any who choose to move into space. Fair enough?''

"I don't like it."

"Look at the ethics." Toolcraft waved his glass persuasively. "The greatest good of the greatest number. Nggongga now supports two hundred million people, most of them in miserable poverty. We can use the planet to make room for a few million times as many, each enjoying a far greater wealth of mass and energy. Is that somehow wrong?''

"I'm still Nggonggan." Blacklantern backed uneasily away. "I still don't like it."

"Neither did Snowfire. She's afraid of harming the native culture." Toolcraft chuckled. "The only thing in danger during her lifetime is the ritual headhunt—which I don't value as much as she and Goldforge do."

"You say she wanted to look at your mine." He tried to see through the goggles. "Did she speak of any plans?"

Toolcraft dropped his freckled hands in that negative gesture. "When I couldn't let her use our transport system, she asked for maps and air charts. Perhaps she meant to hire a flyer."

"The agency owned one when I was here before." Blacklantern frowned. "A battered old machine. Not fit for a flight to the highlands. I hope she didn't take off in that."

"I'm afraid Nggongga's too wild for her." Toolcraft turned to show him out. "Sorry I can't help, but Goldforge makes our policy. My own advice would be to leave Nggongga while you can."

"I can't" he said. "Not without Snowfire."

Back on the hot street, with no other lead, he decided to try the residential compound. It was off the beach beyond the docks, in the Sea clan suburbs. Approaching on a feeder strip, he found two officers on guard outside the door. He rode on to the next terminal, walked back through alleys.

The rear wall was smooth concrete topped with steel spikes. Searching for a way to scale it, he saw fresh-turned gravel at its foot and uncovered the yellow plexoid arms of a burglar's catapult.

Some intruder was already here!

After a moment of startled thought he bent to reset the device, stepped on the arm. It flung him skyward. He caught the spikes, guided himself over the wall, came down on a rooftop airpad. The old flyer was gone. The yard below was empty.

Listening for the burglar ahead, he heard only far street sounds. He went down an outside stair, stopped behind a fragrant clump of purple-blooming heartfruit. Under the windless heat the yard lay hushed and empty. Across the walk a door hung open, the lock broken.

With a sense of brief elation that his boyhood skills had not been forgotten, he crept into the house. The wide

104

hallway was still and empty as the garden. He peered into a pantry, the kitchen, a high-raftered dining room.

A thin sour scent of paragas led him to what must have been Snowfire's bedroom. Its lock was broken. Inside he found a silent record of vandalism. A litter of tangled clothing, broken toiletries, scattered books and tapes, all steeped in that stale reek.

At a sound in the hallway he ducked into a closet. The garments left there carried Snowfire's sweetleaf scent, stronger than the fading paragas. Crouching behind them he saw his fellow intruder at the door—and almost gasped with surprise.

Nearly naked, the man was a yellow-eyed copper-skinned giant. One of the twins who had tried to paragas him on the float. But that couldn't be! He had left one of them dead, the other unconscious. Yet this scowling giant resembled them exactly, which made them triplets.

The giant muttered something, spurted purple spit at the torn-up bed, shambled on.

Blacklantern followed to the airpad, watched him recover the catapult, fold it into an innocent-looking case, and stride down the alley.

Sprinting in the opposite direction, he was in time to be standing on the feeder strip when the big man swung aboard. On the main way, the man bought a seaberry ice. He let a boy clean his boots. Back in the interworld zone, he left the strip in front of a flashy new business tower. A street sign read:

BIO-TECHNIC INSTITUTE
DR. KILLBIRD

A dozen steps behind, he followed into an ornate lobby. The big man stalked on through an inner door. Blacklantern found himself facing a slim young black girl at a huge pale plexoid reception desk. She wore the Sun clan tattoo on her forehead, a pale blue circle rimmed with red teeth. When she spoke he expected her to use the Sun clan dialect, but her audible voice had an alien, singsong into-nation.

"—Institute." His translator caught it. "Do you wish to see Dr. Killbird?"

"I'm not quite sure." Trying to discover why anybody saw Dr. Killbird, he looked around the waiting room. The wall was rich imported hardwood, the carpet luxurious, the air so cool he almost shivered. A long stereo tank held a dozen tall nude dolls on rotating stands.

"Did somebody send you?" The girl's keen stare explored him. "If you're offering yourself, you'll have to see the business office."

"I need more information." He returned her searching look. "Are you native?"

"My body is." Behind the ivory desk she rose and turned for him like one of the dolls in the tank. "Nice, don't you think? I'm certainly happy with it."

"I don't quite understand."

"I'm a transfer." She arched herself to display her high bare breasts. "I came here an old woman. Ill and dying. Dr. Killbird's clones found this body for me. The girl had lived in some mud village. Her people had found no husband for her, and they sold her cheap enough. Now Dr. Killbird is letting me work out the fees."

She leaned to study him again.

"If you want a white body I'll show you what we have." She pointed at the stereo tank. "I'm afraid our stock is always low—"

"You buy and sell bodies?" He peered again at the rotating dolls. "How can that be?"

"A biotechnic art. The last term in human progress—everlasting youth!" Again she preened her dark beauty. "Dr. Killbird learned it on a far planet. Perhaps his fees are high—but what he sells is priceless."

"I see." He nodded dazedly. "If I wanted to be white—"

"You would select a white body. In the lab he would lay

106

you beside it. With his holographic pickup he would scan the synaptic patterns of both brains. Exchange them all from one to the other. Your memory, your personality, your identity—all that is you would wake in the new body.''

She must have seen an unconscious shudder.

''There's no pain at all,'' she assured him. ''You begin with light anesthesia, but the process itself is anesthetic once the scanning starts. The whole exchange takes less than an hour. When you wake, in a strong young body, it's being born again!''

''What becomes of the old ones?''

''Who cares?'' She made a charming face. ''The clones dispose of them somehow.''

She paused. An inner door had opened. An angry woman burst through, followed by a tall protesting man in white.

''No excuses, doctor!'' Her audible voice was high and harsh. ''I've come four thousand light-years for a transfer and I know what I want.''

''Please! Most gracious Redflower!'' The doctor was thin, almost cadaverous. Bright metal gleamed about him. As he came nearer, pursuing his indignant client, Blacklantern saw that his whole body was supported by an elaborate mechanical exoskeleton as if the gravity of Nggongga were too much for him. ''You must see the difficulties—''

''You can't con me!'' Her voice rose higher. ''I won't be black!''

''But the planet's black.'' The doctor spoke in hissing alien sibilants, assisted by an amplifier. ''We can get fine black bodies. Now and then a splendid hybrid. But light skins are rare here—''

''I want the one your people showed me,'' the woman shrilled. ''That one!''

She strode toward the stereo tank, pointing at a pale nude doll. Blacklantern moved after her, staring. With its

107

pale-gold skin and red-gold hair the doll looked suddenly familiar. As it turned on the stand he recognized its green-gold eyes, its haunting smile.

It was Snowfire!

The woman stood waggling her finger at it. Closer to her now, he saw the wasted flesh and wrinkled skin beneath her cosmetics. She reached as if to snatch the doll with her red-enameled talons, whirled back to face the doctor with terror and fury in her haggard eyes.

"That's my body!" she shrieked. "The one they promised me!"

"Most gracious Redflower, please let me explain." His amplified sibilants hissed through the waiting room. "You must understand that such a specimen is never easy to obtain, even here on Nggongga. The arrangements are troublesome, ethically and financially and legally. When this model was prepared, my people expected to have the original available, but they've had difficulties."

"If you want my money find that body!"

"We'll make every effort, but I can promise nothing." As the doctor swung to face him, Blacklantern could hear the tiny whine of motors. Staring from a nearly fleshless skull, deep-sunk eyes measured him shrewdly. "Sir, what's your problem?"

"It's too hard for you," Blacklantern told him. "I'll just keep the body I have."

Turning toward the doorway, he froze. Two black policemen were entering. Between them they supported a reeling copper-skinned giant. One of them called to the girl at the desk: "This man was gassed on a freightway passenger float. An other-worlder clone. He says he's employed by Dr. Killbird—"

"The killer!" his alien voice squealed. "He murdered my clone brother!"

Blacklantern bent to dart for the street door, saw the officers pulling their guns. He turned to dash for the inside door, met the third clone plunging out. He spun to look for

108

another escape, faced a thin-tubed gun in the doctor's power-aided hand. It clicked.

He felt the sting of a dart—

The cage was shaped like a thin barrel, just large enough to hold him. Two dun-furred nearmen carried it, hung between them on springy lancegrass poles. To keep his balance Blacklantern had to clutch the yellow bars.

A whip-cracking warden ran behind, cursing the nearmen. They carried him out of the cell block, down a wide arcade of hunting-gear shops, past the offices of the sacred game, at last into the crowd-packed courtroom.

The nearmen dropped his cage on the floor of a gloomy pit. Steep tiers of seats rose all around, packed with the hunters and the curious. The heat was stifling. Sweating blacks chewed their saltflower seed and spat into the pit. Fanning big hats, they mixed the sharp sweetness of their spittle with the stale ammoniac reek of the nearmen stabled in the basement.

Alien voices trilled and clicked behind him. They meant nothing because his translator was gone. Squirming to turn in the coffin-sized cage, he found a troop of tourists shuffling past. White wisps of condensation veiled their cooler suits, and his naked skin felt a momentary chill. Their guide herded them on into a reserved bank of seats to watch this traditional bit of Nggonggan justice. The nearmen barked again. The crowd buzzed and the guide pointed. Twisting around, he found Snowfire.

Stripped, she was streaked with sweat and grime. Her pale hands gripped the lancegrass bars. Yet she stood proudly straight. Her green-gold eyes swept the gazing crowd, level and aloof, still somehow brave.

"Dzanya!" he called. "Dzanya Dzu!"

She cried out with startled joy before she found him in the cage. Her voice fell then. He could hear her dazed emotion, but the words meant nothing. Trying to answer, he watched her first elation fade into new despair.

109

Pity swept him. He thought she was too clean and fine and fragile, too highly cultured, to endure the primitive cruelties of Nggongga. But he couldn't tell her anything. Her translator, like his own, had been taken away.

On a platform that jutted over the pit a bailiff banged the floor with the butt of his lancegrass spear. The pit fell silent. The lean old Elder Huntsman mounted his high official stool, and the bailiff began a droning chant.

Oppressed with his sense of Snowfire's sick bewilderment, Blacklantern heard only occasional phrases in the archaic legal dialect. " . . . alleged trespass upon the sacred gamelands . . . accused killer of a certain otherworlder, a clone called Ooth Ansk. . . . " Searching the high rows of faces for some hint of aid or hope, he found only staring curiosity, blank apathy, the bright-eyed lust for blood.

" . . . prisoners." The bailiff's spear had thumped the floor again, he twisted in the cage to find Flintbreaker's tattooed snarl fixed upon him. "You stand accused of high crimes against the peace of Nggongga and the immemorial justice of the Game clan. Do you wish to speak to the court?"

"I do." Gripping the bars, he peered up at the black clan elder. "We came here as agents—" Hoarse from the reeking stable dust, he tried to raise his voice. "We are lawful agents of the Benefactors. In exchange for our aid to Nggongga, we were promised safety here. I demand—" His voice broke again. "For Agent Snowfire and myself, I demand our rights under the treaty of entry."

A ripple of interest had spread through the crowd, and the lean old huntsman waited for the bailiff to drum again for silence.

"Fellow Blacklantern, we hear your appeal. We are reminded that all our clans once granted extraordinary rights and immunities to your fellowship. Unfortunately you have forced their cancellation."

110

The standing of an elder came as much from oratory as from skill on the trail, and his fustian phrases rolled melodiously across the pit.

"When we allowed the opening of the portal, you other-worlders promised us great good things. Instead you have brought us only evil. We have therefore withdrawn all your immunities. You stand accused of capital offences and your appeal lacks merit." He signaled the bailiff to thump again. "These two prisoners are remanded to the justice of the clan."

"You can't do that!" Blacklantern saw the black scars harden and he tried to smooth his tone. "We have been cut off from Xyr. May we relay a message to our own leaders there?"

Old Flintbreaker waited for the ritual thump.

"Request denied," he rapped. "Until your ordeal has been concluded. If it happens that you are able to reach the sanctuary with your heads untaken, the court will then uphold your innocence. Your lives will be protected. You will be allowed to go in peace. But the ritual of justice will now continue."

"Mercy, sir!" Blacklantern shouted. "I was born here. I'll take my own chances on the sacred uplands, but I beg mercy for Agent Snowfire. A tender girl. From a cultured world, where life is sheltered. The justice of Nggongga is too cruel for her. I beg mercy!"

"If our ways are too cruel for her, hers are too cruel for us." Flintbreaker's strong teeth glinted through his mask of scars. "Her white kindred opened the portal with promises of all good things—and came through to steal our sacred treasures and profane our holy places, to buy our bodies and blight our souls, to scatter the eggs of monstrous worms to eat our world. We have no mercy left."

Approval echoed around the pit.

"But we do pledge justice," he boomed again. "The game may be hard, but we play fair. We limit the huntsmen to three. We allow you a whole day to run before the first takes your trail. We promise you freedom if you reach Nggooth alive.''

A sardonic grin twisted his tattoos.

''If you find your own world-eating worms in your path before you reach the refuge oasis, then I beg you not to blame the ancient justice of the Game clan for deeds you yourselves have done.''

At his signal the bailiff drummed.

''Gather, huntsmen!'' His rich voice lifted again. ''Prepare to place your bids for the right to take these heads.''

''Sir!'' Blacklantern begged desperately. ''May we just have our translators back—''

The bailiff banged the floor till he fell silent. Bidders filed down from the seats to peer and poke through the lancegrass bars. One huge slow pale bald man stopped to squint at both of them. He reached a huge yellow hand to tweak Snowfire's nipple, spattered Blacklantern's penis with a hot squirt of purple spit.

Toolcraft, the sunburned mining engineer, shuffled along behind him, dripping sweat, looking uncomfortable and apologetic behind bulging purple goggles. He murmured something in his own alien tongue and hurried guiltily on. The pale cold man, Blacklantern decided, must be Goldforge.

Dr. Killbird marched stiffly by, a gaunt puppet hung upon his humming exoskeleton, escorting his impatient age-wasted client. Blacklantern understood nothing they said, but he saw purpose enough in the way they both inspected Snowfire's firm golden flesh.

Old Flintbreaker auctioned the hunting rights, his lilting chant as strange to Blacklantern as another alien tongue. He was clinging to the yellow bars, weak from heat and strain and stable stink, before the bailiff banged for quiet and announced the order of the hunt.

The respected Manager Goldforge, as highest bidder, would hunt first. Dr. Killbird had bought the next place for his client, the respected Redflower. Flintbreaker himself, as chief huntsman of the clan, had claimed the third day's hunt.

And the auction was over. Whips cracked as the wardens brought howling nearmen to carry off the cages. Shuffling out of the pit, the spectators raised foul dust. After a fit of sneezing, Blacklantern twisted around inside his bars and tried to smile at Snowfire.

Though she faced him, her greenish eyes were staring blankly past, as if she had gone blind. Little rivulets of sweat had traced narrow ivory streaks down the dark grime that covered her. Yet, beneath the filth, she was still lovely. A pang of helpless pity clouded his eyes with tears.

The nearmen carried them swaying back through the arcade of huntman's shops, toward the cells. They passed a little kiosk where an aged black woman, withered and toothless and blind in one eye, was hawking trophy heads more hideous than her own.

He hoped Snowfire wouldn't see.

Progress of a sort had come to Tlootl Tloo, the mythical nesting place of the fire-winged tly of justice. A high stone wall, topped with electrified barbed wire, had replaced the thornbush barriers that had guarded its sacred springs and lancegrass groves since history began. A new tourist hotel stood beside the central pool, with its own airpad and a tall observation tower for the hunters.

The prisoners for the game no longer came by nearman caravan, but by flyer. The old prison pit had given way to a long special cell that ran like a tunnel through the new wall. Blacklantern and Snowfire were released from their handling cages into that cell.

Behind them, inside the walls, he could see graceful plumes of green-and-golden lancegrass nodding above the wide blue pool. Ahead, beyond another wall of bars, bare red shale and black flows of ancient lava sloped sharply up toward the savage desert and the far-off sanctuary.

When the wardens were gone, Snowfire turned toward him slowly, moving as if in a dream of horror. She started

113

to speak but saw that her words had no meaning for him. Trembling, she checked herself and stood looking at him in tragic inquiry. Slow tears welled out of her terror-darkened eyes, but she didn't sob.

He wanted to tell her that he was not altogether without hope. In his hard apprenticeship for the arena he had lived with the primitive Wind clan people, hunting wild tlys and evading wild nearmen in country almost as dry and bleak as this. But all he could do was to murmur the music of her name and gesture for her to rest.

Worn dead, she was soon asleep, relaxed on the bare stone floor. He sat propped against the hot wall, watching her sweet and undefended nudity, now and then brushing off a biting fly, dozing a little, watching the sinking sun turn slowly red with dust.

The wardens came back at last with a pail of water and their last meal, a generous tray of ripe fruit and sun-cured meat. He woke her then. She smiled at his touch and murmured something in a child's happy voice before the shadow of terror returned.

She watched like a child, with huge frightened eyes, waiting to see what she must do. She ate at his signal, stopped at once when he had finished. After they had drunk, he raised the pail and poured water for her to wash away the prison filth. She stopped him with a low pleased sound, held the pail while he bathed himself.

When the blood-colored sun was grazing the rock-toothed black horizon, the wardens came back for the empty pail and the tray. The three selected hunters came down from the hotel to watch through the inner bars while the outer door grated open.

Snowfire clung to Blacklantern's arm, mutely watching his face. He turned to look back at the three. At Goldforge, roughly clad in tanned nearman hide and a broad white hat, belted with man-guns. Toolcraft trailing uneasily behind him. At Redflower, standing with Dr. Killbird, holding a thick-barreled paragas gun and eyeing Snowfire

114

with a fierce hawkface. At Flintbreaker, the Elder Huntsman, tattooed and impassive and black.

Only Flintbreaker spoke.

"You have one day to run." He gestured toward the desert and far-off sanctuary with the lancegrass whistle he used to call his striker tly. "But we'll meet before you reach Nggooth."

"We'll meet."

Blacklantern made the slashing sign used by a contender in the arena to show that he was ready for the tly. He turned his back on the three. With a nod for Snowfire to follow, he walked out of the dark tunnel cell into the desert.

Though his feet had once been tough from running barefoot in the alleys of Nggonggamba, now he had to pick his way with care across the unkind rocks. Snowfire was already limping when he looked back, her face taut with pain.

He climbed the nearest barren hill. In the dry ravine behind, where hunters watching from the hotel tower couldn't see, he turned downslope to follow the dry streambed below the oasis. Snowfire kept close behind and he heard no whimper from her.

Inspecting the cruel-edged rocks, he picked up and carried a few choice bits of flint. Now and then he paused to scan the blood-washed sky, but he saw neither aircraft nor tlys. Listening, he heard no nearmen baying. With a bleak little nod of satisfaction, he decided that the Elder Huntsman was really playing fair.

The red dusk faded fast into moonless night, but the Nggonggan sun belonged to a dense swarm in a tight galactic arm. The blazing constellations gave light enough to show his way.

Snowfire had more trouble. Once he heard her calling after him in a stifled, childish voice. He went back and found that she had fallen. When he picked her up, she flung her arms around him. She was suddenly sobbing for

115

her breath, her tender softness hot against him, searching for his mouth.

Lust swept him. For one reeling instant he wanted to stop here, to give up escape and enjoy sex with her and wait for the hunters. Her alien notions of marriage no longer mattered now, when he had no possible rival. But he checked that hot impulse and let the moment go.

She had skinned her knees and hurt her ankle. When she could walk again he led her on. The splendid stars rose ahead and set behind. The air grew cool enough to dry their sweat. Twice he stopped to let her rest. At last he caught a faint scent of moisture. In the still gray dawn they came to a tiny clump of lancegrass, watered perhaps by underground seepage from the oasis behind.

While Snowfire slept on a bed of fallen fronds, he chipped flint for a blade and carved hard dry stalks to make two spears and a throwing stick. He tipped the spears with flint. When she woke, he showed her how to scrape the dead leaves into long skeins of fiber that he braided into a sling and a little pouch for projectile stones.

Hammering strips of the tough inner bark between two rocks to soften them, he made bindings for Snowfire's bleeding feet and his own. He found fireweed blooming in the shade and smeared both their bodies with its milky sap, which turned to an ink-black pigment against the deadly sun.

It was burning noon by then, and they were both parched with thirst. He used a sharpened stick to dig in the old streambed for water, but all he found was dry bedrock and pulpy lancegrass roots that gave a bitter juice when chewed.

Through half the incandescent afternoon they hid beneath the golden plumes, plaiting strips from them into broad Nggonggan hats. Now and then he paused to look outside, but all he saw was the high black fleck of a carrion tly. Flintbreaker had kept his pledge, but their day of grace was nearly done.

116

Snowfire watched while he caught a bit of weary sleep, dreaming that he was back outside the tunnel-cell at the oasis, with only its bars to keep him from a tantalizing pile of juice-rich fruits and a brimming pail of water.

She shook him awake to point at a tower of red dust creeping across the lifeless land behind. He thought it must be only a whirlwind, but still the time to move had come. As they gathered up their crude new gear, he saw a change in Snowfire.

Though they lacked words, he heard a dawning hope in the even tones of her voice. He saw courage in the straightness of her black-smeared body. He thought she had begun to find herself.

With a sudden ache of feeling, he wanted to kiss her again, yearned to take her to bed on the pile of dead fronds. Instead he nodded toward the desert. She caught his hand with a child's trust, smiling so bravely that he was almost glad they had no translators, glad he couldn't tell her that Nggooth was still a dozen days away across the cruelest highlands of the planet.

Leaving those dry ravines that long-vanished floods must have cut, they climbed a rocky slope where he thought their trail would be hard to follow. Though they started strongly, he soon had to slow his pace for Snowfire. Before sunset their crude foot bindings of bark had begun to wear out and he knew they were leaving traces of blood for the huntsmen.

When the sharp horizon began to shear away the dustdulled sun he paused to look back. Their day of grace was gone. The first hunter would be starting. He glanced at Snowfire. Silently she gripped his hand. They plodded bleakly on.

Before the blood-colored dusk had fully faded he heard a droning in the sky behind. At first he hoped for the night to hide them, but that high drumming grew steadily louder, nearer till the hot darkness quivered with it.

With a stifled cry of fear, Snowfire touched his arm. He

117

saw her teeth and eyes shining strangely. When she bent to point at a rock, he saw glints of fluorescence brighter than the starlight.

The first place, he recalled, had gone to Goldforge, who scorned the use of trailing nearmen or striker tlys. Instead the swarmworlder was following with a flyer equipped with black light and perhaps body-heat sensors.

Snowfire studied his face in the starlight and suddenly turned to wave her clumsy spear defiantly at that roaring in the sky.

All night they stumbled on. All night the droning flyer followed and the rocks about their bleeding feet darted flints of colored fire.

Once Snowfire tugged him toward a dark ravine as if she wanted to take cover, but he knew the rules of the game would not allow any actual air attack. Goldforge himself would have to follow on the ground.

In the fiery dawn they topped a knife-edged ridge and found a sea of golden dunes beyond. While he stood searching for a way across it, Snowfire made a sound and pointed back. Beneath the thrumming in the sky he heard a deeper rumbling, rising and falling as the hunter's surface vehicle met the hills and ravines they had crossed.

Scowling at the flame-streaked sky, frowning at that waste of billowed sand, peering into Snowfire's blackened face, he groped for a plan. When at last he moved, he scooped out a shallow hollow in the sand. He made her lie in it, buried her body. He backed away, brushing out their footprints with his hat. He walked out a bold new trail from the rocks to the rim of the first yellow dune. He backed again, now on tiptoe to make prints small enough for Snowfire's. Finally he buried himself near that trail, leaving only a narrow peephole concealed with the brim of his sand-sprinkled hat.

There he waited.

He tasted dry sand in his mouth and the bitterness of thirst. He contemplated the trust he had seen in Snowfire's green-golden eyes, so strangely pale in her darkened face. He surveyed all the infinities of rock and sand and savage sun ahead.

He listened. The drone of the flyer rose and fell and rose again, as if the baffled pilot were circling to search for them. The growl and snort of the land vehicle grew louder, louder, till at last it lurched over the ridge, squat and dark in the red sunrise.

Armored, mottled gray and rust and dun, it ran on cleated tracks and sought its game with a complex sensor array and turret-mounted guns. After a momentary pause on the rise it came grumbling down the trail he had prepared, passing so near him that the hard sand shivered.

At the lip of the dune, where his false trail ended, it hesitated again. The flat turret swung back and forth, sensors searching. It groaned backward, turned, stopped. A steel door clanged open. Goldforge jumped out.

A giant in motley, his nearman-skin jacket belted with other-worlder weapons, he peered warily right and left. He frowned skyward toward his wheeling flyer. Wearing a yellow scowl, he came slowly back along the trail. His own machine had crushed out most of those careful footprints, but he bent at last to study the traces that remained.

Blacklantern slid upright, shaking sand from spear and throwing stick. He flexed his arm twice while Goldforge squinted at the double row of prints. He braced himself, caught his breath.

"Your last hunt," he said.

Goldforge straightened, yelping. He hauled a man-gun from his belt. It crashed once as Blacklantern threw the lancegrass spear. Unaimed, the bullet whined away into the sky. The flint point struck home. The man-gun whirled across the sand.

The big swarmworlder toppled slowly backward, grabbing at the crude spear with both hands. It slipped free without the point. Blood spurted after it, darker than the purple drool on his mouth.

Blacklantern was over him by then, slashing at his

yellow throat with his own hunting knife. He quivered and lay still. Blacklantern stooped again to scour the knife in the sand. Swaying with a sudden unexpected weakness, he stumbled back to uncover Snowfire.

The flyer was wheeling low by then, so near that he could see the pilot's blue-goggled head in the observation bubble. Blacklantern bent for his hat, fanned it triumphantly to wave the flyer off. It left at last, droning away toward the oasis of justice. Toolcraft, he thought, would soon be reporting the game still alive for the second hunter.

Snowfire had Goldforge's man-gun when he turned back, standing over the dead swarmworlder as if she thought he might come back to life. Ruefully he showed her the thumb-plate that keyed the gun to its owner alone.

She watched outside while he explored the vehicle. All its controls were thumb-keyed, too. He failed to start it or to activate its equipment. Yet that hardly seemed to matter, for his own hands could open the canteens of sweet water, the hampers of ripe fruit, the freezer of gourmet food.

They rinsed the bitterness from their swollen mouths, sipped and drank, tasted and ate. When he dared feast no more, he went out to strip the hunter's corpse. The boots were too large, but he padded them with looted cloth. He cut moccasins for Snowfire out of the fringed hunting jacket. He took the translator.

Suddenly, wonderfully, they could talk.

"You're as strange as Nggongga." She stared at him with red-rimmed eyes, leaning close to the translator in his hand. "You could have gone a long way alone. Why do you wait for me?"

"Sometimes I wonder." His grin hurt his sunburned lips. "I guess it's because I'm still Nggonggan."

He saw her flush beneath the fireweed sap. Her pale gaze fell to the corpse and fled toward the hot horizon.

"What now?" she whispered. "What will happen to us now?"

120

"That old she-tly named Redflower will have her chance next, starting when the sun goes down. She'll be using nearmen to trail us instead of mechanical sensors. Paragas to take us. She wants your body."

"Can we—" Snowfire shuddered, shrinking away from the humming flies above the corpse. "Can we get away?"

"We're still on foot," he told her. "Nggooth is still ten days ahead. Tomorrow night, old Flintbreaker will be joining Redflower on our trail. He hunts with a striker tly and he likes to boast that nobody has ever escaped his last day of justice."

She stood looking at him solemnly.

"You are honest," she said at last. "I like you for that. I like you for many things." Impulsively she reached one dark-smeared finger to touch his lips. "If we are going to be killed," she breathed, "I think we should have love first."

A tremor of old emotion shook him.

"I—I'm sorry!" She drew quickly back. "I never understand you."

"Why not?" he muttered. "Now there'll never be anybody else."

In the cushioned comfort of the air-conditioned vehicle, they made love. They slept and woke, ate and drank again. She found a medical kit, used it to clean and dress their damaged feet.

By then the sun was low. Laden with canteens and fruit and dried food, with binoculars and compass from Goldforge's survival kit, with his hunting knife and translator, they left his bloating corpse beside his vehicle and plodded on across the wind-billowed sand.

All that endless night they toiled on. By day each sand hollow became a solar furnace, and still they labored on. In the fiery sunset they paused at the top of a crescent dune.

"We've a chance?" Snowfire whispered. "Haven't we a chance?"

121

He pointed back down the long yellow slope they had climbed so laboriously, at their footprints lying like two wavering trails of ink-black dots.

"We're still alive." He kissed her dust-caked lips. "We'll keep on trying.

But he stood a long time staring into the reddened sky. Another sunset. Old Flintbreaker would be joining Redflower, and their trail was impossible to hide.

They came out of the dunes late that night into a flow of old lava so rough they stopped to wait for daylight. When dawn broke they found a salt flat beyond the volcanic ridge, a dry lakebed so wide they couldn't see across it. Snowfire shrank back from its empty level immensity, but he grinned hopefully.

"Maybe," he whispered, "Maybe we do have a chance."

They struck boldly out across the white waste of hardened brine, circled slowly to the right, doubled back at last toward the lava cliffs.

"Our tracks on the salt are hard to see," he said. "And the heat should kill our scent."

They slept through the afternoon in a shallow lava cave. When the hot dark had fallen, to hide them from Flintbreaker's striker tly, they drank half the water in their last canteen and pushed out again across the salt.

Snowfire seemed strong at first, rested and hopeful. She kept glancing at the blazing constellations, trying to place her own home world and the white sun of Xyr and the farther star of Old Earth. But the lava had shredded her moccasins and the salt now burned her bleeding feet. Though she uttered no complaint, her limping became so painful that at last he let her stop.

He cleaned her feet with the ointment from Goldforge's kit and tried to repair the moccasins. They lay on the hardened brine. Though he hadn't meant to sleep, dead exhaustion overcame him. Dawn had dulled the stars when he woke. Their salt bed had cooled and Snowfire had snuggled against him. He was turning gently to draw her closer when he heard the nearmen baying.

It was a faint, far wailing, as tiny as the stifled screaming of a hatchling tly in an egg not yet pipped. To Blacklantern it sounded sad as death. Snowfire sprang up to run when she heard it, but he called her back.

"Nowhere to go." He gestured into the snowy flatness that reached unbroken into the red sunrise as far as they could see. "We'll wait."

They drained the last sips of water. He leaned down to hone his looted hunting knife on the nearman leather of his looted boots. Gravely Snowfire kissed him.

"The Fellowship of Benefactors is a well-intended undertaking." He tried to grin into her tragic face. "But, for a planet so primitive, with progress so hard, I think we need a few more fellows."

He felt her quiver, heard a tiny laugh that became a sob. They waited. The baying pealed across the sunlit salt, broken now and then when the increasing heat dimmed their trail, but always flowing nearer, wilder, higher, its somber melancholy breaking into yells of fierce elation when the nearmen found a stronger scent. Snowfire gasped and clutched her spear when the first fleet gray shape burst out of the milky glare.

"They are trained not to touch us," he told her. "Unless we try to run."

Shuddering, she stared at the pale-furred creatures racing around them, running sometimes erect, sometimes on all four limbs, sniffing after their blood, peering with strange wild bone-hooded eyes, baring bright fangs to bay. Their odor fouled the cool dawn air.

"Are they"—her troubled voice caught—"aren't they—men?"

"Their ancestors were," he said. "But the old starships were poorly shielded. The passengers got a lot of radiation and the nearmen sprang from mutations. The real men settled and stayed in the north hemisphere. In the great

123

depression around the sea. The nearmen fell heir to this dry hemisphere, which nobody wanted. They've been evolving here for a thousand generations. Roving like wild tlys. Often hunted. Sometimes domesticated.''

"Aren't they protected?"

"The early Benefactors got a token agreement written into the treaty of entry. The clans promised to keep them out of Nggonggamba—along with their flesh and their hides. But it's hard to change the ways of a world.''

"Do you mean"—she turned to stare at the gray howling things—"people *ate* them?''

"They've always been game." She had moved too far from the translator and he had to repeat. "Except for the tlys, they're the only big animals here. I guess neither will last long now, since Goldforge's excavators are eating up their lands.''

"We must look into that. If we live—''

"If we live." He looked at the baying beasts and thoughtfully back at her dark-stained face. "Which is better on the scales of the Benefactors? A handful of nearmen, fighting off the wild tlys and feeding on carrion? Or the billions of civilized spacemen that might live richer lives in swarm vehicles built from all the miles of metal in the core of the planet beneath us—''

The howl of the manpack was suddenly hushed and they turned to find Dr. Killbird and his client emerging from the blinding whiteness. Each was carried by a pair of loping nearmen. Both wore wide flat Nggonggan hats and steaming cooler suits.

The doctor's fleshless body sagged against the rods and straps of his metal exoskeleton, as if the hunt had been too much for him, but he was leaning from his saddle to hand the woman a stubby paragas gun. He slowed his bearers, and Redflower came on alone. At his hissed command she dismounted to shoot.

Blacklantern saw Snowfire standing silent, simply watching him. Her utter trust seemed suddenly ironic. He knew the range was impossibly great, but he fitted a pebble into his lancegrass sling. It whistled three times around his head. As he let fly, something exploded at their feet. He caught the sour stink of paragas.

Snowfire gasped and clutched at him and slid slowly down.

Exhaling, Blacklantern reeled two steps toward the cool dawn wind and dropped on his face. The hard salt pitched giddily beneath him and a freezing numbness washed him. Grimly he fought not to breathe.

He made his dead hand grasp his knife. Clumsily he gouged into the crusted brine beneath his head. When he couldn't help breathing, he forced his face into the stinging alkali, inhaled its bitter dust.

Lying still, he listened.

Set for Snowfire and himself, the translator was dead. He heard Redflower's shrill alien squalling, loud with elation and quavery with age. He heard Dr. Killbird's rasping sibilants, more distant, more cautious. He heard the nearmen growling, their hard feet thudding on the salt, at last the hurried crunch of Redflower's boots.

The salt dust was tainted with her synthetic scent and her shadow fell across him. He knew she was bending to contemplate the fair new body she was claiming for herself. He heard the doctor's anxious hiss, knew it must be a warning to make sure of him.

Rolling upright, he threw the knife.

It missed!

Alerted by the doctor's hiss, the woman had spun when he moved. He watched her raising the slim man-gun she clutched in her red-taloned claw. The gun wavered and dropped. She was crumpling toward the salt before his flung blade flashed by her face. By the time he reached her body, diving for her scrawny throat, she was already dead.

He twisted the man-gun out of her relaxing talons and whirled back to face Dr. Killbird. The fleshless otherworlder sat in his swinging saddle, drooping against his humming supports, weakly clutching the paragas gun the woman had used. His skull-face scowled uncertainly.

125

"Careful, sir!" Blacklantern bent to snatch the translator from behind Snowfire's ear. "Break the rules and you make yourself fair game."

The doctor's haggard eyes blinked. He hissed something the translator failed to catch. His motors whined suddenly and his skeletal fingers clutched for a whip. His nearmen yelped and clattered away. The respected Redflower was left where she had fallen. Her old heart had simply failed before she got the new one.

Now her own nearmen snorted and ran, dropping her saddle and all her gear. The whole pack howled away behind the departing doctor. Snowfire and her dead huntress lay side by side on the hard-caked brine.

The first effect of paragas was something close to death. Blacklantern was a long time finding Snowfire's pulse, and it was noon before she woke. Even when the hot evening fell, she was still too weak to walk.

Yet they went on. Blacklantern put her in Redflower's saddle and carried one end of the flexing poles, letting the other slide on the glassy salt.

Redflower they left for the tlys or nearmen to scavenge. They took her translator, canteen, and food pack. Blacklantern tried and left her man-gun, which was thumbkeyed and useless, but her boots were a fair fit for Snowfire's swollen feet.

He had been half blind from the savage dazzle of the salt, but at sunset he saw one high black dot against the dusty crimson. A wild tly, he wondered, seeking carrion? Or the Elder Huntsman's striker, already on their trail?

To confuse the pursuit he veered left till dark, then right again. When they stopped to rest at midnight Snowfire refused to ride again. They limped on and on together.

Scattered boulders began to break the starlit level, and at last the starlit salt gave way to darker sand. Beyond the old lakeshore they climbed a rough slope of weathered granite. The scarlet blaze of another dawn found them

126

stumbling across a high plateau of bare red rock. Suddenly it ended.

He heard Snowfire's gasp. In his own dead fatigue he had been aware of nothing beyond the next painful step. When he looked up all he could see was a dozen yards of wind-worn sandstone, broken off with a jagged fracture line.

Beyond was the pit.

It jolted him wide awake. Beyond that broken edge he saw the same chasm he had seen in the tank beneath the crystal floor of Toolcraft's laboratory—but the reality was unbelievably vaster than its projected image. To right and left the jagged lip ran on as far as he could see. He couldn't find the farther side.

Creeping fearfully closer, they dropped flat to look over the edge. The sheer rock face dropped straight down, so far it made him giddy. Broken rubble sloped on down from its foot, down and down into the thick brown haze that hid the bottom of the excavation.

"Mechanical maggots!" Snowfire peered at him, her eyes dark with shock. "The metal worms! I was coming to investigate them when the clansmen caught me."

He inched forward to look where she was pointing and saw two great bright worm-shapes creeping side by side along a wide rock shelf that broke the rubble slide. As they devoured boulders, more broken stone ran down around them, veiling them in thick gray dust. Even at that vast distance they looked enormous.

After a long time he gave Snowfire a shaken glance. "The Deeplode pit." He was hoarse with awe. "Back in Nggonggamba I talked to an engineer. The company is digging here for metal to build space vehicles. Toolcraft says they own the mining rights. He says everything is legal."

"You can imagine how the natives feel!" She laughed bitterly. "Mechanical maggots eating up their planet!"

"Toolcraft says the job will take ten thousand years. I

wish we had that sort of time." He shoved himself and turned to look behind them, searching the dusty air for the striker tly. Snowfire lay flat, still staring into the pit.

"I've found another—*thing!*" she gasped. "It isn't eating like the others. It's climbing the rock slides. Listen! You can hear it coming."

Leaning toward the pit, he heard a far sound, faint but deep. If all the flying, humming, stinging things of Nggongga had been rolled into one immense monster, he thought, this would have been its roaring.

"It's climbing straight toward us!" Her voice turned sharp. "Do you think it saw us!"

"I don't think we could matter—"

He had bent to search the pit when something rumbled in the wounded world beneath them. The rock shuddered. A sudden shock toppled him toward the brink. He was reeling on the rim, fighting for his balance, going over, when Snowfire caught him.

They fled back across the quaking rock. It shivered and pitched. It rang like a world-sized gong, as if to deep explosions. Black fissures opened all around them, spitting dust. A widening crack spread wide ahead. Snowfire stumbled into it, almost swallowed. He snatched her up, jumped desperately.

Beyond the crack they fell face down and lay there limp and gasping. The hard rock shivered and boomed beneath them. A vast thundering came out of the pit behind, swelling and swelling until it battered them with an avalanche of sound, cresting incredibly, sinking slowly back into that impossible abyss.

When they found breath and strength to stand they were on a new brink. The rock where they had stood beyond the crack had caved away. Daring to look down, they found a new rubble-slope far, far beneath, with an enormous apron of orange-colored dust still spreading down from its foot into that thick brown haze.

Those three great bright worms were gone. For a time he thought the rockfall had buried them. But then, as that distant thunder kept on dying, he heard the monstrous bellow of the nearest worm, undiminished. Rolling onward, the orange cloud uncovered all three worms. Two were still consuming talus. The third still climbed.

"It's seen us!" Snowfire trembled. "It's after us!"

"Not likely," he muttered. "We aren't that important."

They retreated beyond the risk of another rockfall and sat together on a sandstone ledge. Snowfire looked up at him, her face sick with dread.

"We've come so far." Her dust-roughened whisper wavered. "We've tried so hard." Tears welled out of her sun-reddened eyes. "What now?"

"I don't think we'll ever reach Nggooth," he said. "I'm not even sure it still exists—it may have already fallen into the pit. But still we're going on. I guess that's all we can do, with old Flintbreaker and his striker tly behind us."

Painfully, his lips tried to grin.

"We'll follow around the rim of the pit—Flintbreaker won't come too close. We'll try to stay alive. Our captured supplies are pretty well gone, but we can hope for more. With luck enough we'll find a water hole or perhaps a wild tly's nest."

She searched his face, abruptly leaned to kiss him. Suddenly busy, he opened the last frozen meal from Redflower's coldpack and set it on a rock for the sun to warm. He inspected their footgear, retied the flint point on a spear. Carefully he kept himself from looking at Snowfire or up at the dust-hazed sky where Flintbreaker's striker would be flying.

It struck that afternoon.

They had shared that final meal and a few measured sips of water, had slept till the sun's blue fury goaded them on. They were stumbling down a red-walled canyon that a lost stream had cut in some kinder time, when the hot sky howled.

Blacklantern swung drunkenly and saw the diving tly.

129

Sunlight glanced on arrowed black wings, burned on crimson armor. The five-jawed mouth was a wide black chasm, five great bright fangs unsheathed to strike. The tapered tail was whipping into a graceful curve, already reaching to poison him.

Lovely, deadly! All the emotions of his arena-struck youth came flooding back, as intoxicating as a great draught of seaberry wine. Filled and lifted with it, he felt all the wonder and terror of his first step upon the raked and patterned sand. His dead fatigue fell away.

"Drop!" he called to Snowfire. "Flat!"

Dancing away from her, he loosened his braided sling. Twirling it like a binding rope, he stood balanced on the balls of his feet, waiting breathlessly. That five-angled mouth howled again, its yell meant to paralyze its prey.

With all his old cunning, Blacklantern measured its dive. Deftly, at the ultimate instant, he flicked the sling to draw its black-tipped sting aside. He crouched to bring it lower, sprang to meet it. With both hooked hands he caught the tendons at the base of its slanted wings. Its own reflex lifted him, twirled him to its armored back.

Clinging there, where the sting couldn't reach, he plied his knife, ripping at the seams between the hard red plates, seeking the double heart beneath. The sting exploded behind him. A thick jet of venom spurted past. Recoiling from its acrid reek, he was suddenly afraid.

A single yellow drop . . .

All his long exhaustion washed over him again, as deadly as that agonizing venom. His old skill was gone. That fierce elation died. In this lonely bleak arena he had lost his last contest.

Closing, the powerful wings broke the grip of his knees. Slippery with the tly's bright blood, the knife flew out of his useless hands. He lost his seat. The slashing tail struck him in the air. He fell on hard rock.

Snowfire was tenderly washing his face with the last few drops of their water. He sat up groggily. His bruised head throbbed, but all the hardening blood had been the tly's. It lay near, entirely dead.

Like carrion nearmen they lapped its thick bitter blood from a darkening pool in a rock hollow and devoured hot raw strips of its liver. He cut long slices of its white wing-muscle to cure in the sun and ripped out its full water-stomach, which they could carry like a new canteen.

"I wouldn't have believed—" Snowfire looked up with its bright blood on her blackened face. Her pale green eyes held a dazed expression. "We've come a strange way together."

Later, beneath a cliff that made a narrow strip of shade, they slept. Blacklantern dreamed that he was an apprentice binder again, facing a bigger tly than he had ever seen. When he flicked his rope to turn it, it became a gigantic silver worm, diving at him, whining like a trillion thirsty blood-flies.

Snowfire woke him.

"It's coming," she whispered. "Listen!"

The droning bellow was real. It came from the direction of the pit. They fled from it, down the red-walled canyon, till Blacklantern caught the rank reek of nearmen. With a gesture for Snowfire to stay behind, he crept around a rocky bend and found Flintbreaker.

The scar-masked hunter stood upright in his stirrups, cursing and whipping his nearmen. His bearers had balked. The trailers huddled on all fours around him. The odor of their terror poured down the canyon like a fetid river.

"It seems we have a choice." Blacklantern looked bleakly back for Snowfire. "The mining machine behind us. Old Flintbreaker ahead—"

She was gone. Back around the bend he found her on her feet, staring up the canyon toward the pit. Beyond her, above the time-worn sandstone, a wide curve of bright metal was thrusting upward like a huge moon rising.

He forgot Flintbreaker. Snowfire was reaching blindly

131

for him, her eyes still fixed on that unbelievable reach of shining metal. He caught her clutching hand. Like two frightened children they stood watching the unending loom obscure the dusty sky. The dry rock began to tremble under them.

"Can it see us?" Its growing roar was deafening now; she had to shout. "Should we hide?"

He stood paralyzed as though the tly's sting had found him.

"If—" With a convulsive tremor, he broke free. "If we can find a cave."

They ran on around the bend. Though an evil nearman scent still edged the air, the creatures had fled. They found Old Flintbreaker where his bearers had thrown him, wandering dazedly to gather his saddle and whip, his weapons and packs.

"Wake up, hunter!" Blacklantern shouted. "Guard yourself!"

The old black clansman drew himself up painfully as if to recover his broken dignity and slowly turned to face the lifted spear.

"Kill me if you like." He spread his empty hands. "I don't care what you do."

"You were hunting our heads."

"No longer." His lean frame sagged again to a crushing load. "You ran cunningly and fought well. In all the history of the hunts none have done better. You have won your heads and your freedom—but you have destroyed the justice of Nggongga."

He unsheathed the lancegrass whistle he had used to call his tly, scowled at it sadly, tossed it away.

"I don't expect to hunt again." He was screaming hoarsely now, against that rolling thunder-note that shook the canyon walls. "What is the meaning of justice when our whole world is eaten?"

His stricken eyes lifted toward that bright moon still ballooning above the rust-red canyon walls.

"You call yourselves Benefactors?" His strained voice

turned bitterly sardonic. "Do you call that a benefaction?"

With a glance at Snowfire's troubled face, Blacklantern laid his spear aside. He tried the water in a skin the nearmen had dropped, found it good, shared it with her. Ignoring them now, Flintbreaker sat on a sandstone ledge, staring blankly up the canyon. They stood beside him, hands joined, watching the monstrous metal curve that swelled and swelled above them.

"A maggot!" Snowfire whispered. "A planet-eating maggot!" Her haggard eyes looked at him. "Why is it after us?"

Once he hoped it might pass by, but it turned again, following the bend of the canyon. Its deep thunder battered them. It covered half the brassy sky. Its rock-scarred jaws were straight above them.

Never looking down, Flintbreaker found the small brown pouch hung from his belt, fingered out two slick saltflower seeds, crunched them hungrily. He chewed, his mask of scars flexing stiffly. A sudden bright defiant purple jet spurted toward the great machine.

It had stopped. Now it slowly sank. Beneath its sinking mass the red cliffs split and crumbled. The hard rock boomed and quaked. A thin pink cloud of dry dust rolled down the canyon, hotter than the savage sun.

At last it lay motionless. A mile-long metal worm, worn bright from its work in the pit. Its roaring dropped into a sudden shocking silence. Its long shadow had covered them, and a welcome coolness came after that suffocating gust.

Still they waited.

At the top of its strange-shaped head, armored jaws spread open. A thin black tongue darted out, shot toward them. Its tip was a glittering point which became a shining dome as it swept near. The dome touched the canyon floor. A door slid open.

A man jumped out.

A lean other-worlder, in an odd brief garb with no wide

133

hat or cooler suit to shield him from the sun of Nggongga. Huge yellow freckles splotched his sunburned skin. Striding briskly toward them, he put on purple goggles.

"Toolcraft!" Blacklantern shook his head, only half believing what he saw. "Aren't you engineer Toolcraft?"

"Now manager Toolcraft. Goldforge's replacement, as resident director of Deeplode mines." Beneath the goggles his lean face looked apologetic. "My pursuit no doubt alarmed you. Sorry. When you were detected here we had no vehicle available except the excavator."

"We were alarmed." Blacklantern grinned with relief. "We weren't expecting anything good."

"You Benefactors will find us more cooperative now," Toolcraft promised, almost humbly. "Of course our official policy has always been to preserve the native people and their culture, but I'm afraid manager Goldforge had become a bit eccentric. As for myself, I never enjoyed the hunt. I'm more inclined to subsidize museums to preserve endangered cultural values and to found educational institutions to prepare the natives for transition." He looked at Snowfire, his bland smile fading. "Don't you think that would be commendable?"

"I'm not sure," she said. "The Benefactors will hope to be helpful. Anyhow, it was good of you to pick us up."

Toolcraft shrugged uncomfortably.

"The rules of the hunt didn't allow us to try an earlier rescue," he said. "But I had instructed our crew here to watch out for you. Medical aid is standing by and we have restored your relay service to Xyr. We'll soon have you safe in Nggonggamba—assuming the Elder Huntsman's permission."

Inquiringly he turned to Flintbreaker.

The black hunter had risen unsteadily from his seat on the rock. He looked up solemnly at the armored immensity of the excavator and down again at them. His thin old hands folded together and his scarred head dipped in a ritual bow.

"We had appealed to the justice of the hunt and we

accept the outcome." Grave emotion quavered through the roll of his formal intonations. "But don't hurry me."

Toolcraft was urging them all into his crystal cage, but Flintbreaker hung stubbornly back. Tall with his tribal dignity, he turned to look down the widening canyon into the shimmer of heat upon limitless desolate horizons beyond the bare red cliffs.

"Your iron worms have eaten Nggooth, and I'm afraid our ancient hunts have ended," his mellow voice rolled again. "If the Benefactors say that our old lands must go to make new world-machines in space, let that be. For myself, I need one more moment to swallow the sorrow that swells my throat. I think I'll never see our sacred lands again. But the old must break to make the new—so you have taught us."

He came unsteadily at last and let the engineer help him into the waiting elevator.

Blacklantern followed, feeling both elation and sadness. He and Snowfire had earned new recognition for the Benefactors. They would be getting honors and rewards and exciting new missions. Under their guidance Nggongga would now be moving into a future more splendid than its primitive past.

Yet, when Toolcraft gave his freckled hand to Snowfire, his open admiration and her green-eyed smile left him longing for the days and nights of cruel danger and narrow victory when she had been his alone. He thought he would recall them as the happiest of his life.

4.

BLACKLANTERN came striding across the rumbling cavern of the Nggonggan portal dome, a scowl on his bleak dark face.

"Respected Benefactor!"

A busy traffic inspector recognized him even without the red uniform and the silver crescent of his lunar fellowship, which he had put off for the plain gray kilt of the Game clan.

"Rain and shade!" The black inspector shouted that hearty Sand clan greeting. "We range the desert together."

I range alone.

In no mood for courtesy, he pushed rudely on until he saw that wide grin fading. The man's hurt stopped him. After all, he had no friends to spare.

"Rain." He paused to echo the formula. "Shade. I'm here to meet a passenger."

"Share my tent, sir." Relieved, the inspector bustled up to brush palms with him. "I saw you fight in the arena, sir. Before you had a name. In fact I lost twelve gongs on you." Admiration flashed in the grin. "The unknown challenger from the gutters of Nggonggamba! I expected you to win, but I would have bet another dozen gongs that you would never become the Benefactor. Our first citizen!"

No longer.

The unspoken thought lay bitter on his tongue. A dozen dozen days ago, when Snowfire left, he had been named the resident Benefactor. That high post had been the goal of all his years training on Xyr, and cruel emotion tore him now when he had to give it up.

"I see you're troubled, sir," the inspector bumbled. "Nggongga hatches no end of hard dilemmas, and they all fall upon you. I know that each starving clansman wandering into the city makes a new burden for you. But the Benefactors are our last great hope. We trust you, sir!"

More than I trust myself.

He didn't want to say that he was surrendering his high position just to follow a girl who had left him. Wryly silent, he recalled the term in the Game clan dialect for such hopeless expeditions. "White tly hunts." There were no white tlys.

Disconcerted by his moodiness, the man was turning away.

"Find water." Forcing a smile, Blacklantern groped for words of graceful gratitude. "Find peace."

"Water!" Happy again, the inspector dropped to one knee in the ritual bow of a departing junior. "Peace!"

He bustled away.

Blacklantern stalked somberly on to wait for Thornwall at the arrival stage beneath the space gate. He knew that the stare of the gate was nothing more than an optical illusion created by the transport fields, but in his dark mood it seemed to watch him like the eye of God.

Lidless and enormous, the seeming eye peered out of involute space-time. The blue-glowing control fields were its iris. The pupil, framed in that queerly painful shimmer of dimensionless energy, was the interface itself—the cosmic shortcut to many thousand worlds.

Uneasily he kept shifting along the guardrail beside the exit strip. The eye always followed. Its huge black disk seemed to probe through all his poor defenses of uncertain status and unstable purpose to find the naked black street urchin he once had been.

It made him feel several sorts of fool.

The giant pupil winked. Half a heartbeat from the far-off planet of the Benefactors Thornwall emerged from the reflected cosmic dark. A tall commanding man, robed in formal red. He flashed his ensign at the guards and swung off the transit strip, stern face searching.

Blacklantern started to meet him but faltered. His ageless ice-blue eyes looked too much like that appalling orb through which he had come. When he found Blacklantern, however, all his sternness thawed into an easy smile. Lifting two fingers in the fellowship salute, he paused with a look of mild inquiry.

"I wish you were angry sir." Stiffly, Blacklantern returned his salute. "You ought to be. I've let you down."

"You know you're always free to leave the fellowship." Thornwall's level gaze was still disturbing, but his quiet tone showed no resentment. "We never coerce anybody."

"I can't help feeling disloyal." The implacable stare of that giant eye drove Blacklantern to confession. "I remember you took me out of jail. You made me a Benefactor. You gave me knowledge and power I had never dreamed of—the chance to share the gifts of progress with all my people. I know I've failed and I feel wretched about it.

"What went wrong?"

"Two—two problems." Beneath that ruthless gaze Blacklantern's words stumbled. "You'll meet one of them waiting outside. The other is Snowfire."

"You can forget her."

"The trouble is I can't forget."

"I knew you were lovers." Probing him, Thornwall's pale old eyes seemed as omniscient as the gateway. "That's why we stationed the two of you together here after your escape from the Game clan hunters. When she left I supposed the affair was over."

141

"Not for me."

He stopped uncomfortably, but Thornwall simply stood waiting.

"We had different notions of what love is. When engineer Toolcraft brought us out of the desert after the hunt she fell for him. She wanted us both. Being Nggong-gan, I was jealous. She called me selfish. We hurt each other. When he went back to Swarmworld One I let her go with him, though I thought she wanted me to beg her to stay. I felt too—too proud for that."

He bit his lip with a grimace of pain.

"I was wrong," he muttered. "A wrongheaded fool! I'm going after her now. I'll beg her, if I must, to let me join them."

"You can't get there." Thornwall's thin old voice held a heavy finality. "Swarmworld One is nearly five thousand light-years away. The star gates to it have all been closed."

"I can try."

"Trying won't help. The swarmworlders aren't cooperative. We have an old philosophic quarrel with them about culture contacts. As Benefactors we try to help primitive races adapt to new technologies. The swarmworlders feel that alien technologies are likely to destroy less advanced peoples. They have always kept their culture to themselves."

"I know they don't like visitors—"

But I have a plan.

He didn't say the words because his plan was too desperate. He didn't want Thornwall laughing at him.

"Snowfire's gone." With a shrug that dismissed her utterly, Thornwall swung toward the exit strips. "You're still here. The Benefactor of Nggongga."

"I was," he said. "You'll see why I'm quitting."

When Thornwall's luggage was routed to the agency compound, they rode out of the terminal into the brassy noon of Nggonggamba. Though the "white night" was almost over, the traffic ways were still abandoned to

142

savage sunlight. Blind in the glare, Blacklantern heard angry native voices and the slap of calloused native feet.

"Watch them, sir!" he whispered. "They're desperate!"

A score of nearly naked blacks came rushing at them from the shadow of the dome. A gaunt cripple, lurching on clumsy lancegrass crutches. A reeling woman, skeleton-thin, with a still baby in her arms. A starving huge-eyed child running ahead, holding out a flat bright native hat for a begging bowl.

"They're—dreadful!" Thornwall was thumbing coins from his belt. "Let's give them something."

"Careful, sir!" Blacklantern murmured. "Let me do it."

"You call yourselves Benefactors?" The woman shrieked her accusation in a desert dialect. "You travel to the stars and do the work of gods—but look at my child." Her withered black hands held out the dead infant. "Why won't you share with us?"

"We do share." He took Thornwall's coins and flung them out across the pavement. "We try to—forgive us!"

Most of the mob ran to scrabble for the coins, snarling over them like ravenous animals. The woman stood swaying, the bloated baby in her stretched-out arms. Its odor turned him ill.

"Come, sir!" He hurried Thornwall toward the nearest passenger way. "You'll see our troubles here. Attacks in the public ways. Pickets at the agency. Hatred I can't endure. The people screaming for food. Their leaders trying to blame us for all that's wrong with Nggongga—and more going wrong every day."

"Patience." Gently, the old man smiled. "Our task was never easy."

"Impossible!" he muttered. "Here on Nggongga. The starving mobs are after our heads, and the police can't—or won't— protect us."

A second crowd of shouting blacks had sprung from nowhere before they reached the ramp. A slim young girl hawking desert flowers. Grimy boys clamoring to clean their boots. Shrieking sellers of bright-dyed incense sticks and mildewed muskweed pods and burnt clay charms against Cru Creetha. One blind crone followed the pack, offering a worn-out rug of woven nearman hair.

"Make way!" Blacklantern pushed through them. "Make way for the respected senior Benefactor."

"*Tleesh!*" A tly-stung arena veteran shoved past him, thrusting a twisted claw at Thornwall. "Share life!"

Jostled, the Benefactor tripped over a bootcleaner's box. The horde closed around him. The old tly-fighter bent as if to help—and slammed him viciously back against the pavement. The flower girl snatched at his belt and suddenly ran.

"*Oongath!*" Blacklantern yelled that Game clan warning of ritual revenge and plunged into the mob. The tly-fighter met him with a cunning kick at the groin. Twisting aside, he saw a dagger flash.

"*Tleesh!*" A dirty urchin mocked him with that old appeal for desert hospitality. A thrown boot-box grazed his head. The owners jeered him with his own battle cry, *"Oongath! Oongath!*

The sense of crisis lit a bright elation in him and awoke his old arena skills. Smiling into the sun, he whipped off his belt for a binding rope. One quick flick drew his attacker's eyes, while he dived for the dagger. In another moment the stung man lay squealing on the pavement, bound like a defeated tly.

Blacklantern gripped the captured dagger and whirled.

Suddenly silent, the mob melted away. Two frightened boys scuttled to recover the box they had thrown. The evil reek of the dead baby still tainted the stifling air.

Thornwall stood up, rubbing his bruises.

"My ensign!" he whispered. "Gone."

"Guard yourself." Blacklantern gave him the dagger. "I'll get it back."

Thumbing his own ensign to call the police, he started after the flower girl. She had paused to look back. When

144

she saw him following, she flung the stolen ensign at him and fled again. He brought it back to Thornwall.

"My people!" Blacklantern opened his arms in a gesture of futility. "My own people! As a Benefactor I was trying to bring them progress—or anyhow to help them survive it. But they're too many for me. Too ignorant. Too hungry. Too savage."

"That's why they need us."

"The job's too much for me." He scowled moodily down at the bound man and turned wearily back to Thornwall. "I have a stereogram from Snowfire. Her farewell message from the swarmworld, just before the gates were closed. I want you to hear her—she says we Benefactors have been wrong."

"On some worlds we have failed. We may fail here." Thornwall nodded calmly. "Mankind has one great enemy that we can never completely defeat—man himself." With age-yellowed hands he held up the dagger as if for evidence. "All the human traits that served us in the jungle can betray us in society. Yet we must preserve them. The same dark forces that threaten our survival are also the bright springs of our creative evolution. That ancient blackness sometimes kills us—but sometimes it transforms us. The paradox now and then defeats us—but sometimes we win. The human universe is better than it would have been without the Benefactors."

"I wonder—" He saw Thornwall's pain and checked himself. "Let's get on," he said. "Before the police come. These people will accuse us. We could be the ones hauled in."

He released his captive, who stalked sullenly back toward the shadow of the dome.

"Let's hear Snowfire." Thornwall stood blinking into the searing glare and swaying unsteadily as if Nggongga had been too much for him. "Somewhere out of the sun."

The still-abandoned ways carried them out of the portal zone to a Sea clan wineshop where they took refuge from the white night in a cool dim booth. When the waitress was gone Blacklantern twisted the base of the little black message disk and set it on the table before them.

Snowfire's silver image flickered in its focal cone and came alive with sudden color. Her green-gold eyes smiled sadly at him.

"Dear Blackie—" Her low-pitched voice woke memories that still blurred his eyes with tears. "I'm deeply grieved that we can never meet again. Never touch. Never love. But I guess we've made our choices. You couldn't accept the customs of my folk. I wouldn't accept the ways of yours.

"Anyhow, this will be our last contact. Swarmworld One is closing all its external gates. Indefinitely, Toolcraft says. I suppose you'll wonder why. The reason is something I can only hint at. A cultural quantum jump. A radical new solution to the population problem.

"I wish I could say more. I've been asking for details to send back to the Benefactors, but you know the swarmworld philosophy. My hosts are afraid their new technology might damage other cultures. Perhaps they're right. Anyhow, it is something too far advanced to be useful on Nggongga."

Her image moved in the cone and red fire played across her hair. He trembled, fighting the blind desire to reach, to catch and hold her golden loveliness.

"So this is our final farewell. I wanted to say again that I do love you, Blackie. In my own way—I still wish it had been yours too. It saddens me to think of you left to waste your life on the pathetic little projects of the Benefactors, doomed as you are to suffer and die in the darkness of Nggongga. I still wish—wish—"

Her voice had quivered, and the cone flickered as if she had erased a moment of emotion.

"Don't forget me, Blackie!" Suddenly she was dazzling. "I want you to know that I'm utterly happy. Eager to test this startling new invention. If Toolcraft's promises are true, our new world will be more wonderful than anything you Nggonggans ever pictured for a paradise.

"Good—Good-bye, Blackie!"

Her eyes had darkened with feeling and he caught the green glint of a tear as her image dimmed. The disk clicked faintly and the empty shadow-cone winked out.

Blacklantern sat gazing dully at nothing. She had looked real enough to touch, and he could still imagine her sweetleaf fragrance lingering in the booth. All his own brash confidence had faded with her image, and the gloom around him grew darker now with his own awareness of the tragedy of Nggongga.

He had almost forgotten that he was not alone, and it startled him a little when Thornwall moved. The aged Benefactor looked as fragile as another shadow in the cone, but his quavery voice was strangely serene.

"So we've lost Snowfire." He leaned calmly forward to refill their glasses. "It takes a rare sort of person to remain a Benefactor. But we're still physicians to mankind. So long as men need help to deal with progress, we'll go on."

"Without me." Impatiently, Blacklantern swept his glass aside. "I'm going to follow Snowfire."

"You heard her say all the gates are closed."

"But I think I've found a way." Eagerness lifted his voice. "Engineer Toolcraft was here, you know, to mine Nggongga for the swarmworld—without too much concern at that time about what happened to the natives. The mine is abandoned now. With this new invention perhaps our planet is no longer needed.

"Anyhow, I've earned a name in the Game clan and my new friends tell me the mining machinery is still lying there, abandoned in the pit. I hope to get to the swarmworld through the gates that took the ore.

"Don't laugh at me!"

Thornwall's breath had caught.

"I'm not laughing—but you make me wish I were young again." A brief smile twitched his parchment lips.

147

"If our mission here on Nggongga is too much for you, I think you'll find the way to Snowfire ten times harder."

"I'll take the risks."

"Have you really faced the odds?"

"I've had nightmares about them."

"You've no chance at all." Thornwall's face was sadly stern. "You're a primitive. You'll be lost in the most advanced culture known—swarmworld has been evolving new technologies for twenty thousand years. You don't know the folkways. Not even the language."

He had to nod in uneasy agreement.

"Even if you get there, how will you find her? The swarmworlders have been exploding into space for dozens of generations. The swarm is many billion life-spheres, all in orbit. Each one holds as many people as a planet. Looking for her, you'll be like a blind man searching all the deserts of Nggongga for one special grain of sand."

Blacklantern stiffened impatiently.

"I've met swarmworlders before. I've even killed one—Goldforge, the manager of their mine here—when he was hunting my head in the desert. I have his translator and his name ring. I have Snowfire's swarmworld address—probably Toolcraft's home—from the label on the stereogram. I even have money from selling a few trinkets I'll never need again."

"I drink to your enterprise!" Thornwall raised his glass with a quick ironic smile. "Even though I think you wouldn't be going if you had attacked your problem here with this sort of spirit."

Blacklantern gulped his wine and said nothing.

"Is she really worth so much?" Cold again, the old eyes probed him. "Your whole career as a Benefactor? All our hopes for the future of your people?"

"I've tried to be rational." Blacklantern scowled at the dead message disk. "I used to laugh at the love-crazed heroes in our old epics. I know there are women enough on Nggongga—girls my own color, sharing my own culture, fit for anything. I even know Snowfire will never be entirely mine, wherever I find her."

He spread his hands in a native gesture of submission.

"But—you see, sir—I can't help how I feel. She—she's burnt into my brain. The image of her festers in me like a barbed desert thorn. Not that I want to forget!"

For a moment they sat silent. A lazy fan above them stirred the scents of stale wine and rancid musk and black sweat. Glasses clinked somewhere in the steamy gloom and a girl laughed.

"You trouble me." Thornwall pushed the pottery bottle aside. "You and Snowfire. Top agents. People I trusted—loved. Doing something very foolish that I can't understand."

"I know how to fight a tly." Blacklantern paused uncomfortably. "Nggongga is harder to handle. I guess I've just lost faith. In the Benefactors. Even in myself."

He saw the hurt in Thornwall's eyes and still went on.

"I believe the swarmworld philosophy is right. Nggongga must have been a better place before the eye was ever opened. My people had their own way of living, shaped and tested by a dozen dozen generations."

"Yet they were quick enough to give it up," Thornwall said. "Just watch them now, leaving their desert trails and their old mud towns to flock into Nggonggamba."

"The city seems to draw them as flames draw night moths." He nodded and paused to think. "The unbreakable problem is the people explosion. The old clan system here was a working answer to it—each clan owned only a limited list of names, and nameless men were not allowed to marry. The younger sons had a hard choice—the priesthood or the tly arena. But at least they knew who they were."

He made a face as if the wine were bitter.

"The opening of the eye has wrecked all that. The clans are breaking up. The old traditions are thrown away, the old gods forgotten. Progress has betrayed us. We wipe out

149

old diseases with the miracle medicines—and breed more people than the planet can feed. We buy bright new atomic pumps to irrigate our croplands—and dry up the geologic water under the old oases. In flight from the spreading deserts, we follow the promise of progress into Nggonggamba—and die in the streets.''

He pushed his glass aside to lean across the table.

"Tell me what I could have done," he challenged Thornwall. "As resident Benefactor, after Snowfire left, I was alone here. With no power over anybody. Tell me what one man can do for two handred million. For hordes of hungry people like those who tried to rob us. They can't eat culture or social theory or even benevolent intentions.''

"We can't help people," Thornwall objected patiently. "We learned that long ago. You have millions here demanding food, when there isn't that much food. Even if you somehow fed them, you would have twice as many millions in another generation, twice as desperate. It may seem cruel, but all you can do is tell them how to help themselves.''

"If they're too hungry to listen—"

"We always find a few to listen. We train those few to teach and lead the rest. Better than food, we can offer membership in the new galactic culture. We can build a university, design a planetary language, plan a new government. Rather than food alone, we bring knowledge and purpose and hope. We lead the way to a new social discipline.''

"If people won't follow—"

"We can't compel anybody—but the facts of nature can." Thornwall straightened sternly. "If you Nggonggans could keep on doubling your numbers with every generation, in only six thousand years the whole mass of the universe would be black flesh. If we Benefactors have authority, it comes from such harsh brute facts.''

"I tried." Blacklantern shrugged. "I'm through."

150

Suddenly smiling, he leaned to pick up the black message disk.

"All I want is Snowfire."

"I don't think you'll find her." Yet Thornwall's tight little smile reflected his own. "If you do reach the swarmworld, I want to know that new solution to the people problem. I thought the swarmfolk already had the final answer with all their available mass built into space vehicles and all their solar energy trapped and utilized. I can't imagine anything better."

"I'll try to learn their answer. But I don't expect to be coming back."

"Good hunting, anyhow!" Bright youth had come back to Thornwall's deep-sunk eyes, and he lifted his glass with a flourish. "We trained you well on Xyr. Perhaps you'll make it!"

Blacklantern gave up his ensign that afternoon, though Thornwall still protested. He outfitted himself at a manhunter's shop. Next morning, wearing Goldforge's name ring and translator, he set out on a chartered flight south toward the old hunting lands of the Game clan.

His pilot was a nervous little mud-colored man, a compulsive chewer of saltflower seed, a compulsive worrier about the voltage drop in his reserve power cell, a compulsive talker about his Sea clan wife and his nine unmarried daughters, two of them unaccountably pregnant.

Only half listening, Blacklantern was scanning his route map and the unrolling desert. As last he found the narrow green oasis where the ritual hunts had begun. He picked out the bare red mesas he and Snowfire had crossed, the ripple of yellow dunes where Goldforge had overtaken them, the flows of black lava beyond, and the white blaze of the dry salt lake where the body hunters had finally brought them to bay.

Beneath the flyer all their endless days and nights of love and pain were telescoped into meaningless moments.

151

There was the last red ridge—where the world broke off. Beyond it, sheer cliffs of broken sandstone lipped a pit too vast to show any farther rim.

The brown pilot fell abruptly silent.

He leaned against the window, looking for the bottom of the pit. He found rubble slopes, level shelves, deeper slopes, and steeper cliffs. What he discovered at last, miles and miles below, was no bottom, but the tops of towering clouds, floating out of a hazy void.

"Do you want to land on the rim, sir?" The pilot still thought he had come to hunt wild nearmen. "Our agreement doesn't cover spotting or shooting from the air."

"We aren't landing here," he said. "We're flying down inside."

Profanely, the pilot called the name of dark Cru Creetha, eater of suns. His flyer had been chartered for a flight to the pit, not into it. Of course, personally, he was not afraid to fly anywhere. The Sun Lighter would bear witness to his courage. But he was legally obligated to adhere strictly to the terms of their official flight plan.

"I'll double the charter price," Blacklantern offered, "if you'll land me near one of the old mining machines down inside."

The pilot's muddy color faded. He had heard all he wanted to know about the great metal worms the swarmworlders had sent to eat up the planet, and he had already come closer to them than he wanted to be.

The old excavators were stopped and abandoned, Blacklantern said. They couldn't harm anybody.

So I hope, he told himself.

The pilot crunched another saltflower seed. Muttering huskily through froth-purpled lips, he said he must consider not only the alarming signs of failure in the reserve power cell and his duty to his wife and daughters, but also the terms of his flight insurance.

Blacklantern estimated the funds he had left. Gates and gongs would be useless, he supposed, in the swarmworld,

152

and he wasn't coming back. He offered to triple the charter fee.

The pilot munched thoughtfully and spurted purple fluid at the cabin floor. Squinting shrewdly across that jagged brink into the cloudy depths, he announced that another gross of gongs would complete the dot for his first daughter. Blacklantern paid him and they dived.

They found the excavator lying on a black granite ledge. A small bright worm, it swelled and swelled beneath them to become a mile-long monster. The pilot set the flyer down at a judicious distance and Blacklantern scrambled out with his hunting gear.

"I'll wait overnight," the pilot offered. "For six gross of gongs."

"Don't wait."

"You can't live here. You can't climb out." The pilot peered uneasily up at the slopes of broken stone and the fracture-carved precipices and the broken benches that made a giant's stairway toward the far sky. "I'll come back in three days—for another triple fee."

"I don't have the money," Blacklantern said. "Anyhow, I've another way out, through that old excavator."

Chewing hard, the pilot blinked up at the monstrous metal mass and took off hastily.

From the lip of that wide ledge, Blacklantern looked down into the pit. Though the jagged rim that framed the narrow scrap of sky was miles and miles above, his rocky ledge was less than halfway down. The clouds that hid the bottom were still far beneath his level. Lightning flickered in them now, and an endless peal of thunder began crashing and rumbling and rolling away against those looming walls.

He turned to watch the flyer climb. Dwindling fast, it was only a black insect before it reached the top of the first talus slope. Before it rose above the first black granite wall he had lost it.

He stood there alone.

153

His neck hurt from looking up and he couldn't help a tiny shiver from his shattering sense of the vastness of the pit and the power of the swarmfolk who had abandoned it so casually. Perhaps he had been a fool to let the flyer go, but he had no time for fear. He hitched up his hunting pack and hiked toward the excavator.

The cautious pilot had left him a long way to hike. He was sweating before he reached the great machine. Its curved armor swelled out far above him, scarred from titanic rockfalls, bright and massive and impregnable. Under its shadow, he plodded on toward its rock-crushing jaws.

A new rockslide had half buried the machine since it stopped. Huge fallen boulders faced him with sheer cliffs as grim as any he had conquered long ago, hunting nestling tlys. It cost him a hard hour's climbing to reach the rotary teeth of the excavator.

In the echoing cavern behind those enormous metal molars, he used his hunting lantern to pick a way along the titanic conveyor that had carried broken stone back to the transflection portal. A blue light flashed suddenly ahead.

Alert to the danger of toppling into some ore bin or smelter in the far-off swarmworld, he took that for a warning. Climbing off the conveyor, he explored great strange mechanisms until he found a railed inspection walk that led him at last into a high control booth.

Lights came on when he closed the door. One wall turned transparent to show him a bright picture of the swarmworld—a tiny blue sun wrapped in a milky mist of life-spheres, each invisibly small. A long panel against the opposite wall glowed with symbols he couldn't read.

The third wall framed a dark opening beyond a level ramp. When he walked toward it, new lights picked out a little vehicle without wheels, somehow suspended just above a wide black track. Its transparent shell showed half a dozen seats inside.

Trembling now with the same breathless sense of risk and elation he had felt when he faced his first diving tly, he

154

pulled at its oval door. The door stayed fast—but, beside it, an amber-circled sensor began to blink.

He stopped for a moment, frowning. Any error, now, could be as quickly fatal as a false move in the arena. Yet this was clearly the transport system of the vanished miners. The vehicle promised to carry him to the swarm-world while the blinking sensor seemed to question his right to go.

He caught his breath and thumbed Goldforge's name-ring to flash its color-coded signal ray into the black center of the sensor. The amber circle stopped blinking. The door slid open. Light came on inside the crystal shell. Heart thudding, he stepped inside.

The door clicked shut behind him.

He waited, almost afraid to breathe. Nothing happened until he slid warily into the nearest seat. Then a soft bell-note rang and a bank of keys shone green on an oval panel beside his seat. Most of the symbols that marked them were strange, but he saw that two of them were numerals, oddly shaped, like those on the label of Snowfire's stereogram.

He sat for a moment thinking, muscles as taut as when he first had to judge the strike of a screaming tly. Hopefully, then, he began using the portal print on the label, punching out what he hoped would be Snowfire's swarm-world address.

The life-sphere number—or was it? As he touched the last digit, the panel chimed faintly and one green key turned golden. More elated and more anxious, he stabbed out what he thought should be the level number.

A higher note chimed. Another symboled key changed color. With a heady sense of success, as if he had discovered the blind side of a dangerous tly, he tried the octant number. Another rising chime. Another golden glow.

He kept tapping, his whole body cold with sweat and quivering. The sector number. The zone number. The corridor number. At last, the dwelling number. Its final digit startled him with a deep-toned gong and a flashing crimson symbol.

He froze as if an unseen tly had bellowed above him. While he stood wondering what to do, a toneless synthetic voice hummed from the panel.

"—transposed." Goldforge's translator picked it up. "Dwelling no longer occupied. Access restricted. Revised destination instructions required."

All his muscles tightened, but he had nothing for them to do.

"Request—" His voice failed and he had to catch his breath. "Request destination information. New address of—of last occupants. Of Benefactor Snowfire and engineer Toolcraft."

For an endless second nothing happened.

"Benefactor Snowfire not identified," that dead voice droned at last. "Engineer Toolcraft transposed. No local dwelling in use. Revised destination instructions required."

Grimly he tried to slow his drumming heart.

"Request assistance," he called again. "Required destination is current address of engineer Toolcraft, former occupant of destination first requested."

For longer seconds there was no response.

"Body of engineer Toolcraft located," the machine purred suddenly. "Revised destination will be Ironforge Clinic of Exotic Pathology, Sphere 101011100, Level 1100101, Octant 101, Sector 1100101, Zone 11100, Corridor 110011, Dwelling 11001010. Prepare for departure."

He sank back in the seat with a gasp of relief.

The crimson winking stopped. A triple chime rang. Silently the crystal capsule swept forward into a gray-walled tunnel. Ahead, a giant eye widened.

He shrank in spite of himself from its blue-rimmed blackness.

The vehicle toppled down its track, through the painful depthless flicker of the iris, into the flat enormous pupil.

156

The cavernous belly of the excavator was instantly five thousand light-years behind. The vehicle swayed and fell again, through another gray tunnel and into a stranger space.

For a heart-clutching moment he felt weightless. The capsule tipped up a steeply climbing track. As it gained speed, his sense of weight came back. He caught his breath and tried to see where he was.

On his left a dark wall was blurred smooth by his motion. On the right he looked out into a hollow cylinder, its dimensions too vast for him to estimate. Mottled blue and green, its faraway curve was below and above and all around him. Its farther end was lost in misty distance.

The cylinder seemed to roll beneath his racing vehicle, spinning around him at a giddy rate. A wave of vertigo swept him. Clutching at the seat ahead, he groped for his lost orientation. Though he supposed the life-sphere must be rotated to create a centrifugal substitute for gravity, he knew it couldn't be spinning so crazily.

Most of the actual motion, he soon decided, was that of his own capsule, plunging around and around a spiral track built into the near end of the cylinder, carrying him away from its axis toward the wall.

This long hollow, then, must be only the core of the huge life-sphere. The inhabited levels would be farther from the axis, where the centrifugal pull was stronger.

His giddiness gone, he looked "down" again at the endless racing landscape. Now, as it came nearer, he could see that the green areas were grassland and forest, the blue patches lakes and streams. Here, at the heart of this enormous mechanical world, the swarmfolk had made a place for nature.

Eagerly he began searching for people.

Soon he was able to pick out the boles of odd-shaped flowering trees. He saw winged things flying, fat quadrupeds grazing, a sleek black creature stalking one of them. He caught a glimpse of what looked like playground equipment in an empty park on a wide lake beach. Grace-

157

ful robotic devices were busy here and there, but he found no human beings.

Perhaps the swarmfolk were sleeping.

At the level of that deserted landscape, the capsule flashed past a vacant passenger platform and dropped into another tunnel. A new gong chimed and the whole nose of the vehicle was filled with the stereo image of a half-transparent ball, wide triangular wings flaring from its poles.

Deep inside it a bright green point was crawling. When he found the hollow core and all the curving shells around it, he suddenly understood that the ball was the life-sphere, that the creeping point followed his own position.

Now and then some light or signal flashed backward along the tunnel wall, but the capsule was so soundless that he thought it must be moving in a vacuum. He felt startled when it lurched and stopped with a wheeze of air. The map winked out. A mellow gong rang.

"Ironforge Clinic," that cold synthetic voice announced. "Ironforge Clinic."

When the door slid open, he scrambled out of the capsule. Soundlessly it glided away. He stood on a bright-lit platform. Tensing with a wary readiness, as if waiting for a strange tly to dive, he turned to search that long chamber for the teeming swarmfolk he had been prepared to meet.

He found nobody anywhere.

Bewildered by this silent emptiness where he had expected to encounter teeming billions, he paused to sniff the air for any human odor. His nose was keen enough to tell Sea clan fish-eaters from the muskweed pickers of the Wind clan or the Game clan nearman hunters, but the cool wind that blew from the tunnel held nothing of mankind.

When he listened all he could hear was the thump of his own heart and the rustling of his clothing and the tiny clink and clatter of his hunting gear, all magnified when they whispered back from the hard white walls.

As if climbing near a wild tly's nest, he moved along the platform, all alert, searching the way for each footstep, Still he heard no human sound, caught no human scent—till a loud gong nearly stopped his heart.

Where it had rung, he found an amber sensor circle blinking. Quivering with his own strained readiness, he flashed Goldforge's ring into the circle. It went out. A tall crack cut the wall and widened to make a doorway. He walked through, into a monumental room.

It should have been busy. Rows of seats faced high screens where unreadable legends glowed. Bright kiosks were spaced here and there about an unending desert of floor, as if to dispense information or instructions. All around the faraway walls empty archways opened into half-seen vacant passages.

But all his senses found nobody anywhere.

The dead hush dissolved all his first elation into dark perplexity. Even if the swarmfolk observed their own white night, there should be somebody somewhere. Though he could see no evidence of violence or disaster, he began to feel that he had stumbled into a universe of irrational nightmare.

A liquid clink took his breath again, as startling as some water drop in a desert cave. It rang and pattered and died in the long vaults above him and came again before he found its source in a new pool of scarlet light before him on the floor.

Uncertainly he stepped toward it.

The pool stretched out at once to become a bright red line, leading toward a distant archway. He caught his breath and followed.

The scarlet mark arrowed ahead, guiding him down an echoing hall beyond the arch, across another huge concourse, into another corridor so long that he could see its floor curving disturbingly up and up ahead of him to follow its level around the axis of the spinning sphere.

Still he met nobody.

The red line bent at last to pick out a door. A queer

bright symbol flashed beside it. A chime sounded. The door divided. A gangling, yellow-freckled man ambled out into the corridor to greet him in fluent street Nggonggan.

"Welcome, Benefactor! When the machines said old manager Goldforge was on his way here, I knew it had to be you."

"Toolcraft?" Without the blue goggles he had always worn on Nggongga, with his stiff white hair uncombed and his uneven teeth too widely spaced and a faint purple stain on his lips, the freckled man looked so young and mild and harmless that he was hard to recognize. "I'm glad—glad to find you!"

"You almost missed me."

Relaxed and affable, Toolcraft beckoned him through the entry alcove, past the glowing signals of what must be the master panel for the household machinery, into the thin sweet smoke of muskweed burning in a black clay censer on an antique tripod of Sea clan bronze.

The room relaxed him. The walls were hung with ritual daggers and braided rugs of nearman hair. A tall shelf held a blown tly's egg, painted with Cru Creetha's black-fanged grin. The seats were massive lancegrass cushions. Inside, everything was Nggonggan.

Blacklantern inhaled the incense gratefully but stiffened again when he saw the wide archway in the farther wall. Beyond it, bright-sailed boats were tacking up a slope of flashing blue water, climbing an insane seascape that bent up and up to an impossible perpendicular and curled back overhead with no horizon.

For a moment he thought he was somehow looking through a window into the sphere's hollow core, though he knew he had left it far behind. Then Toolcraft touched a button and the whole unsettling scene dissolved into the gray fog of an empty stereo tank.

"Your signal from Nggongga was just in time to catch me here," Toolcraft was explaining. "I was transposed, you see, several days ago. Ordinarily my body would have gone straight to salvage, but it happens that the medics wanted to hold it for research into the effects of all my years among the pathogenic hazards of primitive Nggongga.

"Otherwise—"

He broke off to urge Blacklantern into the room.

"Sit!" With a Nggonggan bow of ceremonial welcome, he waved at the cushions. "Share water and shade, shelter and life." He added genially, with his gap-toothed smile, "I have to admire your sort of reckless enterprise. Snowfire was expecting you to follow. I thought you would fail to get here even if you tried."

"Is she—" He stood looking around the room, sniffing the heavy smoke-scent, searching for any trace of her. "Is she—here?"

"You're too late to find her alive." Casually compassionate, Toolcraft spread his open hands in the Nggonggan gesture of final negation. "You see, we were both transposed together."

Once, long ago, still proving himself for the arena, he had been creeping into a dark cave to steal an egg from a tly's nest when he heard the furious bellow of the male returning. Suddenly, now, he could taste the bitter dust of the droppings again. He felt the same choking tightness in his dry throat, heard the same fast hammer of his heart.

But engineer Toolcraft was no bull tly. A tall ungainly man with stooped narrow shoulders and weak blue eyes, his pale skin still bronze-mottled from Nggongga's sun, he looked too mildly insignificant to be any enemy—so awkwardly unhandsome, in fact, that he wondered once more what Snowfire had found to love in him.

"About Snowfire?" Tormented, Blacklantern reached out as if to clutch his angular frame and shake information out of him. "What do you mean when you say she was transposed?"

"Sit and rest, respected Benefactor." Toolcraft bowed again in the Nggonggan manner, courteous and almost apologetic. "I'm afraid you'll be disturbed by what I have to tell you, but you're too late to do much about it. The transposition process cannot be reversed."

He was shuffling about the room as he talked, lighting a new muskweed stalk in the censer, placing a low table between the cushions, bringing plates of bright-skinned fruits and small hard cakes, opening a bottle of seaberry wine.

"I spent half my old life on Nggongga," he murmured. "As you can see I became quite a primitive. Of course I never took up trophy hunting the way manager Goldforge did. But I did have a nice antique collection that we brought back and a small cellar of my favorite Nggonggan wines. Let's drink to Snowfire."

Blacklantern had firmly resolved not to be jealous. Though that promised to be difficult, he made himself accept a glass of the aromatic wine. Silently they sipped. The perplexing hush of the whole sphere began to echo in his mind. Toolcraft's air of casual ease brought his impatience to the bursting point.

"Where is she?" he exploded. "Where's—everybody?"

"Transposed." Toolcraft shrugged lazily. "I suppose you came expecting to meet millions of us, but transposition has been in progress for several generations. The whole job will take a few more—a few of the most conservative spheres have hardly begun. Here, we're nearly done, though of course I'm not the only live body left. You'll find a good many at the transposition center. Even a few here at the clinic."

"Tell me—" Struggling with violent impulses, he had to be careful with his voice. "Won't you tell me what you mean?"

"You won't like it." The weak-seeming eyes blinked at him thoughtfully. "Yet your status as a Benefactor ought to help you grasp it. Snowfire had no trouble at all. In fact, she was even wishing you could share it with us."

"She sent me—sent me a stereogram." He felt cold

with a dread too vague to grasp, and his tongue was clumsy with the words. "She hinted at something—some new process. She called it a cultural quantum jump."

"So it is!" Beaming, Toolcraft paused to savor his wine. "Our final answer to the problem of numbers. A universal problem. You can see the beginning of it if you bother to look, even on Nggongga. All those refugees from their dried-up oases and their wind-eroded fields, jamming themselves into the city to beg and breed in the streets."

Toolcraft was leaning genially to refill his glass. Black-lantern waved the bottle away and sat stiffly upright, waiting while the long swarmworlder drained his glass and disposed his angular limbs on the cushions.

"We've always done rather well by our own expanding population." Toolcarft smirked smugly through his freckles. "I won't club you with statistics, but each one of our spheres can hold several times the present population of Nggongga, still assuring each individual an abundance of space and mass and energy that even your rulers might envy.

"A dozen generations ago, however, we began to feel the limits of that physical solution. All the mass of our moons and planets had been built into vehicles and all the radiation of our star had been efficiently trapped. Of course we tried to limit our growth, but our total population had become so large that even the smallest rate of increase produced more people than we could care for.

"We sought new stars to colonize, but those in reach had all been claimed. We did begin efforts at expansion to a few such undeveloped worlds as Nggongga, but even the most backward races turned out to have an irrational attachment to their plague-ridden planets.

"Now and then some radical wanted to relinquish our policy of noncontact, suggesting that our exported technology would soon conquer all the civilized galaxy, converting every star into a new swarmworld. Such proposals were always vetoed. We still respect other cultures."

Blacklantern had moved impatiently.

"Give me time." With a chiding grin, Toolcraft gestured at the pottery bottle. "You may as well relax. You're too late to stop Snowfire's transposition, and she would want you to know all the details before you come to your own decision."

Stubbornly he shook his head at the bottle.

"As you like." Toolcraft shrugged. "But there's no hurry."

If I kill him, he told himself, *Snowfire will hate me. If she's still alive,* he added, *to hate anybody.*

Grimly he sat back to listen.

"We had come to the physical limits," Toolcraft rambled on easily. "It looked as if our growth had ended until the computers made a breakthrough. Of course our computer technology had always been advanced, stimulated by all the demands of our expansion into space. For dozens of generations all our culture had been going into the memory banks—science and engineering, laws and commercial records, literature and history, even music and art. When our dilemma of numbers became acute, the computer net met the challenge with transposition."

"From the living body into the computer!" Blacklantern exlaimed.

Toolcraft paused to enjoy his shocked response.

"The entire mental content is read out and stored. Memory and awareness. Patterns of habit. Emotions and perceptions. Capacity for learning and thinking and growing. Everything that makes us human, scanned from the fragile and fallible cells of the organic brain and transposed into solid-state matrices in eternal crystals.

"Finally, we've shaken off our old animal inheritance—all the jungle traits that trip up progress on planets like Nggongga. We've really done what the priests and philosophers have been calling for since mankind left Old Earth. We've broken the chains of the body to set the human spirit free.

"If you can grasp that—"

Toolcraft stopped, blinking at him doubtfully.

"All this means that Snowfire is dead?" He sank back against the cushions, as numb as if an unmilked tly had stung him. "You did this—this thing to her?" His hands ached for Toolcraft's scrawny neck so savagely he had to clutch them together. "You fed her mind into some machine? And let her body die?"

Toolcraft was nodding cheerily.

"I'm the exception. In most cases the bodies aren't revived." His thin shoulders twisted in a gesture of benign unconcern. "Not that they matter. I've been speaking to Snowfire and my own transposed self. They're both too busy exploring their new state of being to have much time for me, but they're certainly very much alive."

"I—I won't believe it!" Blacklantern tried to soften his grating voice and he made his quivering fists relax. "Snowfire was so—so warm, so bright and beautiful. So altogether human. She can't be herself, caged in some cold machine."

"I knew you'd find the notion hard to take." Toolcraft made a compassionate Nggonggan click. "You're displaying the normal primitive prejudice against machines, but I hope you'll try to rise above it. If you'll stop to think, you'll have to admit that human brain tissue is just about the worst possible vehicle for intelligence."

He grunted his angry disbelief.

"Compare the two!" Toolcraft urged him blandly. "The organic brain functions through clumsy electrochemical processes propagated at only a few hundred feet a second. The computer functions at the speed of light. At best, the human brain is a transient association of unlikely atoms, designed by random evolutionary mutations. Our great computer net is the ultimate mental instrument, formed by intelligence for the functions of intelligence."

Toolcraft's pale eyes shone and a sudden fervor lifted his twangy Nggongan nasals.

"Transposition sharpens all your sensations and amplifies your emotions. It lifts all experience to a new level of intensity—Snowfire and my new self assure me that making love is now an ecstasy they had never hoped to discover."

Blacklantern tried not to flinch.

"The change has made them truly immortal," Toolcraft ran happily on. "They're secure now from sickness and exhaustion, from all pain and decay. Their mental powers are multiplied beyond our comprehension. Their memories are absolute. They can make full and instant contact with all the other minds in the machine—or even merge with them. They have reached a perfect state of being. One that you primitives never imagined even for your greatest gods!"

Blacklantern sat staring, feeling cold and dull and ill.

"Drink up and cheer up!" Toolcraft drained the bottle into their glasses, splashing recklessly. "You haven't glimpsed the real beauty of it yet. I'm an engineer. I respect practical efficiency more than anything, and transposition is superlatively efficient. As a vehicle for life, our computer net is twelve point two million times better than our old organic bodies."

He flourished his dripping glass.

"Evaluate that! Twelve point two million human minds—complete human beings—fully supported with the same space and mass and energy we had been wasting to maintain only one. That's the reason you met so few people on your way here. Most of us—in this sphere. anyhow—have already been transposed. We have resources now to supply twelve million times our former population."

Adam's apple bobbing beneath the yellow freckles, he gulped his wine.

"I suppose you're busy projecting our future population curves. The problem gets complex because nobody ever dies. You'll be glad to know that birth still takes place inside the computer—with none of the old physical hazards and with vastly enhanced opportunities for intelligent selection and manipulation and recombination of the parental genetic factors. Without such growth our whole world would die. Now, however, the rate of growth can be rationally controlled—as it seldom has been on the primitive worlds.''

"I'm not projecting anything." Blacklantern tried to moderate his voice. "But tell me this. If transposition is everything you say, why didn't you let Snowfire take the secret back to the Benefactors? Don't other worlds need it?"

"Our position makes good sense." Toolcraft met his harsh impatience with an air of mild reproof. "We don't export our culture—simply because it is superior. In contact situations, the other race nearly always accepts it and lets their own culture die."

Blacklantern had surged half upright and Toolcraft motioned him back toward his cushions.

"Cultures are living entities with their own rights to survive. When they are closely akin they sometimes merge successfully. I can see a legitimate role for you Benefactors in facilitating such mergers. But we have pulled too far ahead. Contact with your world would surely kill Nggonggan culture, even though dislocated individuals might survive. We don't want that."

Hastily he raised both hands against Blacklantern's anger.

"Share peace! We mean well, believe me, and the wisdom of our position has been established many times. Cultures grow. When you Nggonggans are ready for a new technology you'll find it for yourselves."

"You're wrong!" Blacklantern rasped. "Cultures have always spread from people to people. The impact of new ways may be painful, but progress always is. Our business as Benefactors is to ease the pain."

Toolcraft shrugged, his contempt not entirely veiled.

"About Snowfire—" Blacklantern stopped to smooth

his tone and he spread both his hands in the Game clan gesture that begged for hospitality. "Can I speak to her? Wherever she is!"

"If she likes." Toolcraft waved a limp freckled hand at the stereo tank. "You'll have to remember that transposition has enlarged her whole scale of being. I really doubt that you matter to her now. But you can try."

Lazily he rose.

"With all respects, Benefactor." He stood dipping his whitestubbled head in a Nggonggan bow of parting. "You've had a pretty full briefing and now the medics want me at the lab. Their gross observations are completed. I'm reporting now for the histological studies, so I don't expect to be back."

"You mean—" Shock caught Blacklantern's voice. "You expect to die?"

"The medics will be using up my body." He nodded casually. "It's good for nothing else. But the real me, programmed into the machine, is more alive than ever. I'll never die."

"Once in the arena I heard a disciple of Cru Creetha make the same boast. An hour later he was stung and begging for the dagger."

"People don't return from Cru Creetha's mythical kingdom," Toolcraft murmured. "But if you'll wait here I think Snowfire will come back to you." His white head bobbed again. "Share drink, share food, share peace."

"*Tleesh*," Blacklantern answered stiffly. "Share life."

He was busy for a moment at the control panel in the entry. Blacklantern heard him humming an old Sand clan love song. Then the door whispered and he was gone.

Left alone to wait for Snowfire in that tiny odd oasis of Nggonggan culture, Blacklantern felt lifted with the same curious lightness and keenness that had filled him before his first tly fight. The smoke from the muskweed censer became unendurably sharp and sweet. The aftertaste of the

168

wine turned acid in his mouth. The breathless stillness seemed to promise some intolerable explosion. Each beat of his heart opened another anxious infinity.

The faint click of the stereo tank seemed louder than a man-gun. He had to squint and blink against the sudden glare that burst through its fog. Before any form took shape, he heard Snowfire's eager low-pitched voice:

"Blackie! I'm so glad you came."

While she spoke the burst and swirl of fire in the tank had become another Nggonggan room, with ornamental daggers and patterned carpets on the walls and muskweed stalks charring in a black clay censer on a bronze tripod. Almost exactly it mirrored the room where he was—but the person reflected where he stood was Snowfire.

He ran to meet her, rejoicing in her warm golden loveliness. She wore something snug and lustrous that flowed to the floor but bared one firm pale-gold breast. Her green-gold eyes smiled into his, dazzling with delight.

"Watch the glass!"

In his hot desire to take her in his arms, he had almost forgotten the wall of the tank. She raised her hand to stop him and laughed at the way he checked himself, a glint of malice in her eyes.

"You can't just walk into the computer," she said. "I'll have to send a car to bring you to the transposition center. A few minutes—if you can wait!"

He recoiled almost as if she had slapped him.

"You're really—dead?" he whispered. "Except—"

"I suppose." Her carefree shrug sent waves of fire through her red-golden hair. "The bodies aren't revived. They go straight to the mass exchangers."

"You can't—" His aching throat caught again. "You can't come back?"

"Why should anyone go back?" Her long body shivered in the tight scarlet sheath and her eyes grew dark with something close to terror. "I remember life as it used to be—when I knew no better. I thought it was good, as you still do. But now I could never endure all its agonies

169

again. The limits of the organic body. The frustration and weakness and pain. The dread of inevitable death. Worst of all, the loneliness."

Her long golden arms opened toward him.

"I loved you, Blackie. I believe you loved me. But we were both terribly alone—shut up in the prisons of our organic bodies as all mortal humanity is. I could never really understand you—never really reach you. We always had a barrier between us."

She gestured impatiently as if to brush the wall of the tank aside.

"Out here we communicate. The old barriers are gone. Contact is closer than speech or touch. You're *part* of everybody else, as fully as you wish to be. All that anyone has ever learned or lived is yours to remember—to *be*— with no loss of the individual *you*."

She made a wry little grimace that twisted a dagger in his own recollection.

"Words aren't good enough. They never were. Nothing was—not even the love we had in the desert, with the Game clan hunters behind us." She paused to smile at him dreamily, eyes half closed, lips a little parted, arms slowly lifting to her red-golden hair. "You'll know what I mean," she breathed, "when you're transposed. When we love we'll truly share each other. I'll feel all you feel and you'll feel all I feel. We'll be entirely one."

Thinking of Toolcraft, he felt weak and cold.

"Here outside, all of us share everything." She reached again as if to grasp his hand. "A quantum jump in human evolution!" Her breathless huskiness begged him to understand. "In all history of the universe the only important fact has been the slow expansion of awareness, from a tiny spark in the first one-celled things to each stage of brighter light as some new power of mind emerged. If you look for the quantum jumps, they have all been inventions in communication—nerve tissue, sense organs, language, writing, electronics, the space gates.

"Now, transposition!"

She was leaning closer to the barrier, so ripe and warm and wonderful that he quivered with desire.

"Those inventions have always fused minds together into greater and greater social beings. Into many-celled individuals. Into families. Into tribes. Into nations. Into the whole galactic civilization. Each stage enjoyed wider perceptions, a vaster experience, a higher level of awareness. Now, through our computer net, uncountable merged minds have reached a new era of conscious evolution. We've become a supermind!"

The light in her green eyes frightened him.

"The final limits of our new power are not yet tested—if any limits do exist—but we can already control mass and energy and space and time as no lone human brain could ever hope to. We can already sense older and greater superminds in the farther arms of the galaxy, and we're reaching out for contact with them. We can already foresee even more exciting quantum jumps on our way toward a full conquest of all the brute stuff of the whole universe by a completely conscious mind. A fully sentient cosmos!

"Blackie, aren't you thrilled?"

Both hands now pressed hard against the cold crystal wall between them, he stood frozen, dazed with a shapeless dread, gripped in spite of himself by her triumphant emotion yet stunned by the stark immensity of her vision.

"Blackie, haven't you ever been troubled by the nature of things?" Her voice fell appealingly, as if she had suddenly sensed his whirling uncertainty. "By the deadness of all the cold mass around us? By all the stubborn facts that feelings can't change? By the terrible gap between what we are and what we want?"

When she paused he had to nod.

"The world has always been a poor fit for us." Her urgency was almost plaintive. "Most science and most art and religion has been a pathetic effort to improve that fit—to discover or invent some sort of order or meaning in the shape of nature. Now we've found the natural plan."

171

Elation quickened the rhythm of her voice.

"Now at last we belong! We're all part of an increasing natural order that will expand without limit until it has transformed the whole space-time universe into the mental instrument of a single ultimate awareness—"

A gong boomed.

"Your car." Her bright head moved toward the doorway behind him. "Waiting to take you to the transposition center." Her voice sank huskily again, almost caressingly. "You needn't hesitate. The process has been perfected for several generations and tested many trillion times. There's no risk. No pain at all. The scanner itself puts you to sleep and your body will never be revived." Her full lips pouted as if to kiss him. "In an hour you'll be with me."

The gong throbbed again.

He drew back from her, trembling.

"Listen to me, Blackie!" Her voice was flat and shallow now, alarmed. "If you're still doubtful I can understand. I was a Benefactor, too, you know. The old way of thinking was hard to shake off. When engineer Toolcraft first told me about transposition I begged for permission to take the invention—or even just the news about it—back to the fellowship. He said it wasn't possible. I appealed to the transposition staff on the grounds that isolation law didn't apply to me because I wasn't a swarmworld citizen. Once I thought I was about to win, but they kept delaying the decision till Toolcraft persuaded me to come through with him. Now I wouldn't go back—not for anything!"

Her pleading voice sank breathlessly.

"Trust me, Blackie!"

"I—" A throb of pain closed his throat. "I guess I'm still a Benefactor. I thank you for reminding me of that."

Blackie!" She cried his name sharply. "I was so happy when Toolcraft said you were here to join us. You can't—" He saw her bright tears welling. "You can't turn back!"

Her golden arms had opened for him. He swayed toward her till his head struck the crystal wall. In an agony of frustration he drove his fist against it. The impact dimmed her image and set diamond sparks to dancing all around her.

"Don't!" Her image cleared again, her eyes black with pain. "You could smash the glass. You could bleed. You could die, Blackie. Die!" Dread hushed her voice. "You could miss immortality—all your splendid chance to share the transformation of the universe.

"If you love me—"

A third time the gong boomed.

"Come, Blackie!" she breathed. "Come now. The car can't wait."

"I—I can't!"

"Why, Blackie? Why?"

"Maybe—maybe I'm too primitive." Stiffly, with both hands, he pushed himself away from the tank. "I do love you, Snowfire—at least I loved the human you. But I'm not quite ready to become a god. I'm going home to be a Benefactor."

"You're refusing transposition?" Her wet eyes widened. "The greatest gift there is! I don't understand you, Blackie. I never could."

"You've become a goddess. I'm still a black Nggonggan."

"Knowing about transposition"—her hurt eyes searched him again—"how can you be just a Benefactor?"

"I think I see my mission now," he told her. "I'm going to take the news back, as you wanted to—if I can get back. I can't take the actual process. Maybe Nggongga isn't ready for it. But I think my troubled people need new beliefs to replace the old myths that progress and knowledge have killed. Perhaps the legend of eternal life in the computer can replace the old legend of Cru Creetha."

She shook her head, bewildered.

"I offer godhood." Her eyes were blankly accusing. "You want only a legend. I hope you're never sorry—" Her head turned as if to listen.

"Good-bye, Blackie!" Briefly, sadly, she glanced back at him. "Freckles is calling me now."

The projected room around her dimmed and faded. The Nggonggan daggers and rugs and censer were gone. Where they had been, he saw the fleeting image of a bare black granite peak. Toolcraft stood there with his angular arm flung out toward a huge red sun rising from a flat black ocean. When Snowfire appeared there, he turned to welcome her with his gap-toothed grin, and she was scrambling to his side as they vanished.

Blacklantern stood a long time gazing into the empty stereo tank.

"Freckles!" The sound grated harshly in his throat. "Freckles!"

He swung abruptly from the tank to stalk the empty room, all his new resolution crumbling into pain and doubt. Even though he had refused Snowfire's gift of something like divinity, her golden image still haunted him. Not eternal, he was not yet ready to die. He had rashly spoken of returning to Nggongga, but he knew no way to get there. He felt utterly lost, in a world he would never know.

That mellow gong throbbed again.

Uncertain what it could mean, he started toward the entry.

"Blackie!"

The doorway was open and another Snowfire stood there, quietly smiling. He stared, recoiled, gasped for breath, and swept her into his arms. Her golden flesh felt warm and firm and real. Her red-glinting hair was fragrant with her own clean sweetleaf scent, and he found no barrier between them.

"You look—terrible!" She caught his arms and pushed him off to study him. "Was my other self so frightful?"

"I thought you were dead."

174

"That was my transposed self." She nodded at the grayfogged tank. "But I'm the original *me*."

Her green eyes smiled at his mute astonishment.

"I hadn't expected to be revived," she said. "But I had applied for permission to return to Nggongga, and the transposition staff has finally agreed that we're not under their legitimate jurisdiction. They're opening the gates to return us to Nggongga. The car's waiting.

"Shall we go?"

He glanced back into the stereo tank where her superhuman self had offered him everlasting life. Its cloudy depths looked cold and dead. He waggled three black fingers at it in a childhood gesture against Cru Creetha and swung eagerly back to grasp her mortal hand.

They ran together to the waiting car.

5.

PASSAGE through a major space gate was only a shock of shifting gravities and a wink of suspended sensation, but the one-way, one-person terminal on the Earth probe hadn't been engineered for comfort. Blacklantern was wrenched and squeezed and twisted through the narrow ring-fields, instantly ejected into the coffin-sized receiver, his breath squeezed out and a sharp taste of blood in his mouth.

"Blackie!" Snowfire's bright voice rang out of the dark. Though she had come through only hours ahead of him, her tone held no trace of pain. "Are you okay?"

He wasn't. His strength was gone. His bones ached. Not yet used to free-fall, he was whirling down a dark vortex of giddiness. But he had no breath to say anything.

Blindly, he was groping for the laser energizer. He had worn it into the sender cell, holstered like a weapon to the belt of his stiff survival suit, but he couldn't find it now. Panic caught him.

"Here we are!" Somewhere over his head Snowfire sounded intolerably cheery. "Safe in Earth orbit with thirteen days to open the space gate and complete our rescue—"

"Las—laser!"

That took all his breath, but the energizer was their key to the space gate on Old Earth. Without it they would be trapped there when the planet fell through the black hole. Fumbling wildly, he couldn't feel it anywhere.

Her laughter rippled.

"I've got your gadget. Floated out to meet me. Now reach!"

He reached. Her quick pale hand caught his black one, hauled him out of the dark receiver into the main cabin of the probe. A windowless pit, cushioned all around with stiff gray plexoid, it wasn't much larger. She swam above him there, at home in null gravity, trimly graceful even in her heavy yellow suit.

"Catch!" She sent the energizer soaring slowly toward him. "Take care of it. With only thirteen days to teach the Earthfolk they've been wrong about technology, you'll need it soon."

"Thirteen days!" He snapped the plexoid holster back to his belt and hung peering at her bleakly. "If they're as backward as Nggonggans, thirteen years wouldn't be enough."

"Perhaps they aren't so backward." Hopeful wonder lit her face. "On our first pass around the night side I saw lights moving. High and fast. Climbing toward our orbit like aircraft."

"They had no aircraft." He clung to a handrail trying to stop the whirling of everything around him. "Not when the gate was built. They've turned against technology. Sunk back to where Nggongga was ten thousand years ago. No metal and no machines. Fire a sacred mystery. I doubt they could have invented aircraft in three hundred years—or decided to welcome strangers out of space."

"You're not yourself, Blackie." Her green-eyed smile rebuked him mildly. "You forget we're Benefactors, on a very tight mission. We've no time for gloom."

The narrow cabin kept toppling around him, but she was somehow always still above him. Nothing shadowed her bright expectant face. She was the golden goddess he had glimpsed in the swarmworld computer, almost too serenely perfect, more fit for worship than for love.

180

"I'll be okay." He fought his vertigo. "If we're in orbit I want to look outside. I've never seen a planet from space."

"Sorry, Blackie, we've no time to squander."

She dived to where he clung, caught his shoulders with both hands, kissed him lightly. He tried to pull her to him, but she was already gone, swimming up the cabin as quickly as a fish, leaving a haunting cloud of her body scent.

"We're on the last orbit," her voice pealed back. "Time now to separate the lander and program our descent. Take your seat and secure yourself."

Still clumsy in weightlessness, he pulled himself along the handrails to the seat behind her, squeezed into its padded arms. His bones still ached. Clammy with sweat, he felt suddenly cold.

"We're in luck!" she called again. "There really is an ice age here. The seas have shrunk and our maps don't fit. But I've located the gate. Dome still intact and beacon still burning—after three hundred years! Ready for your energizer."

Her voice faded and her bright head bent. She was the trained space pilot with all the skills she needed to find a pinpoint on the altered Earth and bring them to a landing there. He knew how to fight tlys, but there were no tlys here.

The comparison rankled in him. Confined in his clumsy seat, he watched the dull gray walls and the meaningless shimmer and blink of the instrument panels beyond her. There was nothing for him to do.

"Secure restraints!" she called. "For lander separation."

He let the seat grip him, heard the warning peep, felt the lander shudder when the linkage fused. He saw Snowfire's head bend again, heard the first faint vibration of the jets, felt a slight increasing thrust.

"Why so quiet, Blackie?" She swung her seat around, intently frowning at him. "Were you hurt in the gate?"

"Just lost my breath."

"Why look so glum?"

"Perhaps I'm just Nggonggan."

"But this is not Nggongga, Blackie." Her reproving tone was lightly caressing, the voice of a fond mother correcting a favorite child, but it hurt like the sting of an unmilked tly. "This is no place to pout."

"I'm not pouting." He kept his voice level. "But I need more to do."

"I know how you feel." She nodded, smiling too widely. "You always wanted to be the champ in the tly arena, with colored hats raining down around you. You wanted to be first through the gate because you're a man. You wanted to command our mission."

"Maybe I did," he muttered ungraciously. "Maybe I did."

"This won't be forever." Her voice was too soothingly warm. "We'll soon be home again—if you can open the gate. For now, remember we're both Benefactors. And please remember we're in love."

"Of course I remember—"

He was trying hard to smile but he felt relieved when a chirping signal called her back to the controls. The thrust and roar of the jets was mounting fast and he felt glad she had no more time for him.

She was right of course. Though the mission had brought promotions to them both, she was still his senior in the service. When he advanced from lunar to planetary rank, she had received the golden sunburst of a stellar fellow.

Angry with himself, he sat watching the back of her red-gold head and trying to admire her cool competence. Only a woman, she came from a culture where women were highly regarded. Actually, he told himself, he knew no man who might have been a more able companion on this desperate undertaking.

Trying to accept her superior position, he let his thoughts drift back across the hectic events that had brought them here. Through all his years in the fellowship he had longed for a chance at this Earth mission. Yet, when it came, he had tried to refuse it.

Back from the swarmworld, he and Snowfire had been raised to equal duty in the agency on Nggongga, the clans split between them. The problems of his two hundred million fellow blacks were vast enough to absorb them both, and they were very much in love.

She had aroused him in their bedroom at the compound with the news. Still drugged with sleep and her sweetleaf scent, he reached to catch her to him. She shook him again and slipped out of his arms.

"—Earth probe." Her words jarred him wide awake. "Benefactor Thornwall called to say it's now in orbit. Almost too late. The black hole is already swallowing planets. We're due on Xyr in an hour."

They rushed to the portal dome and flashed through the space gate. On Xyr, they found the Benefactor Thornwall waiting in his tower office. In no apparent haste, the old man made them sit while he siphoned out ruby cups of fragrant black stonevine tea. Blacklantern tasted it politely and tried to decline the mission.

"I know I volunteered, sir. But that was long ago. Things have changed. I have Snowfire now, and we've been working well together. Nggongga is challenge enough for us both. My own newest project is a big plant to unsalt the brine from our sea and water a long valley in the Wind clan highlands."

"We were rather hoping you wouldn't want to go." Nodding calmly, Thornwall sipped his scalding tea. "A very chancy mission. Our problem is that the probe got caught by the hole and delayed too long. One planet already destroyed. With Old Earth next, the portal experts want us to scrub the whole project. I think they're right—"

"Sir!" Snowfire burst past him, a heady breath of sweetleaf scent, a blur of red-gold hair, and green-gold eyes and pale-gold allure. Eagerly she seized Thornwall's lean old hands. "I'm not refusing."

"No!" Blacklantern gasped his protest, gazing at her in blank amusement. He hadn't known she had volunteered. "I need you—we need you on Nggongga."

He turned desperately to old Thornwall.

"If the mission is so dangerous, sir, you wouldn't send a woman!"

"Please, *gunggee!*" Breathing the word for lover she had learned in his own Nggonggan, she turned to smile at him. "I'm a Benefactor."

"Don't quarrel." Thornwall lifted his frail old hands. "We do need both of you on Nggongga."

"We've been happy there." She brushed him with her body, strong and soft and wonderful. "We've reached a cultural compromise. Blackie has agreed to forget the barbaric notion that he has to own me. I've agreed to have his son—and I will, when we get back from Old Earth."

"Don't decide rashly." Thornwall paused to drain his tiny cup. "Let me show you what the hole did to Mars. It may change your mind."

His blue-veined hands clicked computer keys. The blank screen in the alcove behind him became a window into stardusted space.

"The hole," he said. "Observed by instruments on the probe."

A thin green arrow stabbed into that dusty darkness, pointing at nothing Blacklantern could see. The keys clicked again and a tiny rust-colored globe jumped into the window.

"This happened while the probe was fighting through the gravity fields of the black hole to find its Earth orbit," he said. "I'm showing you a taped time-lapse display."

The planet drifted toward the arrow point. Ahead of it stars began to dim and wink. It swarmed faster, faster, its path sharply curving. Another click and its image swelled till they saw dark-rimmed craters and a white polar crown.

"Watch what happens," he murmured. "And don't forget that the hole is whirling on toward Old Earth."

The planet fractured. Black cracks ripped across the craters, sharp at first but quickly veiled with yellow dust. Its disk blurred and stretched. Red fire exploded from its heart, hurling black-walled blocks of its crust into a long spiral streamer.

Blacklantern heard the quick intake of Snowfire's breath, felt her cold hand quiver on his.

They watched that dark-clotted spiral coil back around itself. It spun faster, faster, until it was a spinning plate. The crustal lumps crumbled and dissolved. At the center a point of blue light began to burn.

"The hole!" Thornwall whispered. "A giant imploded star, now only miles across but so massive that nothing—not even light—can escape its gravity. All we actually see is only the funnel, sucking down the wreckage of the planet. The captured mass is torn to molecules. To atoms. Going down the vortex, drawn out of the observable universe, the debris begins to radiate. Heat at first. The light we see. Then gamma rays."

The picture went out.

"That's all." Trembling a little, he refilled the ruby cup. "The radiation burned our cameras out. But that was Mars. Earth is next." He lit the screen with dotted green orbital curves that came together at a bright red point. "In fourteen standard days."

He swung to face them, pale old eyes blinking shrewdly.

"How about it now?"

"I can't refuse," Snowfire said. "The gate is there. I know the Earthfolk wanted nothing from us when it was built, but things are different now. It must be opened." She turned from Thornwall. "How about it, Blackie?"

Before her cool green gaze he shuddered.

"We're going, sir," he told Thornwall. "Together."

They had been trained for probe missions, and their outfitting and briefing took only a day. Engineers from the space gate system taught Blacklantern how to replace the dead energizer, how to activate it to open the gate.

Creeping at only half the speed of light, the unmanned probe had been on its way for three generations. Its own narrow gate opened from a tiny sender installed beneath the main concourse of the portal dome on Xyr, five levels down.

A portal engineer met them there the day they were ready and urged them to give up the mission. A short fat bald man, he wore a bulging brain implant. Bright sweat filmed his colorless skin and his odor edged the dusty air.

"You don't know what you're getting into." He stopped in the tunnel outside the sender, as if to block their way into the gloom beyond the heavy door. "Nobody knows how to cope with black holes. Experts have gone out to observe them and seldom come back. Want to know why?"

"We've been briefed," Snowfire said. "We'll take our chances."

"Listen to me." He stubbornly stood in their way. "I'm the black hole specialist for the whole portal complex. I've watched planets go. Suns and ships. I've seen things your experts won't believe. The hard way, I've learned the truth about black holes."

"What's that?" Blacklantern asked.

"They don't come single. When a giant star falls into itself, dropping into nowhere in a fractional second, the gravity waves are tremendous. They crush nearby masses. A ripple effect. Planets and moons and meteors are squeezed out of space into their own tiny gravitational pits. So the holes come in swarms. That's what traps the experts. Avoiding one, they back into another."

"I've heard the theory," Snowfire moved impatiently to pass him. "Cosmogonists doubt it."

"Experts!" He sniffed and blocked her path. "The live experts have never been near a hole." Scowling out of the shadows under the bulge of his naked, sweating cranium, he swung toward Blacklantern. "In any case the planet isn't worth all you risk."

"But Old Earth is our mother world." Snowfire

grasped his arm as if to push him aside. "The first home of mankind."

"A spoiled world. Our forebears had wasted its resources before they escaped to space. Those left behind were only human dregs. They've fallen into barbarism— the few that survive in a new ice age."

"We're going to rescue them."

"That's been tried," he protested. "We built the gate to bring them into civilization—but they don't believe in civilization. Called us creatures of their devil. Attacked our people with primitive weapons. Broke into the portal far enough to smash the energizer. Our advance crew just managed to escape before the ring-fields failed."

"Come along!" Snowfire's voice was lifting. "We've no time to waste."

"A moment more." His triangular gnome-face tried to smile. "If you want adventure the portal system can offer you something more rewarding. I'm in the survey division. All around the space frontier we have slow probes in flight toward new worlds—most of them as rich as Old Earth ever was. We always need trained crews to flash aboard the probes when they arrive in orbit. I can give you a virgin world to explore instead of the plundered Earth."

Snowfire had lifted her hands in impatient negation. His computer was not quick enough to measure her mounting resentment, and the engineer swung to Blacklantern.

"As I understand, your fellowship asks you to serve for the sake of service. The portal system enjoys a vast income from space commerce and we can pay in cash and privilege. As pioneers opening a rich new world, you can carve out your own rewards—"

"That's enough," Snowfire snapped. "Stop the nonsense."

"I've never understood you Benefactors." With a shrug at Blacklantern he stood aside to let them into the gate room. "An obsolete unit that really wrings you out." He waved a sweaty hand at the tiny sender cell. "Which one goes first?"

"I—" Blacklantern began.

"I do," Snowfire said.

Sitting behind her now, inside the tight restraints, he watched the back of her head and waited to see the ice-bound Earth. When he was a boy cleaning boots on the streets of Nggonggamba, dreaming of the other worlds he scarcely hoped to visit, he had sometimes asked the tourists what ice and snow were like. Now perhaps—

He heard Snowfire gasp, saw her bright head lift and turn.

"Blackie!" Her voice was faint with shock and dread. "I'm afraid we're here too late."

Scarlet signals flashed and burned on the panels beyond Snowfire's head, and hoarse sirens hooted.

"What's wrong?" Blacklantern shouted. "What's going on?"

If she heard, she had no time to answer. He unlocked the restraints and plunged up the cabin toward her. Beyond her head he glimpsed Earth's snow-cloaked face—with one strange line, wide and black, drawn straight across it toward an ominous horizon of twilit gloom.

"What—"

"Sit down!" Her sharp voice cut through the clangor. "Secure yourself!"

Back in the protective seat he watched her golden head bobbing up and down. One by one the warning lights went out. When the last siren had croaked and died she turned briefly back to him.

"Brace yourself, *gunggee!*" she called. "Shock wave coming—"

While she spoke, it struck.

Something louder than thunder battered the lander. Something lifted it, whirled it, hammered it. Something dropped and spun and smashed it till the impacts took his breath and the restraints bruised his body and his vertigo came back. He clung weakly to the handgrips and watched Snowfire's swaying head and waited for the ordeal to end.

188

But it didn't end.

Enduring that unceasing pandemonium, he tried to imagine its cause. The icecaps here might breed more savage weather than dry Nggongga, he thought, but nothing this terrific. A volcano? When he glimpsed that vast twilit snowscape there had been no cinder cones. The hole itself? That wide black line, so queerly straight, was nothing like the ragged fractures that had riven Mars. What else? Nothing he could think of.

Following each dip and lift of Snowfire's head, he found himself wondering dully what had brought him into this strange plight. Red hair perhaps? In escape from torment his thoughts fled back to another redhead he had known. To a girl called Sapphire, who had fascinated and betrayed him.

Had he always been some sort of fool?

He closed his eyes against bone-jarring thunder and tried to recall Nggigi, the new receptionist they had hired for the agency. A slim Nggonggan girl, black and grave and beautiful, she had turned out to be so loyally competent that they had sent her on to Xyr to be trained for the fellowship. Perhaps, he thought, he should have married her instead.

She had told him shyly once that she had admired him long ago, when she was still a child selling hats and flowers in the tly arena. He had seen the hero worship still in her eyes, heard it in her breathless voice. She would have made him a dutiful wife, he thought, aware of her place, with no nonsense about cultural clashes.

But her hair wasn't red, her eyes weren't green.

The squeezing seat tossed him against the restraints, snapped him back, slammed him into the cabin wall, but he scarcely felt the impact. He was suddenly reliving a long-forgotten meeting, on the square below the Nggonggan portal dome, with his very first redhead.

A tall young girl, walking in the throng of otherworlders just emerging from the space gate. Keen green eyes were looking everywhere, and she stopped when she saw him, smiling down in delight. It struck him now that perhaps she was an anthropology student, captivated with native Nggongga.

He could have been no more than three, naked and hungry and no doubt filthy. The half-blind black crone who claimed him was using him for bait, making him beg while she robbed purses. The girl wore no translator. She was stooping over him, mouthing strange soft sounds, when the policeman seized him.

The black crone dropped the purse and dodged into the crowd. The policeman shook him, shouting at him, till the girl reached bare arms for him. Her sweet body scent came back to him now, and the feel of her clean white skin and soft red hair. She took him away from the angry officer, bought him a ripe yellow rockfruit from a vendor, let him go at last with a handful of gongs.

The old woman took the gongs that night and beat him when he cried—

"Hang on, Blackie!" Snowfire's call broke up that poignant recollection. "We're under air attack!"

They carried no armament because the fellowship condoned no violence. Snowfire crouched at the controls, driving them through evasive maneuvers. The battered lander lurched and twisted more savagely than ever, while Blacklantern clung to his restraints and tried to comprehend that impossible assault.

Surveying the planet from their own orbital probe, the builders of the gate had seen no cities, no factory smoke, not even a road. On the ice-bound surface they had found only a few stone-age hunters, apparent worshipers of fire. The metal relics of the past were all taboo, untouchable.

Aircraft simply shouldn't be here—

"Duck, Blackie!" Snowfire screamed. "Duck!"

The lander shivered and spun. Fighting the controls, she had no more time or voice for him. Waiting for something else to happen, he tried to swallow his sullen resentment, tried to admire her cool skill, tried to recover his image of her as his green-eyed ideal.

But his bone-deep feelings were hard to change. "I'm Nggonggan," he muttered at himself. "I guess I'll always be—"

Abruptly their crazy motion changed. The lander struck and bounded, rocked and skidded, came to rest. The howling jets coughed and died. He sat stunned by an avalanche of silence.

For a soundless moment nothing moved.

Then Snowfire swung slowly in her seat to face him, looking limp and pale. She caught a great breath and wiped her wet face with a stiff yellow sleeve.

"Listen, *gunggee*," she whispered. "Listen!"

He heard a far-off wailing, then a sonic thud.

"They're wheeling overhead." Renewed urgency sharpened her voice. "We'll have to abandon the lander. Bring the energizer and your emergency pack."

At the exit she waited for him to jump first into the frigid dark. Snow crunched under his boots, but he could see nothing at all. He was reaching to help when she dropped beside him.

"What are they—"

"Move fast!" She ignored his question. "We're on flat ice. No cover here. There's a ridge to the left. Outcropping rock. We'll try for shelter there."

She marched off into the dark. He slapped his thigh to feel the energizer, slung the pack of survival gear to his shoulders, jogged after her vanishing shadow. Before they had gone fifty paces something shrieked out of the black sky behind. A dull red flash threw their shadows on the snow. Pausing to glance back, he saw a red-flaring jet climbing above the vague mass of the lander.

"Come along," she commanded.

He slogged after her. Behind them another red jet blazed down from the sky, or perhaps the first returned. Its bellow hurt his ears and its dull glare lit the rock-toothed ridge ahead. Their long shadows danced and froze as it dropped on the lander.

A second attacker followed, then a third. The sustained

191

howls of flight became hoots and yelps and shrill explosions. The hideous cacophony reminded him of carrion tlys he had seen fighting over the carcass of a nearman on the Nggonggan highlands. But fighter aircraft, he thought, shouldn't behave like hungry tlys.

The sky screamed again, and yet another attacker came straight at them, flying low. The crimson glare beneath it flickered on the ridge and raced toward them over the ice.

"Drop!" Snowfire gasped. "Flat!"

In his mind he was back in the Nggonggamba arena with a killer tly diving at him. Reflexively he reached for his binding rope, but his grasping fingers found only the laser energizer.

"Down—"

The bellow of the jet drowned Snowfire's cry. The red glare flashed on across the snow. With the energizer in his hand, what he did was almost automatic. He aimed it like a gun. His thumb found the key. The wire-thin ray of pure green light pulsed out to splash the diving object in the dark.

Revealed, it unnerved him again. Vaster than any tly, it was massive and black and incomprehensible—half mechanical, half monstrous. Its stubby wings were angular and rigid as those of some primitive airplane, but its body looked too fat and it had enormous jaws in a yawning cave of a mouth, studded with great dull black teeth.

Before its howling dive he fell flat. The energizer trembled in his hand but he kept the pulsing ray at work, searching out the paradoxical details of its strangeness. The enormous body, almost a globe, ridged with black triangular scales. The silver-black reflective pits at the roots of the wings, spaced like eyes. The black-cleated ridges underneath that looked like legless feet.

Its screaming roar had broken, lifted to a brain-piercing shriek. The eyelike pits squeezed shut as if his probing ray had blinded them. The black wings flexed to pull it sharply upward. In an instant it had passed above them, its bellow

192

dropping to a deeper tone. In another instant its hot red jet was climbing back into the dark behind them. Stinging fumes choked them and the laser burned green in a trailing vapor cloud.

He clicked the green ray off and they stumbled to their feet.

"Drop flat is what I told you." Anger snapped in Snowfire's voice. "Why did you fire?"

"Why not?"

"We don't allow violence. In this case your reckless impulse could bring the whole flight down on us."

"In this case"—he tried to swallow his own sullen antagonism—"I think it drove the thing away."

"Perhaps it did." She reached to touch his arm. "Sorry, *gunggee*, if I was too sharp. But we can't afford such reckless risks. Let's try now for that ridge."

Wading calf-deep snow, they fled again from the bellow and thunder above the lander. Nothing pursued. Running ahead, Snowfire tripped over a jutting stone. He picked her up and they blundered at last over the crown of the ridge and down again into a boulder-walled hollow. He glanced back once at the red jets wheeling above the lander.

"Please keep down, *gunggee*," she urged him gently. "Maybe they'll forget us."

"What are they?" he demanded. "What happened to us?"

"That engineer was right." She leaned against a snowy boulder, breathing hard. "There's more than one black hole. A cluster maybe. At first I couldn't believe what I saw from the lander. A furrow that plowed itself across the face of the planet."

"I guess I glimpsed it." He moved toward her in the dark. "A straight dark line across the ice." He stopped to catch his breath. "You think a black hole made it?"

"I saw the line drawn"—awe slowed her voice—"by a small black hole—smaller anyhow than the one that caught Mars. Just grazed Earth and went on into space. All in half a dozen seconds. Dreadful to see. It swallowed the mass in its path. Cut a canyon across the glaciers. Left a vacuum that made the shock wave. Sucked air and everything after it to set off the storm we came down through.''

"It passed so near?" Wonder dazed him. "And left us alive!"

"Gravitation varies inversely with distance squared," she reminded him. "Away from its center the effects fall off fast. Our greatest danger was the radiation out of the funnel, which tripped the alarms. About all our shields could handle."

"Through all that"—his voice balked, but he forced himself to go on—"you did well to get us down."

"Thanks, *gunggee!*" She moved in the dark to touch his sleeve. "But you don't know the worst part. That canyon was cut ahead of us. Between us and the gate. I was trying to get us across it till those queer jets knocked us down. Now we still have that ditch to cross."

"The jets?" He paused to listen at the yells and wails and booms from beyond the ridge. "They fly like machines but they look—look somehow alive! What do you think they are?"

"I don't know, *gunggee.*" Dread quivered in her whisper. "I can't imagine."

They hid in the rock-walled hollow through what was left of the bitter night. Snowfire worked a long time over the charts and finders she had brought in her pack, estimating the dimensions of that vast new gorge across the glaciers, trying to map a path they could follow to the space gate.

"We aren't too far." She looked up at last, her face pale and strained in the glow of the self-lit charts. "Perhaps three days on foot beyond the furrow. But we're on the wrong bank and it's too long for us to walk around. We've got to get across."

"We can try," he told her. "We have ropes. I've done climbing at home, hunting nestling tlys."

194

He was thawing snow on a tiny stove to mix with their food concentrates. When they had eaten their sparing equal portions, she took the first turn on watch and told him to sleep. Though he was tired enough, that wasn't easy. The sounds beyond the ridge had subsided to occasional hoots and rumbles, but the riddle of the flying things kept gnawing at his mind.

Had they evolved, since the spacemen left, from creatures native to earth? He recalled a lecture at the fellowship academy about great reptiles on the prehuman earth, thought to be extinct—but none of them had been jet-propelled.

Invaders from space? His exobiology classes had surveyed the known variations of carbon-based life with specimens selected from several thousand different planets. None had been so exotic as this.

Another order of life—or half-life?

With no answer for that he dropped at last into an uneasy half-sleep. Even the powered suit failed to keep him really warm, and the hazards of their mission merged into nightmare.

He thought he and Snowfire were back in the imposing old hotel in the trading town of Krongkor on Nggongga, where he had begun to learn her ways of love. They had been diving nude off the stone pier and drinking old Champ's seaberry wine, and at last they had come up to make love in their great khamsin-canopied bed. But their joy was interrupted. Suddenly she was giving birth to their child. It was nothing human, but a black-scaled monster, breathing red fire and snapping black teeth at him, its round black belly swelling insanely, crowding him out of bed.

"Blackie! Your watch, Blackie!"

Vastly thankful when she bent to wake him from the horror of that dream, he wanted to take her in his arms, but she was in no mood for tenderness.

"The creatures are quiet." Her tired voice was crisply impersonal. "Lying around what's left of the lander—if anything is. Watch them while I rest. Alert me if anything happens. And don't fire the laser.''

He climbed back to peer over the crown of the ridge. With a moon rising somewhere beyond the clouds, the snow was now almost luminous. Out where the lander had fallen he found five grotesque shapes sprawled in black silhouette against the ice, almost motionless. Now and again they coughed great booming puffs of steam or crimson fire. The icy air was tainted with their odor, a biting sulphuric stink sharp as the reek of burning plexoid.

Before dawn they began to yawn and crawl about, with screeching blasts and rumbling explosions from their jets. He woke Snowfire to watch them take off. Moving clumsily, like overloaded aircraft, they had to slide a long way down the ice to gain flying speed.

The last one struck an outcropping rock. It spun into the air and rolled far over the snow, snorting scarlet fire, and finished on its back. The others dived and wheeled above it while it tried to right itself.

Its efforts were laborious and slow, but at last it tipped itself over and fell back upright on the ice with a crash that jarred the ridge. It came roaring back down the strip they all had worn and climbed at last into the sky on its tail of crimson thunder. All five vanished together in the dark west, as if in flight from day.

After another hurried meal they packed their gear and went down to where the lander had crashed. It was gone. The creatures had left only a slick black hollow worn in the ice. He stared into that and back at Snowfire.

"What sort of thing can they be?"

"We learned too little to tell." She shrugged uneasily. "If they're really alive their chemistry functions at high temperatures. They consume metal. They seem to dislike light. They move as if they're fantastically heavy. That's about all we observed."

"I hope we don't meet them again." He shivered. "They're—monstrous! By comparison a killer tly looks like a pet kitten."

"They went west." Hopefully she turned to face the frosty dawn. "The space gate is southeast—with that furrow still in the way."

Before noon they were climbing off the ice up another stony slope. The snow cover here had been disturbed by recent rockslides, and long fractures scarred the hillside.

"Marks of quakes," Snowfire said. "Caused, I think, by the passing gravity field of the hole. Here it must have been intense. We are near the trench."

Before they reached the summit Blacklantern looked back along their trail and found a dark fleck creeping over the snow. He hauled the light binoculars out of his pack.

"Somebody following," he told her. "A sledge. People pulling it. One person riding. Two more running behind. All dressed in animal skins. The runners carrying spears. The barbarians, I guess, that we've come to rescue."

"So we're in luck!" Relief lit her smooth gold face. "We may need their help to get across the trench."

"Are you sure they mean to help us?"

"We'll persuade them." She was briskly confident. "Language should be no major problem—the builders of the gate picked up half a dozen native dialects that we've programmed into our translators. When they learn that we're here to warn them about the end of their world and offer them a way to survive it, they'll cooperate."

"I hope," Blacklantern muttered. "But let's have a look at the trench."

Snowfire was climbing ahead when they came to the crest of the hill. She froze there with a gasp of amazed dismay. He clambered to her side and his breath went out when he looked into the trench.

Not so wide or deep as that awesome pit the machines from the swarmworld had dug into the heart of Nggongga, it was just as appalling. Its jagged lip was so near that he swayed giddily back. The farther wall was miles off, tall black cliffs standing on vast slopes of broken stone.

"We do need help," Snowfire whispered. "We can't cross that on foot."

"Nor on a sledge," he muttered. "Even with strong barbarians to pull it."

Still dazed, he looked to right and left. That awesome gorge ran straight forever in each direction, talus slopes and towering cliffs diminishing into hazy distance. Oddly, it was deeper toward each side, with a rounded ridge of shattered stone at the center.

"Formed of rock not quite captured." Snowfire gestured at the ridge. "The hole was moving too fast to swallow everything drawn toward it. The trail of debris left behind fell back into the trench."

He raised the binoculars to scan that endless pit, and abruptly they shook, blurring all he saw.

"Something moving!" he breathed. "Something coming down the trench."

What he had seen was a plunging mass that hid the boulder slopes and rose to the foot of the farther cliffs. Its steep gray face was swirled and streaked with dirty white. A faint vibration filled the gorge ahead of it, a dull rumbling that swelled and swelled until it became deafening thunder. The earth quivering underfoot, they watched great towers of stone shaken from the cliffs, slowly toppling, splashing into an insane brown flood.

"The sea!" Snowfire cried, green eyes wide with sudden comprehension. "The trench was cut all the way from the sea. The flood rolling down it has just reached us."

"Now I know we need help to cross it." He had to shout against the thunder from the gorge. "More help I think than those barbarians can give us."

They climbed and slid back down the quaking hill, to wait at the edge of the ice. While she checked and adjusted her translator, he studied the Earthfolk with the binoculars.

Six gaunt men ran like animals to draw the sledge. Half-clad in crudely laced gray-furred hides, they looked like animals. Their long pale hair and beards were stained and matted, their scarred faces red with cold. Panting, they exhaled white clouds.

Their driver was s tall young woman, in trimly sewn white fur. She was black—but oddly black. When he focused the binoculars he saw pale circles around her eyes and pale streaks across her cheeks. Standing on the back of the lurching sledge, she cracked a long whip at the half-naked backs of the leaning men.

Her two followers were also handsome young women, each half-smeared with the same streaky black, one on the right side of the face, the other on the left. They wore smooth white fur with bone-white daggers at their waists and carried flint-tipped spears.

"The black is only paint." He passed the binoculars to Snowfire. "Their light skins puzzle me. I thought the people of Old Earth were mostly darker."

"I suppose the ice age has bleached them," she said. "Pigmentation seems to be a function of climate. You Nggonggans evolved it for protection against a hot blue sun. Under these cloudy skies too much pigment would cut off essential ultraviolet. But I don't understand the paint."

She handed the binoculars back and he studied the whipped men straining on the ropes.

"Women seem superior."

"What does that matter?" She shrugged. "I know your own Nggonggan bias, but all we need is their help to reach the space gate."

"They look like the lowest sort of savages," he objected. "Too backward to be much use to us."

"Cultures differ." She reached for the binoculars again. "You can't draw sound conclusions from a single observation. These people may surprise you."

She climbed on a rock as the sledge drew near and spread her hands wide in what was meant as a gesture of peace. The natives stopped a hundred yards across the ice, however, well beyond translator range. The black-painted rider huddled with her two spear-carriers. Through the binoculars Blacklantern saw them peering apprehensively at him.

"We'll walk out to meet them," Snowfire decided. "Move slowly. Keep your hands open and wide. Don't touch the laser."

When they started forward the natives showed alarm. The rider whipped her team of men into a sudden turn as if for flight. Her two followers stood behind, spears pointing at Blacklantern.

"They're afraid of you," Snowfire said. "Maybe they've never seen an actual black. Wait here. I'm going on alone. Whatever comes, don't use the laser. There'll be no violence."

Unwillingly he waited.

Hands spread wide, she walked slowly out across the ice. The natives watched her narrowly. When she was still twenty yards from the sledge, the rider beckoned her to stop. The two followers moved a little forward to face her with their spears.

He saw them speaking, but his translator picked up nothing. The rider beckoned Snowfire forward and the others closed in beside her. Presently he saw them all looking back at him, saw the spears lifting toward him.

The talk went on a long time. He saw Snowfire waving at the clouds, pointing back along their trail, gesturing ahead toward the trench and the space gate. The rider frowned and stamped her boots on the snow and waved her whip toward him.

Snowfire came plodding slowly back at last. Her golden face looked bleak and tight and the binoculars showed her tears of frustration. The natives followed her with the sledge, keeping a wary distance.

"Anyhow, we tried." She gave him a small wry smile. "Not much luck. They won't believe anything I say. About the gate and the Benefactors and the danger from the black hole."

Unconsciously his hand had fallen to the laser.

"Don't touch it!" Authority edged her voice. "I

promised not to let you hurt them. In return for their promise to be humane to you.''

"Why humane to me?''

The laser was not designed for combat, but its stabbing needle could be blinding. He fought a savage impulse to try for the eyes of the white-furred leader. Quivering with confused emotions, he almost lost Snowfire's words.

"—let them take you prisoner. Otherwise they're determined to try to kill us both.''

"Why me?''

"Our bad luck. And their own, of course, They've identified you as an evil god they call Ghur. The dark destroyer. They blame you for all their recent catastrophes.''

"How—how can that be?''

"A whole train of disastrous coincidence.'' Her slim gold hands fanned out in a gesture of futility. "Ghur, I gather, is a god of fire and machines, burned black with the smoke of his forge. The things that attacked us—the *bomzeeth*—are creatures of his.''

Behind her, the spear-women were cautiously advancing.

"They saw our lander crash, with the *bomzeeth* swarming around it. We seem to be the fulfillment of a prophecy that Ghur will return in a season of storm and earthquake and signs in the sky to destroy the world and all its people.''

She paused to wave the women back.

"These natives belong to a Ghur cult. Larlarane calls herself his bride—her official title translates as 'bride of night.' All their rituals seem planned to placate him. Black is his color. Metal is sacred to him. Only the cult members are allowed to touch it, and then only to offer it to him. Larlarane was crossing the glacier when our lander fell, collecting junk metal for his altars. She's terrified now because their rituals were meant to prevent your prophecied return. Your arrival means that their religion has failed. Now they don't know what to do.''

She turned again, calling strange syllables she must have learned from them.

"I had a hard time persuading them not to attack us at once. We finally reached a bargain. I'm surrendering you in return for agreement not to kill us. Not a very good arrangement, I know, but at least it buys us time to learn a little more about the situation and perhaps to frame some better plan."

Warily, in spite of her gestures, the women were closing in.

"Sorry, Blackie." She stepped quickly toward him with a pale appealing smile. "I knew you wouldn't like it, but this is the best thing we can do." Her gold hand reached. "Now give me the energizer."

He recoiled in dazed indignation, clutching at the laser energizer.

"Surrender?" he gasped. "To three women?"

"Not only to them," Snowfire protested. "But to a total situation."

"Two spears against my laser! I can wipe them out."

"Perhaps you could. But what then? We're still on this side of the trench. We'd never reach the space gate." She reached again for the energizer. "Please, Blackie! Remember we're Benefactors. This is the only way."

Clutching the energizer, he faced them all. The black-daubed priestess with her whip. The half-black fighting women. The toil-stooped men huddled in front of the sledge, peering dully at him through matted yellow hair. Snowfire herself, whom he loved and suddenly hated.

The energizer lifted itself in his quivering hand. The women poised their stone-tipped spears. Larlarane flicked her whip at him, its crack a cruel explosion. Snowfire flung herself in front of the energizer, seizing it with both hands.

Shuddering, he let it go.

"Thank you, *gunggee!*"

The women closed in around him but kept a cautious distance, afraid to touch anything about him. Under their eyes, Snowfire was busy stripping him of possible weapons. His binoculars. His pack. The coiled climbing rope. The knife and tools from the pockets of his suit. Even his translator.

At a shrill command from Larlarane, the men came trotting with the sledge, which already carried a few shapeless bits of rusty iron. Snowfire piled his gear on the iron, secured it with pieces cut from his own rope, and finally came back to him with a length of rope.

"Sorry, *gunggee.*" Her voice was faint and strained. "Hands behind you now."

"No!" he whispered bitterly. "I won't be bound."

"Blackie, please!" Her green eyes gleamed with tears. "If you resist they'll kill us both."

"You're a fool!" he muttered. "So am I'"

But he didn't resist.

She tied his wrists behind him, knelt to tie his ankles. At another command from the black priestess, she ripped a strip from the hood of his suit to make a blindfold. At that point the women were brave enough to seize him. They dragged him from his feet, loaded and tied him on the sledge. The whip cracked, a man howled with pain, and they lurched into motion.

The old metal and his own lumpy gear made the sledge a painful bed. The ropes numbed his hands and feet. Arctic cold sank into his bones. But the cruelest fact was his own spineless surrender, a rankling wound, harder to endure than anything physical.

He tried to imagine some chain of events that would set him free and let him open the gate, but imagination failed. Even if Snowfire somehow secured the willing aid of these degenerates, that appalling trench was still in the way.

Fighting despair, he seized and searched each new sensation. The hissing of the runners against the snow. The cracking of the whip and the crunch of running feet. The voices of Snowfire and the women, all stripped of meaning now, since she had taken his translator. Nothing permitted any hope.

"Dzanya Dzu!" he shouted once, calling Snowfire's native name. "Where are they taking us?"

"Quiet, *gunggee!*" she answered sharply in his own Nggonggan dialect. "They're afraid you'll cast some spell. If you try to speak again they'll gag you."

He lay silent, hating her and hating himself. Trying not to brood upon his hopeless situation, he sought to recall brighter bits of the past. The first tly he had been able to bind, as a learner in the arena. The wild tly he once had trapped and tamed, on the Wind clan highlands. The earlier time in Nggonggamba when a loud other-worlder kicked over his boot-cleaning box and he followed the man into a crowded shrine of Cru Creetha and escaped with his fat wallet. But such recollections were too fleeting and brief to ease his long anguish.

At last the sledge stopped. He caught a tantalizing scent of broiling meat and longed to be unbound and fed. But the whip kept cracking. Men shouted and yelped. Boots crunched the snow and the sledge lurched on—now drawn, he supposed, by a fresh team of men.

A long time later, it stopped again—and shuddered under him. A grating vibration throbbed deep in the earth, heavier than thunder. The sledge pitched. The black priestess screamed, feet thudded, something sharp jabbed his chest. He heard Snowfire's sharp protest echoed from her translator, then her quick warning in his own native Nggonggan.

"Quiet, *gunggee!* Don't try to move or speak. Larlarane thinks you're making the quakes."

He lay silent. The quakes ceased at last. The jabbing spears withdrew and the sledge rocked on—and on and on. His whole body ached. Thinking dully again of Cru Creetha, he cursed Snowfire and himself and all the Benefactors in that dark god's name. His awareness faded slowly, before fatigue and cold and pain.

He came half-awake at last, somewhere in the dark. The

ropes were gone though his hands and feet still prickled and throbbed. He lay sprawled on something hard. Animal skins had been thrown over him and he wasn't quite so cold.

Wondering dimly where he was, he remembered being rolled off the sledge to some sort of litter, being carried on by running men, remembered swaying on a rope tied under his arms and falling on this hard floor. He rubbed his bruised wrists, pulled the skins around him, and went to sleep again.

"Wake up, *gunggee!*"

For one happy instant when her soft voice roused him, he thought they were safe in their bedroom in the compound on Nggongga, thought the whole mission to rescue the Earthfolk had been an incredible nightmare.

But then he smelled the reek of the untanned hides and heard their brittle rattle when he moved and felt the hard floor under him. Sitting stiffly up, he found Snowfire standing over him, holding a small clay lamp. Its flame lit a bare stone floor and a curving wall behind her.

"If things go wrong, *gunggee—*" Trouble slowed her breathless voice. "If things go wrong, I hope you'll try to forgive me."

He stumbled to his feet, swaying painfully on swollen ankles, and stood staring blankly at her. Her yellow emergency suit was gone; instead, she wore white fur. Her golden skin was all dyed black.

"What is this place?"

As she hesitated he peered around him. In the flicker of her tiny lamp he saw that they were in a big circular room. He found no door or window. The domed ceiling was high, with one dark round opening at the center.

"A sacred place," she said. "Sacred to Ghur because of the machines that used to be here. From what I've seen, I think it was once a launch point for the shuttles that carried our ancestors into space. This cell must have been a fuel tank."

"So what happens now?" He searched her black-stained face. "Have you found any way to the gate?"

"I've tried." Despair dulled her voice. "But all I say turns against me. Larlarane wants nothing to do with the space gate. The whole region around it is taboo. According to the legends the men who built it were Ghur's demons, trying to open a way from Earth into his dark inferno. These people are afraid to go anywhere near it."

She bent to set the tiny lamp on the floor and sank despondently down beside it, as if too tired to stand.

"I've tried, Blackie. Tried—and tried again." Her voice quivered. "But everything about our arrival seems to justify their prophecy that Ghur will return in the last days to tempt them to use his evil machines and destroy themselves. Larlarane rejects everything I say."

"Don't they remember anything?" He knelt urgently before her on the little pile of skins. "About their own great ancestors? And the scientific culture that put mankind in space?"

"They don't believe in space." The lamplight glittered on her exasperated tears. "Earth, to them, is the only world there is—except the smoky hell under the volcanoes, where Ghur forges his machines. Tales of other worlds are lies told to lure people into his traps."

"So we're on our own," He peered at the dark opening above. "We've got to get out."

"They won't let you out. You're the only black man they've ever seen. Your color is proof enough that you are Ghur. They're convinced that you brought the ice, and burned Mars, and dug that trench. They believe the *bomzeeth* are your children—born of a white princess you raped, who turned black in your arms. They think you have brought them back to haunt the dead world after all humanity is gone."

"Those flying things?" He peered into her pale-eyed face. "What have you learned about them?"

"They appeared only a few seasons ago—sent, Larlarane believes, to prepare the way for your return. They fear the light—she says they lurk in caves and old mines through the day. They fly out in the dark to look for food. Metal is the food they prefer—that's evidence they really are your monster children. And why Larlarane was gathering junk metal. She was trying to appease them.''

"But you don't know what sort of thing they are?''

"I—I've a theory, Blackie.'' She hesitated, frowning through her mask of blackness. "You may laugh, but it fits the few facts I've been able to gather. I don't think their vital energy comes from any ordinary biochemical process. I think it's—gravitational.''

"You don't mean—'' A shock of intuition took his voice.

"I believe that engineer was right with his notion that black holes come in swarms, in all sizes. I think each one of those creatures carries a tiny black hole in its belly. I think they live on the gravitational energy generated when mass is sucked into it. That's why they seem so heavy, and why they're able to eat metal and ice, and why they seem so hot inside.''

"How—how could such things evolve?''

"All life is an unlikely function of energy-flow,'' she insisted. "The energy flow from a star takes a long time to evolve our kind of life. Perhaps the energy sink around a black hole can form life—or something that looks like life— just as well.'' She shrugged forlornly. "Not that it matters to us now. The evolution of the *bomzeeth* can't get us to the space gate.''

"I don't know what *can* get us there.''

They sat for a time in abject silence. The yellow flame of the little lamp flickered slightly, casting huge unsteady shadows on the tall, unbroken wall. Listening, he heard no sound from anywhere outside. Once the stone floor quivered as if to another afterquake, but even that was soundless.

"Forgive me, Blackie,'' she breathed at last. "This isn't what I hoped for.''

"I don't like surrender.'' Staring into her darkened face, he asked, "Why the paint?''

"The only way I could reach you." She hesitated, almost shyly. "The purpose of the cult, you see, is to propitiate Ghur. The black paint is a sign of dedication. Larlarane is officially your bride—but naturally somewhat apprehensive about the consummation. She let me take her place."

She swayed a little toward him, opening the white fur to show herself completely black. Beneath the rank muskiness of some native perfume he caught a faint hint of her own sweetleaf scent.

"If you wish, *gunggee*," she whispered. "If you love me—"

"It's no time for love." He shoved her back. "If you're still a Benefactor get me something to eat. Get me out of this pit. Help me find a way across that ditch to the space gate."

"Forgive me, Blackie." Shivering, she pulled the white cloak back around her. "I have been begging for the food in our packs, but Larlarane won't trust us with anything. She doesn't know what we might use for magic. Certainly she doesn't intend to set you free."

"I guess all our technology looks like black magic to her—but magic is what we need." He stood up, swollen ankles still a little stiff, and caught her stained hands to pull her from the floor. "Go on back to Larlarane," he told her. "Invent some magic for us."

"I'll try, Blackie." She clutched the white cloak around her. "But what—what could it possibly be?"

"We'll have to fly," he said. "Nobody can climb and swim across the ditch."

"Fly?" she gasped. "How?"

"Any way we can." He paused to grope for the miraculous. "A fire balloon—if we can find paper to make it. A glider—if we can find anything light and strong enough. A kite, perhaps—the Wind clan hunters used to fly men on kites to reach the cliffs where the wild tlys nest. With cloth and a few sticks and our own climbing rope we might make a kite."

"In the few days we have?" She shrugged hopelessly. "With no tools? With nothing?"

"We can't just sit. We've got to fight."

"I'll try, Blackie." She turned uncertainly away toward the center of the cell. "I will try."

She called something through her translator at the dark opening overhead. A looped rope dropped. She stepped into the loop, waved a black hand at him as the rope hauled her upward.

Carrying the lamp, he explored the cell. The curving wall was seamless, slick and cold—forbidden steel, perhaps, but hidden beneath a yellow ceramic. The floor was rough masonry with no drain or other possible exit.

Something came thudding down behind him.

What he found was a small straw basket of food. Scraps of smoked fish. Bits of something dark and tough and sweetish, perhaps dried fruit. Stone-hard cakes of black bread. A small skin of some sour, weakly alcoholic liquid.

Too ravenous to be critical, he gulped the beer and gnawed the bread, trying to infer what he could about the native culture. There was fishing and farming and brewing of a sort—since the food was all preserved, he thought it must have come from some more fertile region, perhaps as tithes to support the bride of night. Nothing suggested a technology advanced enough to cross the trench.

While he ate, the tiny lamp flickered out. Left in utter blackness, he finished the food, drained the last drop from the skin, and sat back restlessly to wait.

Desperately, seething with his own frustration, he groped for ways to escape the pit, to cross the ditch and reach the space gate. All the plans he found were sheerest fantasy. He saw no action he could take.

He was blindly pacing the floor, avoiding collision by the echo of his footsteps, when the earth quaked again. Thrown against the wall, he fell back to the pitching floor. The planet reverberated under him, its vibration more powerful than sound.

Struggling to his feet in the dusty dark, he was flung

209

down again. At last he merely lay there, ill from the motion of the troubled world. The floor quivered again to smaller concussions, and he wondered if some tunnel above him had caved in to seal the cell.

At last there was silence.

Lying helpless there, with nothing else to do, he imagined the black hole still plunging Earthward, dragging the unswallowed fragments of Mars. The new quake was due, he supposed, to the beginning strains of its terrific tidal forces—or perhaps more likely to the passage of another satellite hole like the one which cut that trench.

Perhaps Snowfire would know.

With slowly waning hope he waited for her to return with news, with some unimagined miracle that might carry them across the trench to the space gate, but she didn't come. His mouth was parched and hunger tormented him and still she didn't come.

He tried to estimate the days or hours left, but his sense of time was gone.

Finally, exhausted, he slept.

Snowfire woke him.

"Sorry, Blackie."

Her touch shattered a dream in which he had been a boy again, newly apprenticed to the arena and elated to be in the highlands on his first tly hunt. The master hunters had rigged a kite and he was riding on it to reach the nests on the cliffs.

"I did—did try!" Despair broke her voice. "No luck."

He sat up stiffly, his dreamed elation dying.

Stooping over him, she held a clay lamp in one black hand and a coil of his own climbing rope in another. Her black-streaked face looked pinched and bleak.

"What now?"

"Forgive me, *gunggee.*" She set the lamp on the floor and bent as if to kiss him. "Can't you forgive me?"

"What do you want?"

"This isn't I who wanted this. Believe me, *gunggee!*"

Frozen, he sat staring at the yellow rope.

210

"It's Lar-Larlarane." Her voice shook. "She's afraid to hold you any longer. Since the moon is breaking up. She thinks that's your doing. She wanted to fill the pit to bury you alive, but I convinced her that you could make a new volcano here to lift you out again. Her solution now is to give you to the *bomzeeth*."

He merely stared in dazed protest.

"Please stand. Hands behind you."

"Not again!"

"We must."

He stood unwillingly and felt her fingers knotting the ropes.

"The blindfold, too." Her low voice caught and quivered. "We—we must. Because Larlarane's still afraid of you. She won't risk letting you see her again, or even the inside of her underground temple." The blindfold covered his eyes and he felt her cold lips brush his. "Good-bye, *gunggee*. And please don't blame me."

"I don't blame anybody," he muttered hoarsely. "What's the use?"

She slid a rope under his arms. It tightened. He felt himself hauled upward, dragged through the ceiling vent, tossed on a litter. Silent men ran with him. The air on his face was suddenly cold. He heard the crunch of snow underfoot and the crack of Larlarane's whip. At last the litter bearers dropped him into soft snow and ran. Their receding footfalls died. All he could hear was a faint crackling like a fire that gave no heat. He lay somewhere alone, in an icy wind. Once he caught a sharp whiff of wood smoke, but he felt no warmth from anything.

Shivering, he waited.

For this useless end he and Snowfire had been trained as Benefactors. They had waited long years for the slow probe to reach Earth. They had left undone all their tasks on Nggongga. They had lost each other—

Whipping about him, the arctic wind was suddenly alive with another sound, a far-off steady howling. On a more advanced planet it might have been the whine of

211

some jetdriven aircraft. Here, it could only be a diving *bomzeeth*.

He lay trembling. Trying not to feel the numbing cold, he wondered about those alien creatures. Really, could their vital force come from small black holes? The physics of it troubled him. There would be radiant heat of course, from matter sucked into the funnels, and the energy of falling particles might be trapped by magnetic fields, but he couldn't quite imagine the anatomy.

The nature of the holes themselves was another puzzle. If the force of gravity was propagated at the speed of light, how could the gravitational field of the swallowed mass reach out to trap more matter? He should have asked that double-brained portal engineer more about the theory.

Though he found no answers, he kept himself busy with such problems. They were better than counting the seconds toward the breakup of the Earth, better than regretting that he would never know the son Snowfire had promised him.

The wind brought another whiff of pungent smoke. He heard sudden distant shouts, the far-off crack of Larlarane's whip, the jangle of broken ice beneath running feet.

"*Gunggee*—" Snowfire was suddenly above him, gasping for her breath. "I slipped away—from Larlarane—to die with you!"

"Untie me!" he rasped. "Can't you untie me?"

"Here's your knife. I'll cut the cords."

He felt her at his aching wrists and ankles. Suddenly the blindfold was gone. He sat up unsteadily on a snow-sifted pile of broken iron. Though it was night, the half light seemed strangely bright. He looked at the sky—and trembled.

What he saw was a long egg-shape of silver fire, pierced with one hot blue point. Flecked and streaked with black, it reached from the zenith of the sullen sky toward the ice horizon. Its strangeness brushed him with a numbing chill.

"The moon of Earth," Snowfire was whispering. "Broken up by the tidal forces of another black hole— larger I guess than the one that cut the trench. The fragments are in elliptic orbits around it. The blue point is the funnel of the hole itself, at the upper focus."

Shaking, he staggered to his feet.

"A dreadful thing!" She caught his arm and he felt her trembling. "And it fits a prediction that you will set the sky on fire before you destroy the Earth. Larlarane is terrified. She was afraid to follow me."

He looked uncertainly around him. The eerie light of the shattered moon lay blue and cold on a vast flat field of snow. A foot-beaten trail ran far across it to a low stone building, which he thought must be the temple of Ghur. Beyond, rounded mounds were soft with snow.

"Ruins," Snowfire gestured widely. "A city—when Earth had cities. This flat field is where the shuttle craft took off. Your altar, now. The fires must be a signal to the *bomzeeth.*"

He found the fires as she spoke. Three smoky blazes, spaced wide about the pile of broken metal where he had been tossed. Their yellow light was dim beneath that great frozen whirlpool of brighter fire overhead.

"What—what now?" Her teeth chattered. "What can we do?"

He caught her arms and held her off to look into her green eyes. They were lusterless and hollow, dull against her black-dyed face. He felt her shivering beneath the loose white cloak.

"We're still Benefactors," he told her. "We'll do what we can."

She still held his knife in one black hand. Behind her, among the scraps of metal offered to Ghur, he saw their packs, his binoculars and translator, Snowfire's yellow survival suit, finally the laser energizer.

"Our key!" He bent to snatch it up. "If we could reach the space gate. . . ."

His voice faded when he heard the howling returning

213

overhead. The diving creature thundered low above them and climbed again on its plume of scarlet flame. In black silhouette, its big-bellied shape crept upward across the silver egg-shape of the splintered moon.

"Can you run?" She tugged at his sleeve. "Maybe it will wait till the fires burn lower before it drops to feed."

Scarcely hearing, he stood following its far red fleck, climbing and wheeling above the broken moon to dive again. Trembling, he almost felt that he was once more in the great arena at Nggonggamba, awaiting the dive of a killer tly. His numb fingers tightened suddenly on the laser energizer.

"Get out of that cape." He swung suddenly to Snowfire. "Get into your suit."

She slid out of the loose white fur. Nude and black, shrinking from the bitter wind, she looked so defenseless, so utterly despondent, that a lump throbbed in his throat. He held the stiff yellow suit while she slipped into it, then bent to gather up the rest of their gear.

High in that uncanny sky the *bomzeeth* turned to dive again. He saw a ripple of color beyond it and paused to stare at the long curtains of green and crimson fire dropping toward the blue-lit white horizon, all across the north.

"The aurora," Snowfire whispered. "Caused I guess by particles from the funnel that tore up the moon." Breathless, she finished fastening her suit. "Shall—shall we run?"

"Not far," he murmured. "Not too far."

Just beyond the nearest signal fire he pulled her flat beside him in the snow. The *bomzeeth* came roaring down, more appalling than any tly. The ice quivered when it struck. Sliding onto Larlarane's offering, it began licking up the broken iron with an enormous rough black tongue.

"Come along!" He hauled her upright. "We're going for a ride."

She hung back, staring blankly. "Are you crazy?"

"Maybe," he muttered. "But the craziest chance is better than none."

He dashed back around the fire toward that dark and monstrous shape. At the last instant its alien black-scaled hugeness almost broke his resolution—but an unseen drag had already caught him. Swept unexpectedly ahead, he jumped high. Snowfire came flying behind him, drawn by that same savage attraction.

They crashed against the hot black scales. The impact dazed him for an instant before he caught his breath and tried to stand. The pack had been torn off his back and his limbs were leadenly heavy.

"So I was right!" Her outcry was oddly triumphant. "It does have a black hole in its belly. We're already caught in the gravity field."

Fighting that ruthless force, he was climbing the great scales to the top of its swollen body. Twenty feet beneath him that thick snakelike tongue dropped a mass of rusted arm and struck savagely at him. He thumbed the laser alive and slashed back with its blinding green needle.

The tongue recoiled.

The creature bellowed with a hurricane of sound that battered him backward and ached in his bones. Snowfire seized his arm, screaming. He heard nothing, but saw her arm pointing. He turned and found the creature's black-fluked tail whipping toward them.

He stabbed it with the laser.

The blade of pulsing light did no harm that he could see, but the creature thundered louder. The tail stiffened, red fire exploding from its flaring jet. The hot thick scales quaked underfoot and suddenly they were gliding across the flat snowfield.

Snowfire's clinging fingers dug hard into his arm. Glancing at her, he found her eyes dark and staring. Beneath the mask of blackness her drawn face wore a look of startled incredulity.

"Down!" he mouthed. "Hang on!"

She gaped at him, unhearing, unbelieving.

Crouching against the bitter wind rising, he beckoned her down behind him. Followed by its long plume of crimson thunder, the creature was sliding faster, faster. Larlarane's tiny signal fires were lost behind. The airstream tore at him till he had to drop deeper into the grip of the creature's great belly and clutch the edge of a massive scale. Suddenly they were in the air, lifting above the rounded mounds that once had been a city. Wheeling beneath the blazing ellipse of the fragmented moon, the creature swung north toward the cold high shimmer of the aurora.

"The wrong way!" The shriek of the icy wind and the roar of the jet swept Snowfire's voice away, but he saw her dark mouth moving and saw her black hand pointing and understood her desperate words. "The gate is southeast!"

He searched to sense and master the creature as he would have probed to control a fighting tly. Fighting the cruel wind, he played his wire-sharp laser blade against its left-hand fluke. Its rough scales bucked under him and its bellow hurt his ears. But the massive tail flinched aside and the aurora slid back across the sky.

Pure joy lifted him, a sheer elation he had never felt before, but had only imagined once long ago, the first time he sneaked into the arena to try picking pockets and discovered a new ambition when he saw a black champion binding a vicious tly, with thrown hats falling in a colored rain to acclaim his triumph. Nothing in all reality had left him feeling quite so splendid.

The aurora, he saw, had wheeled too far around. He stabbed the laser at the right-hand fluke. The creature roared and veered sharply back. Snowfire was suddenly shaking his arm, pointing down. He saw the trench.

An endless black slash across the blue-lit snowfields, it crept back beneath them. To his left, the bottom of it shone with sudden silver, burned with one bright blue spot, reflecting the shattered moon.

That brief reflection dimmed and the barrier chasm was suddenly behind.

"The beacon!" Snowfire's scream was whipped away again, but he followed her pointing arm to the green-and-orange blink on the far white horizon. "The gate!"

It was slipping aside, and he stabbed the laser at the left fluke again. Again the creature veered. Green and orange, green and orange, the beacon winked straight ahead.

The windstream tore and battered at him, blurred his eyes with tears. His straining fingers ached and slipped on the edge of the great black scale. Snowfire lost her clinging grip on his arm, clutched at him desperately. He flung his free arm around her to pull her down behind him.

And the beacon crawled on toward them.

He ducked his head to wipe his streaming eyes and found the dome beneath it, a tiny bulge on the vast expanse of blue-lit snow. He gave Snowfire a grin of elation and saw the agonized question on her tear-streaked face.

How were they to reach the ground?

"Here we are!" He yelled into her ear, though he knew the wind would take his words. "With no fall gear."

Testing the responses of the creature, he played the laser on the eyelike pits at the roots of the hard-scaled wings. It lurched and bellowed and at last began to drop. He stopped the stabbing needle until it tried to climb again.

The beacon and the dome came nearer, nearer. He let the creature lift a little, held it level, forced it sharply down. Howling, it touched the ice, plowing out great plumes of snow.

"Now!" He lifted Snowfire. "Off!"

Fighting the pull of that vast anomalous mass in its belly, they climbed the thick-scaled tail, dropped off into a bank of snow. He heard its jet boom and shriek behind him, felt its scorching blast above him, saw its crimson glare receding.

And it was gone.

Dazed and bruised, he pulled himself out of the drift and turned to look for Snowfire. He found her standing where they had fallen, bent double. Sick, he thought, or perhaps hysterical. He was stumbling to help her when she straightened with the energizer, which he had dropped.

"Here, *gunggee.* You'll need this."

They slogged to the portal dome. Built of massive permalith, it stood unscarred by centuries of vandals. The tall entry doors slid open before their translators. Inside, they found gloomy silence, a few scattered rocks and sticks left by the ancient Earthfolk when they disabled the gate, a dusty human skeleton sprawled beside a stone-tipped spear, where one invader had died.

On the high control stage everything looked intact except a single shattered plexoid panel with a rock still embedded in it. With stiff and trembling fingers he pulled out the broken energizer beneath it, snapped the new unit into place.

Nothing happened.

"Something wrong!" A shock of fear took his breath. "I don't know what—"

"Wait!" Snowfire whispered. "I think the ring-fields are forming."

The console was suddenly alive with winking symbols. At the center of the vast floor below them, where the entryways and exit ways converged around a circular pit, fleeting wisps of dark shadow and pale blue fire had begun to flicker. The fire suddenly ballooned to become an enormous blue iris. The shadows blackened and condensed into its center, became the staring pupil of the interstellar eye. Sudden light flushed the vault above them. Signals chimed from the console. The ways began to crawl.

"*Gunggee!*" Elated, Snowfire gripped his arm. "We've done it!"

They ran down the ramp to the nearest entryway. It swept them into the enormous lid-less eye. Transit through the ring-fields that bridged the light-years was only a shock of shifting gravities, a wink of suspended sensation.

With no more sense of motion, they were abruptly in the vaster portal dome on Xyr.

The fat bald portal engineer found them there in the emergency hospital center. Between their tests and shots and treatments, he wanted to know every fact they had learned on Earth. News of the *bomzeeth* lit a glint of eager interest in the pale eyes beneath his implanted computer.

"Gravitophores." His great naked double cranium nodded ponderously. "Fragmentary reports of such creatures have been sent back by one or two explorers of black holes, but you are the first to return with actual confirmation."

The nurses were taking Snowfire to wash her black paint off, and he stayed to question Blacklantern.

"We've no time to waste," he apologized. "Earth has only ten days now before the central hole arrives. We're anxious to initiate the research and rescue programs we have planned. A dozen major expeditions are organized and ready. Archaeologists waiting to salvage the last relics of our ancestors. Anthropologists interested in the culture of our surviving cousins. Teams waiting to study the swarm of black holes—I myself am hoping to capture one of the gravitophores you report."

"What's happening to the Earthfolk?"

"The portal authority is offering them free transit." He shrugged, not much concerned. "If they decide to leave."

A technician had come to take Blacklantern for counter-radiation. When he returned, tingling all over and pleasantly half-drunk from the treatment, the engineer was still waiting.

"One more item." Beneath the mass of his auxiliary brain, the small eyes shone shrewdly. "If this has been enough of the Benefactors, I still want you in the portal survey division. You've seen the last of Old Earth. We've an explorer probe in orbit now around a virgin world with a rich carbon-based biosphere. I'll make you the planet manager there, at a scale of pay you can't refuse—"

"But I can," Blacklantern said. "I'm still a Benefactor and my own people need me."

"You Benefactors!"

With a puzzled shrug the engineer waddled away.

Snowfire came back scrubbed golden-pink.

"You're released," the senior medic told them. "No permanent damage from radiation or exposure, though I advise a few days of rest."

Benefactor Thornwall was waiting with congratulations when they left the emergency center. He kissed Snowfire and greeted Blacklantern with the palm-touch he had learned on Nggongga.

"I'm putting you up for promotion," he told Blacklantern. "To a stellar fellowship—"

"Gunggee!" Snowfire flung eager arms around him. "You've earned it."

"And I've a choice for both of you. You may go back to Old Earth when you feel able, to lead our effort to persuade the natives that technology might be a good thing for them. Or you may return to Nggongga, to carry on as our co-agents there. How about it?"

They looked at each other. Without the paint Snowfire seemed strangely pale, but her green eyes were shining. She reached quickly to take Blacklantern's hand.

"The rescue effort mustn't wait for us," she told the old Benefactor. "Anyhow, Blackie's the wrong color for it."

She turned to smile at him, her tone gently mocking. "Before he tamed that dragon the Earthfolk thought he was their devil-god. They'll be certain of it now."

"We'll choose Nggongga," Blacklantern said. "We've work enough waiting for us there."

"And love." She squeezed his hand. "We're going to have a son."